BOOKS BY HELENA NEWBURY

Helena Newbury is the *New York Times* and *USA Today* bestselling author of sixteen romantic suspenses, all available where you bought this book. Find out more at helenanewbury.com.

Lying and Kissing

Punching and Kissing

Texas Kissing

Kissing My Killer

Bad For Me

Saving Liberty

Kissing the Enemy

Outlaw's Promise

Alaska Wild

Brothers

Captain Rourke

Royal Guard

Mount Mercy

The Double

Hold Me in the Dark

Deep Woods

THE DOUBLE

HELENA NEWBURY

1

HAILEY

I FELL for Konstantin Gulyev long before I ever met him.

That hard, tan jaw with its perfect shadow of black stubble was etched into my mind from staring at it day after day. I spent so much time looking at his lips, the top one hard and stern, the lower one soft and sulkily pouting, that I knew what they'd feel like brushing against mine. I knew him so well, I could tell you whether the shirt he was wearing came from his tailor in Russia or his tailor in New York, from the way the snow-white fabric stretched over the broad slabs of his chest.

There are other crime bosses in New York. Even a few other Russian ones. But none are as notorious, none have produced as many myths and legends as him. *They say he takes three women to bed each night. They say he kills his enemies with his bare hands. They say his mansion has a vault stocked floor-to-ceiling with gold, and the government doesn't dare try to arrest him because he has so much money he could crash the economy...*

That last one, at least, isn't true. I know because I'm on the FBI team assigned to bring Konstantin down, and we *are* trying. We're just failing. His organization is huge and unimaginably strong, protected by guns and bribed officials and encryption. He's untouchable and he knows it.

Watching him was my job. It had become my obsession.

As his limo entered the deserted construction site, I was a tiny speck in the distance, perched in the darkened window of an abandoned building over half a mile away. But the camera's long lens brought me close enough that I could see the rivets on the limo's license plate as it prowled across the muddy, churned-up ground, the tattoos on the bodyguard's hand as he opened the limo door. And then I was looking at *him*. Konstantin.

He was impeccably dressed as always but he didn't even glance down as his Italian leather shoes were ruined by the mud. He ignored the rain that hissed from the slate-gray sky and soaked his hair. With his coat billowing out behind him like the devil's black wings, he marched over to where the other man cowered beneath an umbrella. He stopped so close, and he was so tall, that the other man had to look up into the rain to keep eye contact, blinking and spluttering, his face bone-white with fear. I held down the camera's shutter button, taking a flurry of shots.

Everyone is scared of Konstantin Gulyev, from the small-time crooks at the bottom to the white-collar crooks at the top. You don't run for mayor in this city unless Konstantin says so. Rumor is, you don't run for *senator*.

Smuggling. Gambling. Guns. Protection. Billion dollar construction contracts obtained through bribes. He's not *a* criminal, he's *the* criminal.

And we—the FBI—can't prove any of it. That's why I've been watching hfim for two years.

And at some point, during that time... I started to get obsessed.

It might have started when I was listening to his phone calls, every long *r* and hard *k* of his Russian accent earthquaking down my spine to pool in my groin. Or when I was in a building across the street, a telephoto lens bringing that brutally handsome face so close, it felt like I could reach out and press my cheek against his dark stubble. It might have been the time I was in the next hotel room, my palm pressed to the wall, feeling the vibrations as he fucked his girlfriend up against the wall, his muscled body slamming into her no more than a foot from me.

He's pure *bad,* given human form. And he's not just my enemy, he's my nemesis. I've run surveillance on plenty of criminals and Konstantin is the only one I haven't been able to bring down. I should hate him. But....

But there's something about his raw, dark power that pulls me in and holds me. He terrifies me and yet I can't look away. I knew that, if we ever actually met, he'd utterly destroy me. But he's as hypnotic as a tornado, as tempting as a cliff edge.

He looked up.

I froze.

I knew that he couldn't see me. I was dressed in black, my camera was painted a dull gray, and I was deep in the shadows, up on the tenth floor of an abandoned building. But none of that mattered, not with him staring right at me.

Konstantin's eyes are like no one else's. At first, you think they're utterly devoid of color, a pale gray that puts me in mind of a winter sky about to unleash a truly biblical ice storm. But if you look long enough, if you really concentrate, there's the faintest hint of blue there. Just enough blue to give you some sort of forlorn hope. Just before he crushes it completely.

My brain knew he couldn't see me, but my body didn't. I stared into those frozen eyes and a wave of heat broke over my face and rippled down through my body. My lungs ached, but I didn't dare breathe. I wasn't half a mile away, anymore. I was *there,* right next to him, close enough to touch. I could feel what he felt: the rain hitting my scalp, the wind whipping across my cheeks. I could feel the heat of his body, we were so close. He could just reach out and grab me, one big hand on the back of my neck, slamming me against the huge, warm wall of his chest, panting into his pec. Then a nudge with his knuckles under my chin, gently tipping my head back....

I swallowed. God, he had the face of a king, like you'd carve him out of freakin' marble. That elegant nose and those cheekbones, balancing that strong jaw just enough. Powerful. Commanding. *Gorgeous.*

He'd lean down, those lips descending towards mine—

"We gotta go," said a voice in my ear.

I'd lost all awareness of the room I was in. My soul was down there in the rain with Konstantin and as I looked up from the camera, it had to rubber-band all the way back in. I rocked unsteadily on my stool, blinking behind my glasses, my face turning scarlet at what I'd been imagining. "...what?" I croaked.

Calahan was standing next to me. "They want everyone back at the office," he said.

Sam Calahan is my best friend, and my opposite. I'm small and the way I hold myself makes me look even smaller; he's a hulking beast of a man. I'm just a surveillance specialist; he's a bona fide field agent with a whole slew of high profile cases under his belt. And where I don't even run in the hallways, Calahan breaks the rules *a lot.* Ever since I've known him, he's been one reprimand away from getting fired. We work well together. He doesn't mind me being quiet and weird and I do my best to reign him in so he can keep his job.

He's always sort of rumpled, like he's been up all night, but he manages to make it look *good:* tousled black hair, a stubbled jaw he rubs when he's thinking and a worn suit that fits that hard body just right. Hell, he's *hot.* There were times, early on, when I was yelling at him that *no,* he really *shouldn't* defy orders and run off to Mexico to single-handedly chase down a suspect, that he'd narrow his eyes and sort of smolder down at me and I'd swallow and—

And then he'd look away and nothing would ever happen. And then one night, after too many tequilas, he told me the story of the woman he lost. Her death shattered him: he's broken in a way I don't know how to fix and it breaks my heart because if ever someone deserved to be happy, it's Calahan. Since that night, we've settled into *friends* and that works.

I put my eye back to the camera's viewfinder. "In a minute," I murmured. Konstantin had turned away again, still talking to the other guy. I was praying for a shot of something incriminating: an envelope of cash changing hands, a crate of guns. But I knew it was a long shot. *You're too damn smart, aren't you?*

"*Now*," said Calahan. "It's Carrie. She says it's an emergency."

I looked up, startled, and then scrambled to pack away my gear. Carrie Blake was the head of the entire New York office of the FBI. Taking down Konstantin was her number one priority, so for her to pull us from surveillance, something huge must have happened.

As we left, I took one last look over my shoulder. Without my zoom lens, Konstantin was just a dot in the distance, but I still couldn't tear my eyes away. It's like an aura he has: he sucks you in. Everyone knows him, everyone talks about him. He dominates any room he walks into.

And me? I'm the perfect person to watch him. No one notices me.

My name is Hailey Akers, and I'm the closest to invisible a person can be.

Carrie Blake is in her fifties with long, gray-blonde hair. When she wears it down, it gives her a kindly, Earth-mother look. Right now, though, she had it pulled back into a ferociously tight ponytail and her eyes were bright with gleeful excitement. "Who can tell me who this is?" she asked, bringing a photo up on the conference room's big screen.

Calahan and I looked up at the screen... and my hand shot up into the air. Then I remembered *this isn't school* and flushed and tried to make it look as if I'd just been pushing my glasses up my nose. "Um, Christina Rogan, ma'am. Konstantin's girlfriend." They'd been together about four months, now. She was beautiful, with big blue eyes and glossy, sleek black hair, but I didn't really like her.

A few weeks after they met, Konstantin had taken her on a business trip to Monaco. I'd watched through the security cameras as Christina strutted empty-handed through the airport while one of Konstantin's maids struggled along behind her, pushing an overloaded trolley filled with her luggage. Christina had kept turning around to snap at her to *hurry up* and the poor maid had almost been in tears.

"Correct, Hailey." Carrie grinned. "About two hours ago, while Christina was on a shopping trip in Milan, *this* happened."

The picture changed to show a wrecked sports car, its hood wrapped around a lamppost.

I drew in my breath. "Oh my God! Is she okay?"

Everyone else around the conference table stared at me, startled. Christina was *the enemy*. Then Carrie softened and gave me one of those *Oh Hailey* looks I get a lot. "She's fine," she said. "Bumps and scrapes."

I flushed again. I can't help it. I'm just a surveillance geek, not a field agent, and I'm not hardened like the others.

"What this gives us," said Carrie, leaning forward over the conference table, "is a unique opportunity. I managed to pull some strings with Interpol and they've told Konstantin that Christina's injured. Nothing life-threatening, but she'll need a series of operations. He's not expecting her back in the US for three weeks." She walked over to the door and showed in a man in his fifties with curling silver hair and a shiny bald pate. "This is Doctor Franklin. He runs the plastic surgery team who assist with our witness protection program. He'll explain."

Doctor Franklin took up position beside Carrie. "We're going to take one of our female agents and use plastic surgery to make her the exact double of Christina. Then we're going to send her back to Konstantin in Christina's place."

There was total silence for maybe five seconds. Then the table exploded into a chorus of disbelieving *what's?!*

Calahan's bass rumble drowned out the others. "That's *insane!* You can't make her look *exactly* the same!"

"Actually, we can." Doctor Franklin had the excited grin of a child unpacking a new toy. "As long as the subject has suitable bone structure and she's the right height and build, she can look identical. And the beauty is, Konstantin's been told that Christina's sustained facial injuries. He's *expecting* her to have had plastic surgery. That'll explain any minor differences."

My head was spinning. Would someone actually do that? Change their whole face? And then strut straight into the life of one of the most terrifying men in the world and... *Jesus, she'll have to sleep with him!* My mind snapped to a very specific, graphic image: some nameless female agent on her back, legs open, with Konstantin's muscled body pinning her to the bed, his ass rising and falling—

Just as my face went hot, Calahan spoke again. "Who?"

"Me," said Alison from further down the conference table. "Carrie briefed me before the meeting. I've already volunteered."

I twisted around to look at her. Alison is like my cooler, prettier, older sister. She has long, shining black hair and is so good at martial arts, the FBI uses her to help train new recruits. If anyone could impersonate Christina and come out alive, it was her. But the idea of my friend in that sort of danger made me go cold inside.

Calahan agreed. "It's way too risky. Alison would have to mimic Christina perfectly. Voice. Walk. *Everything.*" His voice rose. "If *one thing* goes wrong, she's dead!"

"I know it's dangerous," said Carrie. "But just think what Alison will be able to accomplish. All criminals confide in their girlfriends— in a few weeks, she'll know every detail of his business. And she'll be right inside his home: she'll be able to get into his paperwork, his laptop... we'll get all the evidence we need to bring him down." Her face turned grim. "And we need this. We're running out of time. Every day, Konstantin takes over a little more of this city."

She brought another image up on the screen, a map of New York with neighborhoods drawn in three colors: blue were controlled by Luka Malakov, a rival Russian mafia boss. Green were controlled by Angelo Baroni, an Italian Mafioso. And black were controlled by Konstantin Gulyev. At first, the three colors were roughly equal: the three powers had been in an uneasy truce that had kept the violence to a minimum. But as Carrie fast-forwarded through the last twelve months, the black expanded like a shadow falling across the city, squeezing out the other two. "We're at crisis point." said Carrie.

"Another month, maybe two, and Konstantin's expansion will force the other two into an all-out gang war. We *cannot let that happen!*"

Calahan and I nodded grimly. Hundreds of innocents would die in the crossfire.

And for Carrie, this battle was personal. Konstantin might wage war with the other crime lords, but as the head of the FBI in New York, *she* was his real enemy. The two of them had been locked in combat for years: she'd make arrests and gather evidence and raid properties and he'd trot out alibis and expensive lawyers and slip free every time. When we interrogated one of Konstantin's men, sometimes he'd deliver a message, always scrupulously polite, usually gently mocking. *Mr. Gulyev says: you'll have to try harder than that.* Rumor had it, they'd actually met face-to-face once, at a cocktail party, and exchanged words. I would have loved to be a fly on the wall for that.

"We *have* to do this," said Carrie. "We'll never have an opportunity like this again and it's our only shot at stopping a gang war. Doctor Franklin will operate on Alison tomorrow. Hailey, I want you to pull together all the information you have on Christina. I'm also having Christina flown here so we can question her. The Italian authorities found cocaine and amphetamines in her car so she's looking at jail time unless she strikes a deal with us and cooperates. That'll be all."

As I left the conference room, Calahan grabbed my arm and pulled me into the stairwell. "We can't let them send Alison into Konstantin's bed!"

"I know! But...." I gave a helpless shrug. *What can we do?*

He pressed his lips together and looked furtively around. I started to get a bad feeling. "Konstantin's in Boston tonight, at some political fundraiser. He's staying the night in a hotel." He looked at me carefully, watching my reaction. "So he'll have a hotel room."

I sighed. "If it was that easy, we'd have arrested him years ago. We'll never get a warrant to search his room. Most of the judges are on his payroll."

Calahan just looked at me.

My jaw dropped. "You want to search it *without* a warrant? You mean *break in?* Anything you found would be inadmissible!"

"I know! But maybe we can find something that'll give us an advantage. A date, a place... something that'll let us plan a bust. Then we can talk Carrie out of this plan."

I gawped at him. "*What if you get—*" He made *shh*-ing gestures and I lowered my voice. "What if you get caught?! You'll go to jail!"

"I won't get caught," he said levelly. "Not if I have someone keeping watch."

My stomach dropped to my feet. "Oh God. No. *No!* Absolutely not. I am not running off to Boston with you on some illegal, unsanctioned...."

I trailed off. Calahan was looking right at me, open and sincere, and I could see the pain in his eyes. I remembered what he'd told me about his past. *He can't lose someone else he's close to.*

"Please," he said.

He was my best friend. I couldn't let him go alone. And Alison is like a big sister to me. If doing this kept her out of danger.... I sighed and my shoulders slumped in resignation. Then I pushed my glasses up my nose. "Okay," I said. "Let's go."

2

HAILEY

"FIND ANYTHING?" I asked for the tenth time.

Calahan's voice was stressed and breathless in my earpiece. "Still nothing."

This was *not* going well.

I was in a hotel room, staring at my laptop screen, using the hotel's security cameras to keep tabs on Konstantin. Just across the hallway, Calahan was frantically searching Konstantin's room. We were way behind schedule. The plan had been to get into Konstantin's room as soon as he went downstairs to join the party, but one of the hotel security guards had been patrolling the hallway and we'd had to wait for him to leave. Calahan had only made it into Konstantin's room a few minutes ago and we knew Konstantin would come back upstairs any moment.

"Anything?" I asked again.

"*No!*" snapped Calahan. I could hear the bangs as he pulled open drawers and slammed them shut. "Where is he?"

"Still in the ballroom," I said. I watched as Konstantin prowled the room. I could actually see his power in the way the crowd parted ahead of him, reverent and fearful, in the way people turned to stare at him and then whispered in his wake. As I watched, Konstantin locked eyes with someone right on the other side of the room... and *scowled.* Just a tiny narrowing of those cold gray eyes, a tightening of those gorgeous lips, but it was enough to make the man on the receiving end go pale and stumble backwards, then flee the room entirely. The sheer, raw *power* of the man....

I knew Konstantin would start back upstairs any minute. He was at the party for business, not fun, and the second the last shady deal was done, he'd go back to his room to work. I've never known anyone so intensely focused. He never took a vacation. He didn't seem to have any vices at all... or if he did, he kept them hidden within his mansion.

"Come on!" I told Calahan. "Get out of there!"

"Just keep watching him," said Calahan stubbornly. "I want to check the closet."

I gritted my teeth, my foot *tap-tap-tapping* on the floor with stress. If we didn't pull this off, Alison would have to go undercover. And if we got caught, we'd be going to jail. I focused on Konstantin to try to take my mind off how high the stakes were.

But staring at Konstantin had its own problems. His back was turned to me, his dinner jacket stretched tight over his broad back, the fabric sweeping down elegantly in a vee to that tight, toned waist. The fabric was so expensive, so perfectly black, that it looked as if he'd had it made from a piece of the night sky. I imagined pressing my hand against his back, my palm caressed by the silky smoothness of his jacket and then the heated throb of the hard muscle underneath. The size of him, so much bigger than me...it would be like touching a bear, a lion, knowing that he could twist around in a heartbeat and end me....

I reached out and brushed my fingers against Konstantin's back, but all I could feel was the hard plastic of the screen. For a second, I wished....

I wished I could get close to him. Just for a second.

Then I realized what I was thinking and I went cold. *Am I going crazy?* After two years of watching him, had I forgotten who he was? The man was pure, undiluted evil.

And he was suddenly moving, crossing the room in huge strides. My throat went tight. "He's on his way!" I managed. "Get out of there!"

A sudden intake of breath from Calahan. "I found his laptop!"

"*I don't care!*" Impatient, Konstantin wasn't waiting for the elevator. He was taking the stairs three at a time. "Get out now!"

"It's booting," said Calahan. I heard him tapping keys. "Hardware key? What's a hardware key?"

I flipped through cameras, tracking Konstantin as he moved. "*He's on our floor! Move!*"

Calahan cursed under his breath. Then I heard the laptop close.

"*Hurry!*" I begged.

"I've got to put it back where it was," muttered Calahan. "Or he'll know we were here." I heard the rustle of clothes and then the closet doors closing and footsteps. "Okay, coming out—"

I checked the cameras and my heart nearly stopped. "*Wait!*"

Calahan's footsteps stopped as he froze.

"We're too late," I moaned. "He's in the hallway! He'll see you coming out!" I could feel the blood draining from my face. This was way worse than getting caught by hotel security. Konstantin was likely carrying a gun. If he found Calahan in his room, he'd shoot and then claim self-defense....

Konstantin arrived outside his room. I imagined Calahan standing on the other side of the door: they were practically face to face. There was only one thing to do. "*Hide!*" I told him frantically.

I heard footsteps in my earpiece as Calahan turned and ran. His breathing suddenly went echoey. *The bathroom. He's hiding in the bathroom.*

Konstantin opened the door to his room. I held my breath...but there was no yell of shock, no gunshot. Calahan must have gotten out of sight just in time. Konstantin went inside... and closed the door.

I sat there frozen, staring at the screen. Calahan was trapped. And as soon as Konstantin went into the bathroom, he was dead. I started to panic, breathe. *What the hell do I do?* I wasn't a field agent like him, I just did surveillance. Should I call the cops? Call Carrie? We'd broken into a hotel room without any sort of warrant. We'd be arrested, our careers would be over, and Konstantin would find out he was being watched. He'd be too suspicious for Carrie's undercover plan to work. *We've blown the whole thing!* And even if I did call for help, it probably wouldn't come in time. Konstantin would find Calahan any minute.

Unless....

My eyes lifted from the screen. I looked towards the hallway, and Konstantin's room.

Unless someone distracted Konstantin while Calahan slipped out.

My heart came to a juddering halt. Go in *there?!* With *Konstantin?!* I couldn't be a diversion, I've spent my whole life *not* getting noticed.

But if I didn't do this, Calahan was dead.

I ran for the bathroom, stripping off my suit as I went. I didn't have a plan, I had an idea, and I didn't have time to worry if it was a good one or not. Naked, I turned the faucet on the sink on full and dunked my head under. When I lifted my head, I caught a glimpse of myself in the mirror and froze. *This is crazy.* This needed someone like Alison, someone pretty and confident and brave. But all there was, was me, with my mop of frizzy hair the color of dirt, freckles and scared brown eyes blinking behind thick glasses.

And low down on my side, an ugly, raised scar. The reason I learned to be invisible.

I grabbed one of the fluffy white bathrobes and pulled it on, then ran out into the hallway, slamming our room's door behind me.

I lifted my hand to knock, then faltered. *What the hell am I doing?* This was *Konstantin.*

But this was Calahan's only chance. I knocked.

Distant footsteps, coming closer. My legs twitched with the need to *run, run!* But I made myself stand firm. My vision swam, the door distorting. I felt giddy and weak.

He threw open the door.

And I was face to face with Konstantin.

3

HAILEY

I'D THOUGHT that I was used to him. I'd spent more time staring at this man than most married couples spend together. But it had always been from a distance. However close the camera lens had brought him, it was nothing like being in his presence.

I'd known he was big because I'd seen him tower over other men. But looking down on him from a rooftop was very different to looking up at him from two feet away. Being in bare feet made me even smaller: the top of my head barely reached his shirt collar. I had to crane my head way, way back to see his face. And...God, he filled the doorway, his shoulders almost brushing the sides, his chest a wall of solid muscle that filled my view. His body was beyond intimidating: he could easily pick me up with one hand.

But that was nothing compared to *who he was*. That knowledge was like a cold blackness pushing in from every side, sapping every bit of strength and warmth from me. After years of anonymity, of staying safely at a distance, suddenly I was in direct contact with everything the FBI fought against. His branch of the Russian Mafia had the wealth and power of a small country and he could bring the entire weight of it down on me. My death would take a mere wave of his hand. I was too scared to breathe.

And then I looked into his eyes.

At first, all I could see was cold. He was glowering down at whoever had dared disturb him and the chill in those gray eyes made my chest contract. *He's looking at me.* After two years of watching him, *he* was looking at *me.* I couldn't speak. I just stood there staring up at him from behind my glasses.

Then he blinked, just once, as if surprised. His eyes crinkled. Confusion... then *fascination.* At that moment, his eyes didn't look completely gray. There was just the faintest hint of pale blue.

Suddenly, I could breathe again. And when I inhaled, the air carried the heat of his body and the clean, rich smell of him. I'd always been so far away, I'd never imagined him having a scent, but it was amazing. Vanilla and something I couldn't identify, sharp and citrusy and *cold:* I imagined bright red berries that grew only in Russia, frozen solid in a fierce winter and then crushed to extract their essence.

What's going on?

I fought it, but my eyes were darting helplessly over him. For two years, I'd had to gauge his body under suit jackets and coats. Now, his jacket was gone and he'd undone a few buttons on his shirt, his bow tie hanging loose around his neck. There was a tantalizing triangle of smooth, tan skin, with just the hint of the tops of his huge pecs. I could follow the shape of them as they pushed out his shirt, and there was just enough light in the dim hallway to make out the shadows of his nipples. There were other shadows, even darker, just below his collarbone: Bratva tattoos. My eyes roved lower. There was a hint of alternating dark and light: the ridges and valleys of his abs. Then the dividing line where soft white shirt disappeared into the black of his tuxedo pants. God, his waist was so tight, and the way he flared out, his hips and quads loaded with power....

The blood was rushing in my ears, my heart pounding. That look in his eyes had made the fear drop away *just enough...* it was still there, but it had disappeared beneath a tidal wave of raw, hot need.

I knew I was attracted to him. But through the lens of the camera, he'd been toned down and abstracted, a faded photocopy. Now I was getting the real thing.

I swallowed, breathless, and looked up at his face. I was seeing a million new, tiny details now. It was as if my senses had been starving for him all this time, surviving on just distant glimpses, and now they were gorging themselves. I'd seen that strong jaw a thousand times, but I'd never noticed how the dimple set off all the iron hardness: I had the crazy urge to run my finger down his chin and press it. And that pouting lower lip, so arrogant.... I'd thought of him as looking like a king but I'd never appreciated just *how much:* there really was something regal about him, something grand and imperious. *King* didn't cut it.

I felt myself teetering on that cliff edge again. And all I wanted to do was step out into space.

He stared at me, his face hardening. But his eyes kept that faint hint of blue, that tiny touch of warmth, however much he tried to frown it away. I swallowed. *Emperor.* That described it better. Konstantin was like a Roman Emperor, lord of the entire freakin' world. And when he looked at me like *that,* there was some deep, shameful part of me that piped up *and I'm just a lowly...*

I pushed the thought away. I had *not* just thought *slave.* But the twisting, thrashing, squirming hot mess I was inside said otherwise.

"What?" he asked. Just one word but in that amazing Russian accent I knew so well from listening to his phone calls. It was even better in real life, an aural kiss, the long *w* like a press of the lips and the sharp *t* a lash of the tongue.

I pushed my glasses up my nose. My voice ran on autopilot. "I'm really sorry, but I have the room across the hall and I went out to go to the ice machine and the door closed behind me and I don't have my key. Could you please call reception for me?" I gestured down at my bathrobe. "I don't want to go all the way down there like this."

He frowned even more deeply. And then his gaze left my face for the first time and did a slow slalom down my body. When his eyes came back up, I swallowed. They'd gone glittering and hard, but absolutely blazing hot, gray-blue diamonds melting in a furnace. I glanced down.

Shit. I hadn't had time to belt the robe properly as I crossed the hallway. The belt had slipped completely undone and the two sides of the robe were just hanging. With his height, he could look straight down onto the upper curves of my breasts, revealed almost down to the nipples. And a slice of skin was visible all the way down my body: the valley between my breasts, my belly, my navel and then on down to—

Things fell off into shadow around there. I wasn't sure how much he'd seen. I grabbed the sides of the robe and tugged them firmly closed, then knotted the belt like I was securing a lifejacket. When I looked up again, his eyes were still blazing, but now they were... *disapproving.*

He didn't like that I'd covered myself. A hot rush of excitement sluiced down through my body. Then I went almost dizzy with the shock of it. *What's going on?* No one has ever looked at me, especially not a man. I've spent my entire life trying not to be noticed.

"Please?" I asked. Unexpectedly, that shameful heat twisted inside me again. Reacting to the sound of me begging him.

He didn't move back out of the way. But he leaned a little to one side and lifted one arm up, opening up a tight little doorway.

I squeezed through, my wet hair brushing the underside of his arm, my wrist sliding along his side. Beneath the thin cotton of his dress shirt, he was a wall of hard, hot flesh. I'd never known anyone so *solid.*

The first door we passed was the bathroom and I tried not to even glance at it. *Hold on, Calahan....*

I kept walking. There was a *whump* behind me as Konstantin closed the door and I faltered. That was it: I was sealed in here with him. What if he started to suspect who I was? What if he already *did* and he'd just wanted to lure me in here so that we were private? The fear came back. The urge to just turn around and bolt for the door was almost irresistible.

But if I wanted to save Calahan, I had to go further in. I had to get

Konstantin as far from the bathroom as possible. So on shaking legs, I carried on walking.

I entered the living area. The suite was huge and opulently furnished, with big leather couches, an open-plan dining area and three more doors that I guessed led off to bedrooms. No wonder it had taken Calahan a long time to search it. I walked right to the far corner. I needed to get Konstantin over there, too, so that he couldn't see the bathroom door. But he hung back, circling me at a distance. His eyes were still molten but there was caution there, too. Suspicion. "It's just you, in your room?" That accent...rough black rock carved by a razor-sharp blade until its surfaces shone like silver. "No husband? No boyfriend?"

I did what I always did when someone asked me that: I flushed, looked at the floor, and gave a little snort and a shake of my head, like, *don't be silly*. But when I focused on him again, he'd tilted his head to one side and was glaring at me, his eyes even hotter. Disapproving, again. As if he expected me to have a boyfriend. And he really, *really* didn't like me putting myself down.

I blinked at him in shock from behind my glasses. A slow-motion explosion of warmth was going off in my chest. The scariest guy in the world had somehow just made me feel better than any guy ever had.

I swallowed. "What about you?" I looked around. "This place is huge. Are you here with someone?"

He gave a slow shake of his head, still circling and watching me. "She is... indisposed." His English was perfect. If he'd wanted to, I think he could have gradually eliminated the Russian accent and passed for some CEO from Boston or New York. But I got the impression he had no desire to pass for anything. He was proud of what he was.

I looked into his eyes. Was he missing Christina? He didn't look sad, exactly, more frustrated that she wasn't there. Surely he must be worried, thinking of the woman he loved lying in some Italian hospital. A pang of guilt went through me. *Isn't this wrong?* We were lying to this guy. And soon, when Alison went undercover as

Christina, we'd be deceiving him on a whole new level. He was a criminal. The end justified the means... right? I pushed my glasses up my nose as I debated—

And saw him abruptly stop circling and just *look* at me. *What? What did I do?*

Whatever it was, it ended his suspicion. He marched across the room to me. Closer and closer. *Okay, he's going to stop now.* Closer. *Closer*—

He came to a stop with his calf pressed against mine. Leaned forward—

I held my breath.

He plucked the phone from the desk behind me and straightened up, leaving me red-cheeked and flustered. *What did you think he was going to do?!*

But he didn't back away as he made the phone call. He stayed right there, his leg touching mine, the heat of him throbbing into me. I listened as he explained to reception what had happened. *She's locked out of her room. 503.* I stood there drinking him in, seeing all the little details I'd always been too far away to make out. I'd known that he wore a ring on his right hand, for example, but now I could see it was old and worn, the engraved silver dark with age. The style of it didn't go with his crisp, modern clothes at all.

The receptionist must have asked him a question because Konstantin put his hand over the phone and said, "Name?"

And without thinking, I said, "Hailey Akers." I was almost embarrassed by it. It was as dull, as *normal* as *Konstantin Gulyev* was exotic and exciting.

And then it clicked that *I'd just told him my real name.* My stomach lurched and my skin flashed hot with panic. I'd make the worst undercover agent ever.

Konstantin hung up the phone, which involved leaning in towards me again and reaching around behind, his forearm gliding across my lower back. "A few minutes," he told me.

From across the suite, I heard a very faint *click.* The sound of the door to the hallway being very quietly closed. Calahan was out. I tried not to let out a huge sigh of relief. "Thank you," I told him. "I'll go wait outside my door."

Konstantin hadn't yet straightened up from replacing the phone. So when his head snapped up in surprise, he was suddenly looking into my eyes from less than a foot away. That frown that was becoming familiar, that scorching gaze: *that is* not *the right answer.*

He wanted me to stay. Even though he had a girlfriend. The idea rippled down through my body. *But you have Christina! She's beautiful and sexy and—* I was shocked and outraged and confused... and flattered.

And then he seemed to catch himself and he straightened up, tugging his shirt straight and gesturing towards the door. Leaving me to walk past him and show myself out, as if he didn't want to tempt himself by getting too close to me again. My heart was crashing against my ribs. *Me?* I'd never tempted anyone before. And I was weirdly relieved to find out he wasn't a cheater... as if that could possibly matter, given who and what he was.

I was so distracted that when he suddenly said, *wait,* I didn't pick up on the abrupt change in tone. I turned around and I think I actually smiled.

Then I saw the expression on his face. Something had just occurred to him, something awful. Something he didn't *want* to be true.

"What were you going to carry the ice in?" he asked.

I blinked stupidly. "What?"

He started walking towards me. I must have been imagining the blue in his eyes because all I could see now was merciless gray. "You were going to get ice from the machine when you got locked out. So where is the ice bucket?"

Shit. I opened my mouth, but nothing came out. My brain was scrambling for an explanation and finding none. "I—"

And that did it. Not the lack of an answer but the guilt that was clear in my eyes. He stormed across the room, closing the distance between us in huge strides. I twisted around and grabbed for the door handle—

His hand captured my wrist and I let out a scream as I was yanked backwards, right off my feet. Then he flung me against the wall and a second later his body was crushed against mine, pinning me there, each pant of anger pressing his pecs into my breasts. Those frozen gray eyes bored right into my soul.

"Who are you, *Hailey Akers?*"

4

HAILEY

THE FEAR. Oh, God, the fear. I'd blown everything. I shook my head, trying to deny everything, but that only made him angrier. He snarled and grabbed both wrists in one huge hand, trapping them against the wall high above my head. "What was the plan? Kill me? You have a knife under there, a needle?" He hooked his fingers under the belt of the robe and tugged and the knot came apart, the whole thing going loose around me. I struggled, flushing. "Or were you just here to open the door for a hitman?" He glared at me. "It wouldn't be the first time a pretty woman's tried to do that."

Pretty?!

He pressed my wrists harder into the wall. "*Who are you?!*" he roared.

I squeezed my eyes shut in terror. I wanted to weep because it was all so *wrong*. I'm not a sexy assassin or a hitman's girlfriend or even a proper FBI agent, I'm—

"*I'm no one!*" I sobbed.

The pressure on my wrists eased a little. When I opened my eyes, he was swimmy and blurry behind a film of tears. I blinked them away and saw the anger slowly fading from his face. For a second, his eyes were blue, gentler, than I'd ever seen them. "You really believe that, don't you?" he muttered.

I just panted and stared at him, stunned.

He had that look again he'd had in the hallway. *Fascinated.* He'd seen something in me that cut through all that coldness. I wasn't a threat, anymore.

He released my wrists, but he didn't step back, yet. My arms slumped down to my sides and that made the robe slide down over one shoulder. His eyes followed it, tracking over my shoulder, my collarbone, the slope of my breast.

Our breathing slowed, the adrenaline leaving us. And the mood shifted.

When his eyes flicked back up to my face, I saw that glittering, furnace-like heat again. I realized just how close our bodies were pressed. My breasts were pillowed against his chest. Our breathing had fallen into sync and every time we inhaled, the tight pressure, the rub of hard against soft, was almost unbearable, sending streamers of heat snapping and twisting down to my groin.

For the first time, both of us seemed to become aware that his leg was between mine. His clothed thigh was against my bare one and, even as I registered it, I could feel his cock hardening, thickening, the heat of it pressing against the very top of my inner thigh, the head of the bulge nudging up against my pussy lips. I swallowed, going weak. The heat was continuous, now, strumming faster and faster through my body, and every time it reached my groin I could feel it turning to slick moisture.

He glanced down again. The press of his chest was all that was stopping the robe from slithering the rest of the way down my arm and off. If he moved just a little....

He looked at me again. For an instant, he almost looked helpless. *Konstantin? Helpless?*

And then he closed his eyes and uttered some Russian curse under his breath. When he opened his eyes, he wouldn't look at me. He stepped back and, to my amazement, he very gently gripped the robe and pulled it back up my shoulder and into place. Then he took the two edges in his hands and wrapped them around me, and finally tied the belt in place, as carefully as if wrapping up a doll for Christmas.

When he'd finished, he stared at the floor for a second, those muscled shoulders rising and falling as he fought to control himself. Finally, he lifted his head and looked me in the eye. The cold was *almost* back, just a hint of stubborn blue remaining. "I am going to do something a man like me never does, Hailey Akers. I am going to apologize." He looked me right in the eye. "I am sorry."

And then he opened the door and gestured for me to leave. I was a teary, shaken, turned-on mess, but I didn't know what else to do, so I stepped out into the hallway. One of the hotel reception staff was approaching with a keycard to let me back into my room.

Konstantin's voice stopped me just as I reached my door. "Hailey?"

I turned around. His hulking body filled the doorway, one big hand gripping the frame. "I don't know why you were really in my room. But from now on, stay away from men like me."

He closed the door. A moment later, the woman from reception let me back into my room. And the very second my door was closed, Calahan grabbed me and pulled me into his arms.

For nearly a minute, he just hugged me, his arms locked around my back. My cheek was against his chest and I could feel how angry he was, his breath trembling on each inhale.

He suddenly pushed me back to arm's length, his hands gripping my upper arms so hard it hurt. *"Are you fucking crazy?"* he snapped. "Have you got *any idea* how dangerous that was?"

I'd never seen him so scared. I knew that was where the anger was coming from so I just nodded meekly. Then, "I wasn't going to leave you in there."

He glared at me. Cursed under his breath. Then he pulled me tight against him again, stooping a little so that his stubbled cheek was pressed to mine and I was looking over his shoulder. "You're okay?" he asked, his voice raspy with fear. "He didn't hurt you? He didn't...*do* anything to you?"

I shook my head, clutching him tightly. But my heart was booming in my chest. He'd done plenty to me. I was a wreck, scared and shocked and turned on and... *God, did that really happen?* Had I...*connected* with the guy we were meant to be bringing down?

He'd nearly kissed me. Hell, when he was standing there with his leg between my legs...I felt my face go hot, just at the memory of it. And I'd wanted him to. I *still* wanted him to.

I squeezed my eyes closed. *Idiot!* I was lucky to have got out alive. What I still didn't understand was why he'd let me go. What had he seen in me that made him soften?

I'd thought that I knew him, after watching him for two years, but I'd been utterly wrong. For a few minutes in that hotel room, I'd glimpsed a different man. One I didn't understand at all.

5

KONSTANTIN

I STOOD in the hallway of my suite, staring at the door without seeing it. I was seeing *her*, tracing the soft curve of her neck in my mind, seeing over and over again that sudden flash of half-nakedness when her robe had slipped open outside my door, that hypnotic valley between her breasts, leading my eyes right down to the shadowy curls between her legs.

With any other woman, I would have assumed it had been a deliberate move. A seduction. But with Hailey....

I'd never met anyone quite like her. She was so different to the preening, conceited women I usually met. I loved her shyness, her awkwardness, and the way she pushed her glasses up her nose was just *preléstnyj*—what the Americans would call *adorable*. The innocence, the *goodness* radiating off her was so strong, I could taste it. It was why I'd let her into my room. Why I'd had to work so hard to stop myself from just grabbing her and kissing her.

There's no better temptation for the devil than an angel.

But I'd held back. *Twice*. And God, the second time, when I could feel the warmth of her naked pussy caressing the head of my cock.... Pulling back from her had taken all the strength I had.

I told myself it was because I was faithful. And it's true: unlike a lot of Russian men, I don't cheat.

But I knew that was an excuse. Christina and I are together for convenience. A mutually beneficial arrangement. I don't love her and she certainly doesn't love me. The real reason I hadn't kissed Hailey, the reason I'd warned her away from me, went much deeper.

To build an empire like mine, you must be hard. Nothing but hard. I've seen the consequences of allowing innocence and love into your life. There must be no weakness.

And Hailey? I knew it. I could feel it.

Hailey made me weak.

6

HAILEY

I WAS NEVER meant to be in the FBI. My life started out on a completely different path.

I grew up in a little town in Wisconsin. My mom was a seamstress and ran a dress shop selling her handmade dresses. My dad was an artist who painted landscapes. We weren't rich, but we were happy, and lived in a rickety old house with a big garden that backed onto fields. I ran around barefoot in grass that came past my knees and made friends with the rabbits and birds. My mom was pretty, with long golden hair, and my dad had a prickly, dark brown beard and played the guitar under the stars. When I painted pictures of our family at kindergarten, I always knew I could make the color for my muddy brown hair by mixing their two hair colors together. I got my freckles from my dad, and my short sight. But I didn't inherit his artistic ability. No matter how hard I tried, I couldn't paint like him. "You just haven't found your thing yet," he used to tell me. "You will."

Then one night, when I was eight, my dad went out to pick up milk and didn't come home. The police arrived an hour later to tell us he'd been shot dead by a guy who'd robbed the convenience store.

It was like my mom's heart had been ripped out. For two years, she got thinner and paler, and I got more and more worried about her. Then a guy called Tanner stopped at the dress shop to ask directions, and everything changed.

They went out for three nights in a row, but then Tanner had to go: he lived in New York and had only been passing through. A week later, he was back, and then it was every weekend, and that unsettled me because I wasn't sure I trusted this guy. He drank, and he made jokes about everyone in our little town being bumpkins. And when he got mad, he'd yell and curse and kick stuff in a way that scared me. But my mom's face lit up whenever she saw him and I just wanted her to be happy. So I smiled and kept quiet.

Six months later, they were married. We sold everything except my dad's paintings and moved into Tanner's cramped New York apartment. The first evening, Tanner took us up to the roof, holding hands with my mom and grinning as we looked out over the city, but I remember feeling sick. Not just from the drop—I *hate* heights—but from the endless gray blocks around me. I couldn't see any green anywhere.

I hated my new school: I was the weird country kid. The only nature was a tiny neighborhood garden where the grass was yellow and crunchy, as if the city was making it ill, and all the kids stared at me when I took my shoes off.

Pretty soon, we realized that Tanner was into some bad stuff. He dealt some drugs and the apartment was full of stolen stuff he was trying to sell. He wasn't good at it, though, losing more money than he made. My mom opened a dress shop and somehow made it work, even in that lousy neighborhood, but there was still barely enough money to pay the rent. Then she got ill and the doctors diagnosed her with lupus. When it was bad, she couldn't work and money became even tighter. Tanner turned sour and resentful: his four nightly beers turned into six and then eight. He'd get wasted and yell at her.

And then the yelling turned to hitting. Black eyes she tried to hide with make-up. Cracked ribs that made it painful to breathe or talk. I hid in my room and looked up at the magazine pictures I'd used to paper the walls, far-off places like Colorado and Alaska, full of green and blue, and I tried to dream myself there.

When I was ten, my mom tried to leave him and run back to Wisconsin. Tanner caught us halfway and put my mom in the hospital, and told her he'd kill both of us if she tried to leave him again. He'd failed at being a criminal, failed at being a provider. He didn't want anyone to know he'd failed at being a husband, too.

A few weeks after that, Tanner rolled in drunk and collapsed into his armchair. He yelled for my mom to bring him a beer but she was in bed with a bad flare-up of the lupus, barely able to walk. I was in their bedroom, looking after her, and I saw her struggle to try to get up, gritting her teeth in pain—

"No," I told her, tears in my eyes. "No." And I pushed her back into bed and went out into the hallway, ignoring her protests. I went to the refrigerator and *I* brought Tanner his beer.

When he saw it was me, he cursed me, saying I was just as much of a waste of space as my mother. And when I got close enough, he hit me for the first time, an open-handed whack across the face that shook my teeth and made me see stars.

But from that night on, I brought him his beers and food, and cleaned the house. Anything to keep him away from my mom, who was getting sicker each day.

He hit me. He kicked me when I was down. Once, when I was thirteen, I dropped a hot skillet and it left a scorch mark on the linoleum. Tanner picked it up, pulled up my T-shirt, and pressed the hot edge of it against my side to teach me a lesson. I heard my skin sizzle like steak dropped into a pan. I knew I couldn't go to the ER, so I treated the burn myself, and I still have the scar. It *did* teach me a lesson, though. The less he saw and heard me, the less he hit me.

And so I became invisible. My self-confidence disappeared. Every day, I heard how worthless I was, the words driven into me with his fists. He laughed at my dreams of green, faraway places and ripped down the pictures I'd taped to my walls. I was glad I'd hidden my dad's paintings at the bottom of my closet or they would have been destroyed or sold. I retreated into myself, dressing in shapeless hooded tops and jeans, making myself as neutral and easy to ignore as possible. Boys looked right past me. Teachers forgot I was even in their class. I took a job at a grocery store to help with the bills: my mom was barely able to keep her store open, she was sick so much.

When I was eighteen, I went up to the roof of the apartment block. I was so lonely, so beaten down, I was at the point of jumping. But I was worried about my mom. If I left her alone with him, he'd start beating her again.

That's when I saw it, balanced right on the edge of the roof. A bird's nest, with a mother bird perched on the edge, feeding her young. It was the most beautiful thing I'd ever seen, and I was *so close:* the birds were completely unaware of me.

And I realized that my invisibility was good for something. I was so quiet, so unobtrusive, I could get closer to animals than anyone else.

I started to head out into the city, slipping unnoticed through abandoned buildings, finding bats and stray cats and mice to watch. Being around those little bits of wildlife was just enough to keep me sane.

One day, exploring a derelict factory, I found I wasn't alone. An old African-American guy, his hair gunmetal gray, was photographing the birds I was watching. I was cautious at first. I was amazed someone had even noticed me. But he was friendly and, over weeks and months, we became close. His name was Rufus and, back in the day, he'd been a war reporter. His apartment was covered in yellow, faded photographs of Iraq, Kuwait, and Sarajevo. He gave me one of his old cameras and, from the first moment I tried it, I was hooked. My invisibility meant I could get close to the animals I loved, and the camera meant I could share what I saw with the world. A few weeks in, Rufus looked at a photo I'd taken of a nest of newborn mice, cuddled up together for warmth. One had opened his eyes and peeked up at me and, reflected in those big, black orbs, you could see the New York skyline, the big bad city they were about to go out into. "You're a natural," Rufus told me. "You have an eye for detail."

I'd finally found my thing.

For two years, my life was protecting my mother at home, working at the grocery store to earn money for rent, and a few precious hours each day learning from Rufus. He asked about the bruises and I knew he was mad that someone was hurting me. But I also knew Tanner would kill him if they fought, and Rufus was becoming like a father to me, so I kept quiet.

Then, when I was twenty, Tanner died, stabbed in a bar fight. I knew I should be sad, but all I felt was relief, which made me wonder if I was a terrible person. I thought my life would change, but my mom and I were still stuck in New York: we didn't have the money to risk shutting down my mom's store and re-opening it back in Wisconsin. So I kept working, learning, looking after my mom, hoping one day I could get somewhere green again. I dreamed of becoming a wildlife photographer.

One night when I was at Rufus's apartment, there was a yell from outside. One of the local dealers was beating up a woman, right outside the door. When Rufus went to help, I grabbed his arm. He was almost seventy, for god's sake!

But he turned to me, one hand on the doorknob, and said, "Someone has to do something."

And before I could stop him, he ran outside and pulled the dealer off the woman. They rolled on the ground together, then the dealer got on top, raising his fists....

By the time the cops arrived, the dealer had run and so had the woman. And my friend and mentor was lying dead on the ground. The cops knew the dealer: everyone in the neighborhood did. But they claimed there wasn't enough evidence to bring him in. The truth was, they'd been taking bribes from him for years.

At Rufus's funeral, I was the only mourner. I stood there with rain mixing with my tears, the hot, bitter injustice of it filling me from the inside out until I thought I'd explode.

I wasn't brave. I was no one.

But someone had to do something.

So I took my camera and packed a bag with food and water. And for three days straight, I followed that dealer like a ghost, hiding in alleys and on rooftops, documenting his every move. My eye for detail let me get the little things that would make a difference: the scratches on his car that proved it was his, as he pulled away from picking up a package of drugs. The tattoo on his hand, as he handed over bribe money to the cops.

I sent the photos to the head of the Vice Unit, going over the heads of the bribed cops. A few days later, the dealer was arrested. But another dealer moved into his territory. People were getting hurt. Kids were being recruited to sell on street corners. And no one else in the neighborhood could do anything.

I began to take them down, one by one, hiding in the shadows and getting the photographic evidence the police couldn't and sending it anonymously to the Vice Unit. In six months, I helped bring down four dealers. I bought a burner phone that couldn't be traced back to me and gave the number to the police in case they needed to ask for more pictures of someone. But when it rang, it wasn't the police. It was a woman called Carrie Blake, and she worked for the FBI. She persuaded me to meet and, over coffee, she asked me if I'd like to come and work for them. "You have an amazing eye for detail," she told me. "And you get shots no one else can. How would you like to bring down some *really* bad guys?"

I knew I was nothing like an FBI agent. I wasn't brave, or heroic. But my mom's medical bills were piling up and the FBI paid a lot better than the grocery store....

So I went to work at the FBI's New York office as a specialist and met Sam Calahan, and Alison, and Gwen and Kate, and they were *real* FBI agents, cool and confident field agents who kicked down doors and pointed guns—even Kate, who was only a little thing of 5'2", but could take down a bad guy better than anyone. They tolerated my quietness and they all became friends, especially Kate, and I really missed her when she moved to Alaska.

Carrie became like a second mother to me and I worked hard, surveilling anyone she pointed me at. In my first year, I got the goods on every bad guy I was told to watch. I was good at my job, but I was still hiding behind a camera lens, invisible... and very, very lonely.

Then one day, Carrie showed me a grainy black-and-white

photograph of the most gorgeous man I'd ever seen. *This is Konstantin Gulyev,* she told me. *And you and I are going to bring the bastard down.*

For two years, I tried to do exactly that. I watched his every move, listened to his calls, but he was too smart, too careful: I couldn't get the evidence we needed to bring him down. And I started to find myself drawn to him. I couldn't understand why. He was a criminal, and criminals had killed or hurt everyone I'd ever loved.

Then there was Boston, and what happened in his hotel room.

And now, everything was different.

7

HAILEY

THE MORNING AFTER Boston, I needed three vanilla Americanos just to keep my eyes open. After we'd packed up my equipment, Calahan and I had made the long drive from Boston back to New York, but heavy rain and howling winds had slowed the traffic and what should have taken five hours took closer to seven. I'd only arrived home an hour before I had to get out of bed again and I'd spent that hour lying awake, going over and over what had happened in Konstantin's hotel room. I was still shaky from how close I'd come to getting killed. But there was that look I'd seen in his eyes, right at the end, when I'd told him I was no one.... At that moment, he'd stopped being terrifying. He'd seemed almost...*protective.*

And the way he'd looked at me, when we both realized his leg was between mine....

Under the covers, my hand had crept slowly down, over my stomach, and into my panties. It had started off slow and gentle, just a way to calm me down so I could sleep. But it gradually got faster and more urgent, little details driving my fingers faster and faster. The feel of his pecs against me, the way his muscled leg had spread my thighs, the hot hardness of his cock through his pants...

My heels dug into the mattress, my knees came up, and suddenly I was rocking and gasping, my thighs crushing my hand between them. And then, panting in the aftermath, *what the hell is wrong with me? This is Konstantin Gulyev!*

Now, slumped at my desk, I was struggling to stay awake. Calahan had been silently brooding all morning. I knew he was worried about Alison. We both were. She was at the hospital right now, and any minute the operation to transform her into Christina would be starting. Thanks to us failing in Boston, in a few weeks she'd be sent right into the lion's den.

I busied myself pulling together everything we had on Christina. Compared to Konstantin, we knew very little about her. She'd suddenly appeared in his life about four months ago, sexy and glamorous and always dressed in amazing designer clothes. I stopped for a second, staring at a photo of her and Konstantin as they prepared to board a private jet. That bit of my brain that noticed details was scratching at my mind, trying to tell me something was off, but I was too tired to figure out what I was seeing. I kept going and only stopped again when I came to a close up shot of Christina. She was gorgeous, but there was something about her I just didn't like, a cruelty in those clear blue eyes....

Wait, am I jealous? Is that why I don't like her? I felt myself flush and got on with my work. Alison was going to have to mimic every detail of this woman: the way she walked, the way she spoke. I started going through the most recent photos of Christina, taken by an Interpol team while she was in Milan. One, taken shortly before the crash, showed her climbing into the sports car, the wind lifting the back of her loose blouse to reveal—

I jumped to my feet, my eyes wide.

"What?" asked Calahan, immediately alert.

I grabbed my phone. "We have to call Carrie," I said as I dialed. "We have to stop the operation!"

He grabbed *his* phone and called the hospital, but the receptionist refused to pull Doctor Franklin out of an operation to come to the phone. And Carrie's phone went straight to voicemail. I knew she was at the hospital, keeping watch over Alison. The hospital must have made her turn it off.

I looked at the door. The hospital was less than a block away. "Keep trying," I told Calahan. And ran. I pelted down the stairs to the street and then along the sidewalk, dodging tourists and street food carts. By the time the huge, gray bulk of the hospital loomed up ahead of me, I was red-faced and panting, and wishing I'd joined Kate on all those runs through Central Park she used to do.

I asked a startled nurse which operating theater Doctor Franklin was in and then crashed through the doors. Everyone around the operating table looked up in shock. Masked and gowned, Doctor Franklin looked very different, but I'd have known those big, bushy white eyebrows anywhere. And yes, that was Alison on the table, her face a mess of marker pen lines.

"What the hell are you doing?" snapped Doctor Franklin. "Get out of here! You're not sterile!"

I leaned against the door. "*Stop,*" I panted. "Stop the operation!"

"What? Why?" Doctor Franklin looked towards a window for help and I saw Carrie standing on the other side, equally confused.

"Christina has a tattoo," I managed, still out of breath. "Low down on her back. We didn't know it was there."

Doctor Franklin sighed. "You came in here for *that?!* That's not a problem, we'll give Alison the same tattoo when we're done with the operation."

I shook my head. "But she already has a tattoo in the same place!"

Everyone froze.

"You're sure?" asked Doctor Franklin, after a few seconds.

I nodded. "About a year ago, some of us went to a karaoke bar and Alison danced on the table. Her top rode up and I saw."

Doctor Franklin cursed. "Help me roll her on her side," he told the nurses. They did, and when he lifted Alison's robe, we saw the tribal band she had across her lower back.

"What does Christina have there?" Carrie called through the window.

"A bird," I said forlornly.

"Could Alison's tattoo be removed by laser?" asked Carrie desperately. "And then the new one tattooed on?"

Doctor Franklin shook his head. "A tattoo that big would take a whole course of treatments to remove. There's not enough time."

A bang made everyone in the operating theater jump. It was Carrie, slamming her fist against the glass in frustration.

The whole undercover operation was off.

Back at my desk, I stared at my monitor without seeing it. Our once-in-a-lifetime chance was gone. Our only shot at taking Konstantin down.

We could go back to watching him, but I knew we were never going to get lucky. Konstantin was too damn smart. Carrie's plan had been our one chance to turn the tide. Now the FBI was going to lose, all because there were no female agents who could do the job. It had to be someone from our team: we were the only ones who knew Konstantin well enough to stand a chance of passing as Christina. Alison had a tattoo in the wrong place and Kate, even if we brought her back from Alaska, was way too short. And those two were the only women on the—

I suddenly caught sight of my reflection in my monitor and my heart seemed to stop.

No. No, that's insane.

But I was the same height as Christina. And the same build. And I didn't have any tattoos.

I can't be her. Christina was glamorous and cool. She was the center of attention everywhere she went. The complete opposite of me. *I could never pull it off.*

But.... I looked around. Not just our little team, but the whole of the floor looked despondent. Konstantin was going to cover this city like a black cloud, blocking out the sun. Another month, maybe, and he'd grow so powerful that the other crime bosses would be forced to fight him. New York would see the sort of violence it hadn't experienced since the 1930s. Hundreds of innocents would die. And when Konstantin eventually won—and I was certain he would—we'd be looking at a city run by a criminal. He'd have too much power for anyone to stop, even the FBI.

I thought of Rufus, my mentor, about to go outside. *Someone has to do something.*

But... *me?* I'd have to lie, constantly, every day. I'm a terrible liar. And even if I was the best liar in the world, how could I keep up the act with Konstantin when—

My skin went hot. When I felt like *this* about him?

And if I lost focus for one second, if I did something Christina wouldn't do, or *didn't* do something she *would* do, and he found out I was spying on him, he'd kill me. There'd be no mercy this time.

I imagined being in the mansion with him, cut off from my friends and with no backup, maybe for weeks or months. The fear hit me fully, then, like someone was pumping ice water steadily up through my veins. *This is Konstantin Gulyev we're talking about.*

A little voice inside me whispered, *no one has to know you thought of this.* Carrie hadn't even considered me for the mission. All I had to do was keep quiet and the mission would stay cancelled.

But...I'd know. When people started dying, when Konstantin took over... I'd know.

I forced my shaking legs to stand and walked to the elevator.

Carrie's office is right up on the top floor, which gave me far too much time to think. I nearly stopped the elevator three times and walking down the long hallway to her door was the hardest thing I've ever done. *This is crazy. I'm not brave enough to do this.*

By the time I reached Carrie's door, I didn't dare stop to knock: if I stopped, I'd just turn around and run. So I barged in and then stood there, eyes wide and chest tight.

Carrie was sitting behind her desk, in the process of unwrapping a sandwich. An antique clock was just chiming one. She looked up, startled. "Hailey?"

I couldn't speak.

She stood, trying to fill the awkward silence. "I always shut myself in here at this time and turn my phone off. It's the only way I get to eat." She walked over to the floor-to-ceiling windows of thick, bulletproof glass that formed one end of the room and looked out at the fantastic view of New York. "For five minutes, I just stand here. Reminds me what we're fighting for."

Today, though, she didn't look inspired. She looked defeated. She loved this city and its people and most of them never even knew her name, or the lengths she'd gone to to protect them.

If New York has a guardian spirit, it's Carrie.

And now she'd lost. She let out a long sigh and dropped her eyes to the floor—

"I can do it," I blurted.

Carrie turned to me and looked blank, which made me falter. That's how completely unsuitable I was: she didn't even understand what I meant.

"I can be Christina," I told her.

She cocked her head to one side... and then her jaw dropped. "You —" She looked me up and down and I could see the battle on her face. She wanted it to be possible but she also *didn't* want it to be possible. She's really grown to care about me. "No. No, I mean.... No, you're not tall enough."

"I am. I'm exactly the same height as Alison and Christina. They just wear heels and I... slouch." I stood up straight.

Carrie looked ill. She called in Doctor Franklin, maybe hoping he'd rule out the idea. But he cupped my head in his hands, felt my jawline, compared a photo of me to a photo of Christina..., and nodded. "It would work," he told us. "Any tattoos we should know about?" I shook my head. "Any scars?"

I froze. Calahan is the only one who knows about my childhood. We were working on a case involving children and one night I just broke down and told him everything. He got this fiercely protective look in his eyes and I think he would have gone straight out and hunted down my stepfather if he was still alive.

But if I was going to do this, they had to know. I lifted my suit jacket and my blouse to reveal the ugly burn scar on my side.

Doctor Franklin stooped and took a look at it. "Not a problem," he said cheerily, and scribbled something on a clipboard. "We'll say some hot metal burned you while they were freeing you from the wreckage."

Carrie's reaction was completely different. She must have read the pain in my expression because for a second, she looked as if she was going to wrap me up in a hug. She settled for taking my hand and squeezing it tight. She held my gaze for a moment longer and then sighed and shook her head, still undecided. "You have no undercover experience," she said. "You're not even a field agent."

"But I do know Konstantin," I said quietly.

"Hailey... you'd be his girlfriend. You'd have to—"

I flushed. "I know."

"Do you have a boyfriend?"

For a second, I flashed back to Konstantin asking me the same question. I shook my head. Men don't notice me... except him.

Carrie closed her eyes. "I—No. No, this is beyond crazy. No."

"It's the only chance we have," I said.

She stared at me for a moment, then whirled around and stalked over to the window, wrapping her arms around herself as if the view suddenly made her cold. "I can't ask you to do this," she said at last.

"You don't have to." I said. "I'm volunteering."

She turned and pinned me with a look. "Hailey, there's not a shred of compassion or warmth in that man. If he suspects, even for a second, that you're not Christina, *he will kill you.*"

I took a deep breath... and nodded.

Carrie pressed her lips tight together, deciding. Then she nodded. "Alright, then. We'll get the operation organized. You get down to the detention area. She just arrived. You better start getting familiar with her."

It was time to meet Christina.

8

HAILEY

I DIDN'T GO IN right away. I stood in the room next door to the interrogation room, watching her through the one-way mirror. How was it possible for someone to look that serene? Christina was sitting on a metal chair at a metal table, both of them bolted to the floor, in a featureless underground room. She was facing serious prison time for the drug charges. And yet she sat with her legs elegantly crossed, her chin resting on her perfectly-manicured fingers. She looked as if she was posing for a lifestyle magazine photo in the lobby of some luxury hotel. *I can never be like that.* I couldn't believe our bodies were even the same. If that was true, how come she could look so lithe and leggy, and I always felt so short and dumpy? And I was sure our breasts were different. Hers were small and pert and perfect, like some Hollywood actress's. I've always been self-conscious about mine because they're on the big side, for my frame.

My heart was hammering as I walked to the door that led into the interrogation room. I'd never interrogated anyone before. I understood why Carrie wanted me to do it: it was *me* who was going to have to impersonate her. Or maybe she was trying to make me see that I wasn't cut out for this at all.

I gathered up all my confidence and marched into the room, trying to do it like Calahan would. I needed to get answers out of this woman.

But as I crossed the room, Christina looked at me. Just a glance out of the corner of her eye, as if I wasn't worth turning her head for. Her eyes tracked up and down my body just once... and she gave a tiny sniff of disgust and looked away.

I faltered, mid-step, my face hot with shame. Suddenly, I was back in high school: the weird country kid who all the cool kids sneer at.

I steeled myself and walked over to the table. I couldn't let her intimidate me. I was going to have to *be* her.

But as I started to sit down, she nodded towards the mirror and said, in a clipped, polished accent, "How long were you watching behind that mirror before you plucked up the courage to come in?"

My face went hot all over again. My mouth opened stupidly, but I couldn't deny it. I'd completely lost all authority here. "My name is Hailey A—Akers. I need to ask you some questions about Konstantin."

She grinned and put her feet on the table. Her shoes were scarlet, the straps covered with tiny, glittering jewels and her legs were flawlessly smooth. Her voice was really something: moneyed and cultured, a razor dipped in honey. "I already told the Italian police, I don't know the details of his business."

Calahan had once told me that, to get a suspect to tell you something, you should lean forward like you're sharing a secret. I leaned in to her. "I want to know about your relationship with him."

She pushed her face close to mine. "*Do you?!*" she gushed, loudly enough to make me jump. "Do you want to know about my *relationship* with him?" She studied me again: my dry, dull hair, my cheap suit, and my flat shoes. "Is that the closest you get to a man? Do you want to take notes about Konstantin's *big, thick cock* plunging into me? Do you want to know how it feels when he's pounding me from behind?"

I couldn't look at her. I stared at the desk, my cheeks scarlet.

"Oh, look at you, that *is* it, isn't it? God, have you been fantasizing about him?" She leaned even closer and whispered. *"Does that get your poor little FBI pussy wet?"*

I leapt up from my chair as if burned.

"He's the most exciting thing to come your way in years, isn't he?" asked Christina. She mock-cried. *"Poor. Little. Haiiiiiiley.* All she wants is a man and she can't get one, so she rubs herself off thinking about what the *big, bad mafia boss* would do to her if he got his evil hands on her."

I drew in my breath but it went shaky and gulpy. I realized my eyes were filling with tears.

"Oh dear," said Christina innocently. "Did I hit a nerve?"

I very nearly ran. But if I folded now, I'd never have the strength to come back in here. I took two long, shuddering breaths. "Look," I said desperately. "I know you want to protect him. I get that you're loyal to the man you love, but you—"

"Love?!" Christina sounded genuinely bewildered for a second. Our eyes locked. Then she burst out laughing, her shrill peals ringing around the room. *"That's* what you think? You think it's all fluffy toys and walks in the rain?! You think I love him? You think he loves *me?"*

I tried to get her on my side. "You're beautiful. Why wouldn't he love you?"

She looked at me as if I was an idiot child. "Because a man like Konstantin isn't capable of love."

"Then why are you together?"

"Why do you think? It used to be a different woman every time, but then some girl played him, distracted him while her hitman boyfriend sneaked in. Having me is easier and safer."

"And you...."

"I get to live like a queen, Hailey. I get a bottomless credit card and shopping trips to Milan." She smirked at me. "You think I'm a cold-hearted, evil bitch?"

I hesitated, then nodded.

"That's what makes me perfect for him."

～

I walked out of the interrogation room still stinging from how she'd humiliated me and still trying to work out how the hell I was going to pull this off. She was sexy, glamorous, ruthless... I was nothing like her. She was the perfect match for Konstantin.

And the revelation that they weren't in love with each other! So it was just convenience, just about sex and money? I couldn't even imagine that sort of relationship and I was going to have to live it.

I headed up to the tenth floor, but slowed when I reached the hallway outside Carrie's office. I could hear a familiar, deep voice yelling. No, *bellowing*. Oh God. I could make out a quieter, more measured voice between the rants: Carrie. I could only make out the odd word but I heard my own name several times. There was a thump that sounded like a big, male fist coming down on a desk. That triggered a threat from Carrie about *gross insubordination* and then, as her voice rose, *exception this one time because you're clearly acting on personal feelings."*

I flushed.

Calahan stormed out of Carrie's office. As he passed me in the hallway, he spat one word from the corner of his mouth. *"Garden."*

I ran after him. *I should have talked to him first, as soon as I volunteered.* But I hadn't been able to face telling him. Some FBI agent I was.

The garden is where Calahan and I go when one of us has had a bad day. It's a big, oddly-shaped section of neatly-mown grass with a monument in the center. There's no shade or trees or benches, it's designed to be ornamental rather than a place to hang out. But in summer, if you don't mind getting some funny looks, you can sit on the ground, close your eyes and feel the grass against your fingers and it's a little bit like being back in Wisconsin.

Now, though, it was fall and the sky was an ugly gray. I pulled my jacket tight around me: it was too cold to be outside. But the garden had another advantage: it was private.

Calahan had managed to bottle up his rage all the way there. Now he finally unleashed. "You're out of your fucking mind!" he snapped.

"I know what I'm doing," I told him. I was pretty sure that was a lie.

"This is *Konstantin*. He scares the other crime bosses. He scares *me*." He grabbed my wrist and hauled me with him as he stalked across the grass to the monument. "Look. *Look!*"

I looked. The monument is a big slab of black marble with a list of names etched into it in gold. The names of agents who've fallen in the line of duty. "You want to be one of them?" he demanded.

I relived the sickening fear when Konstantin had grabbed me and pinned me against the wall: the brute strength of him, the coldness in his eyes. I felt myself crumpling. Of course this was a mistake. I needed to tell Carrie I was backing out.

But if I did that, we'd lose this fight. We'd lose our city. And all those people who died in the coming gang war... that would be on me.

Someone had to do something. I was the only one who could.

I turned to Calahan. "If it was a guy they wanted to impersonate, and you were a match, would you do it?"

He sighed in exasperation and glared at me. But one thing Calahan always is, is honest. "Yeah," he said at last. "But I'm *me*. You're...."

He looked away, glaring off into the distance for long seconds. "You're my friend," he said at last.

I reached up and pulled him down to me and he wrapped me up in a hug.

Back upstairs, Doctor Franklin started talking me through the operation. "We need to shave the bone a little here," he said, drawing on my nose with a magic marker. "And your chin needs to come in just a touch." He was almost gleeful and I found it unnerving. *I'm just a project, to him.*

"Will it be... permanent?" I asked.

He tilted his head to one side as if he hadn't even considered that.

"Some of the changes *could* be reversed, in theory. But with each surgery, there's a risk of weakening the underlying bone structure...."

I nodded, feeling ill. I was going to look like Christina forever. Why did that bother me? It wasn't as if I was pretty.

"We'll tweak your cheekbones," said Doctor Franklin, still drawing. "And... *here* and *here* and... *there!*"

He handed me a mirror and my stomach lurched. My face was a mess of marker lines. I could barely see *me,* anymore.

I glanced down, remembering something. "I, um...I think my breasts are bigger than Christina's," I said awkwardly.

Doctor Franklin shook his head.

I bit my lip. He was the doctor, but I knew my own body. Her hips and waist might be the same, but I swore I was at least a cup size bigger. "Maybe we should check—"

"I assure you," he said stiffly, "You're exactly the same."

I nodded meekly.

"You'll need laser eye surgery," he told me. "Christina has 20/20 vision."

I hadn't even considered that. No more glasses.

"At the same time, we'll use a different laser to destroy the brown pigment in your eyes, turning them blue."

There was a sudden, unexpected wrench, deep inside me. My dad had always loved my brown eyes, saying they matched my mom's. "Okay," I said in a voice that didn't sound like mine. "That's fine."

For three days, while Doctor Franklin made his preparations, I sat behind the one-way mirror and watched Christina. A whole host of FBI interrogators tried to question her, but none of them could get anything useful out of her. I didn't understand why she was being so loyal to Konstantin, since she didn't love him. Fear of what he'd do to her?

I put my weird brain to work, noticing the details that made her *her:* the way she ran her hands through her hair when she was thinking, the way she walked, slinking around the room, trying to distract the male interrogators with her ass. Out of sight of everyone, feeling ridiculous, I started to mimic her.

At first, I had no luck imitating her voice. She'd grown up in a very respectable Boston neighborhood, a long way from Wisconsin. Her accent shone like a polished scalpel, making mine feel clunky and dull. Then there was the confidence: where I mumbled and *umm*ed, the words poured from her mouth easily, seductive and teasing one moment, cruel and cold the next.

But one thing I've always been is patient. I recorded her talking, put on some headphones and played it on loop with my eyes closed, repeating each sentence as if I was learning a language. And slowly, very slowly, my tongue learned the new shapes of words.

The mimicry became almost abstract, like a game. I almost forgot why I was doing it. Then, on the morning of my operation, something happened that brought it all home to me.

Carrie called me aside and pressed a rectangle of foil into my hand. "We found these in Christina's luggage," she told me. "I thought you should know, in case you needed to make an appointment with your physician."

I looked down at my hand. It took me a few seconds to recognize them as birth control pills. "Mm-hmm," I said, all cool professionalism. "Thank you."

But when I walked away, my legs were shaking. Suddenly, it was all real: I'd be having sex with Konstantin. And not the tentative, *let's take it slow,* step-by-step sex of a new couple. He thought we'd been lovers for months. He'd expect me to just jump into bed and—

Heat mingled with fear rippled down my body and I had to stop and lean against the wall for a second. *Am I really going to do this?*

At that moment, Calahan ran up to me, holding a phone. "We've got a problem," he said. "Konstantin called the hospital in Italy, demanding to speak to Christina. The doctors have told him she's about to have surgery, but he's insisting. Says he'll send someone over there if he doesn't get to speak to her."

"We could let him speak to Christina," I said. "Tell her to say everything's fine."

But Calahan grimly shook his head and I realized he was right. Once she had the phone, we wouldn't be able to stop her shouting a warning to him. She didn't know our plan, but she could tell him she'd been arrested. That would blow the whole thing. But what other choice did we have?

Calahan held out the phone.

My eyes bugged out. "*No!* I'm not ready!"

"You have to! We're blown if you don't!"

I stared at him in horror... and then nodded weakly.

Calahan muttered into the phone: "*Put him through.*" Then he handed it to me and I ducked into a side room where it was quiet. A click. A hiss.

And then I was speaking to Konstantin.

9

HAILEY

I ONLY HAD a second or two. I willed my throat and lips into Christina's cool, precise voice. "Hello?"

I thought that it would be the same as speaking to him at the hotel. I'd forgotten that then we were strangers; now, we were lovers. His low voice rumbled from the phone's speaker directly into my ear and from there straight down to my groin, shockingly intimate. Three words that were so normal, but he made them a confession, a grudging admission of... *weakness?* "I've missed you."

I swallowed and closed my eyes, trying to focus on shaping the words correctly. "I've missed you, too."

His voice tightened with anger. "The doctors wouldn't let me speak to you."

"I'm about to have surgery," I told him. "I won't be able to talk, while it heals. But once I'm healed, I'll be able to come home."

"I've been remembering the night we met." Oh God, that *voice.* I knew I needed to focus, but it was so easy to get lost in that Russian accent. *Remembering* was like a string of pearls, the silky bump of each *m* caressing my brain. Then the hard fall of each *t,* like a playful slap on the ass. His voice always had a physical effect on me, but when he spoke like *this,* low and growly and intimate, it was taken to a whole new level. I realized I was crushing my thighs together.

And then I had a horrible thought: I had no clue what happened, the night they met. *Shit!*

"You looked so small, by the side of the road," murmured Konstantin. "So lost." His voice tightened for a second. "Your boyfriend...."

I was piecing the story together as quickly as I could. Christina's boyfriend must have dumped her there, and Konstantin found her. "My boyfriend was an asshole," I told Konstantin. That felt like a safe response.

"He didn't know what he had. But I did. As soon as we got home... do you remember what I did to you?"

"Of course I do."

"Tell me," he said, his voice urgent with lust.

Shit! I had no idea. I flailed around for an excuse. "It's not very private here," I lied. "There are doctors all around me."

I could almost see his brow furrow. "That never bothered you before. You *like* people listening."

Great. Of course sexy, confident Christina would be an exhibitionist. In desperation, I tried the truth. "I'd rather hear *you* say it," I told him. "You know I love your voice."

There was silence for a second and I wondered if I'd slipped up. But then, "First of all, I stripped off your clothes. Your dress in the lounge. Your bra on the stairs. Your panties, I tore off on the bed."

I swallowed. *"Mm-hmm."* I knew I had to concentrate. One slip and he'd realize something was wrong. But his voice was rough chunks of black rock floating on a stream of molten silver. It coursed straight down my body, pooling between my legs. God, I could *feel* his big hand tearing at my panties, the elastic stretching and then snapping.... I pressed my thighs hard together and leaned back against the door.

"I took hold of your ankles and pushed them *up* and *back.*" He emphasized the word and I could almost feel myself opening, feel the cool air of the room hitting my folds. "I took your breasts in my hands and rubbed, very slowly, back and forward, until your nipples were scraping my palms."

My cheeks were scarlet, my breathing tight. I could feel the heat, throbbing between my thighs, turning to slick moisture. I knew he was describing *her,* not *me,* but it didn't matter. With his voice, it *was* happening to me... right now. I could feel the rough touch of his hands on my breasts and under my bra I could feel the nipples tightening and rising—

"I put my face between your thighs and I started licking you. Just the tip of my tongue, parting those lips—"

I glanced around the room. I was alone and there were no windows.... *No. Jesus, no, don't be stupid, I'm not going to—*

"Then I pushed deeper."

Deeper, said in that accent, was almost a penetration itself. It seared into my mind, making me gasp. The heat in my groin became a needful ache. Crushing my thighs together wasn't enough.

"Tasting you, plunging up into you while my hands squeezed your breasts."

I glanced down at myself. *No!* I was in the middle of the FBI building, of course I couldn't—

"I licked at you until you arched your back off the bed and came. And I made you come again and again. Until you begged me. Until you screamed and kicked and sobbed and *begged* me to fuck you."

The ache in my groin was almost painful. I squeezed my hands into fists. "*Mm-hmm.*"

"And then, only then, did I put my cock against you. Do you remember how soaking wet you were? I put the head against you, and you were *tight,* you weren't used to me and you weren't sure you could take me."

Oh God. I hauled my skirt up my thighs.

"But you *did* take me. All of me. Right. Up. Inside. You."

I plunged my hand into my panties and started to rub myself.

"And I fucked you slow and deep and then hard and fast. Until you clawed at my back and screamed. Until I felt your tight little pussy clench around me as you came for me."

I pressed my lips tight together, but I couldn't make my climax completely silent. It came out as a guttural sound in my throat, a helpless, shameful admission. I folded forwards at the waist, my hand trapped between my thighs, rocking and rocking against my slick fingers as I rode it out. By the end of it, I was so shaky-legged, I could barely stand.

I realized he'd gone silent. He was listening. He knew exactly what I'd been doing. I drew in a long, shocked breath. *Did I really just do that?* I hadn't intended to.... I frantically pushed my skirt back into place. *God,* the control he had over me, just with that voice....

"Go and have your surgery," he told me. "Get well. And come back to me." And he hung up.

10

KONSTANTIN

I HUNG UP and stood for a moment at the window. The mansion's overgrown gardens were below me, but I didn't really see them. I was thinking about Christina. About my weakness.

It was at night that I missed her most. In sleep, it's more difficult to maintain control. Before Christina, even with vodka to knock me out, I used to have vague, troubling dreams: cold, black water that sucked me down and leached the warmth from my body until there was nothing left.

I'd fuck women for the release, but I wouldn't let any of them share my bed and I wouldn't ever see the same woman twice. That would be weak.

Then I found Christina by the side of the road and took her back to the mansion. It was only ever meant to be a one night thing. But after sex with her and a shared vodka, I dropped into a sleep so deep, the dreams couldn't reach me, so deep I was still sluggish and groggy the next morning.

By pure chance, I'd met my ideal partner. Christina was as cold and ruthless as me. Cruel, even, in ways that I wasn't always comfortable with, and jealous. But those qualities meant she had no problem with who I was and what I did. She even seemed to relish my reputation. She didn't love me and I didn't love her. She didn't need conversation or romance, she didn't care that I shut myself in my office all day, tending to my empire. She didn't mind my obsession, my taking New York street by street, neighborhood by neighborhood, grabbing more and more and *more* power, anything to fill that yawning, black void where my heart used to be.

We were perfect for each other. And so I asked her to stay. I knew I'd never be close to her, because I'd never be close to anyone. But I gave her money and clothes and she seemed satisfied with that.

Since she'd been away, the dreams had returned. I knew that needing her—needing anyone—was a weakness, but I couldn't help it.

Talking to her on the phone, hearing her breathing tighten as she rubbed herself, had left me iron-hard in my pants. Getting through the next three weeks was going to be hell.

When she came back, she'd better be ready. Because the moment, the *very second* her plane landed, I was going to race back to the mansion with her and hurl her on the bed.

11

HAILEY

I T WAS TIME for the operation. I was perched on the edge of a bed in a hospital gown, waiting for Doctor Franklin. Calahan sat in a chair next to me, holding my hand, and brooding.

I looked in the mirror on the wall. *This is the last few minutes I'll ever be Hailey.* I was trying to contain my panic, but as the minutes passed, it rose higher and higher in my chest. When it reached my mouth, I suddenly blurted, "It's just a disguise, right?"

Calahan had been glowering at the floor. His head snapped up to look at me.

"Just like wearing a mask," I reasoned, but my voice was cracking. *One I can never, ever take off.*

Calahan jumped to his feet and put his face close to mine. *"Tell them,"* he ordered. "Tell them you've had second thoughts. This is *fucking insane!* You don't have to do this!"

All of the doubts I'd been nursing bubbled up inside me. This *was* insane. I wasn't even a field agent. I couldn't impersonate someone as glamorous and sexy as Christina. The attraction to Konstantin made this even more dangerous. To pull this off I'd have to stay objective and detached and how could I do that when he could just look at me and make me melt? One mistake and I was *dead*—

Doctor Franklin burst through the door, followed by an anesthetist. "Sorry we're a little late," he said cheerfully. "Let's get started."

Calahan squeezed both of my hands, hard, and gave me a pointed look.

I opened my mouth....

And thought of all the people who'd die in a gang war, if Konstantin wasn't stopped.

I swallowed.

And lay down on the table.

The anesthetist swabbed my arm and I felt the prick of a needle. "Count backwards from ten," he told me.

I reached seven, Calahan's worried face blurring and distorting in front of me.

And then nothing.

12

HAILEY

I SPENT FOUR DAYS in a fog of heavy painkillers, my whole face swathed in bandages and tubes in my nostrils to make sure the swelling in my new nose didn't suffocate me. At one point, the coverings over my eyes were briefly removed and a machine shone a vivid crimson light into them. Then darkness returned.

At last, the fog seemed to lift. I was aware of being sat up and then the bandages were being unwound from my face, layer by layer. I opened my eyes. Everything seemed blindingly bright, after so long in the dark, but then it settled and snapped into clear, crisp detail. Doctor Franklin was leaning over me, brushing his fingertips down my cheeks, and smiling with satisfaction. Calahan was there, looking grim. Carrie, too.

"Everything worked," said Doctor Franklin. "And you're doing fine."

I nodded. "Can I see?"

He passed me a hand mirror.

I brought it up to my face and—

Wrong.

Wrong on an instinctual, primal level. *Wrong wrong wrong wrong wrong.*

It was as if reality had skipped sideways, like a train jumping onto a different track. For twenty-five years, I'd looked in mirrors and seen *me*. Now someone else was looking back at me from the glass and the raw shock and loss was like being punched in the gut. I'd lost *me*. My ears were ringing and I realized I was screaming, and couldn't stop. *Where was I?!*

Calahan grabbed one arm. Doctor Franklin grabbed the other, brisk and efficient where Calahan was tender. Behind them, Carrie had one hand over her mouth, her face pale.

"Hailey, you're having a normal reaction to major facial surgery," Doctor Franklin told me. "Try to breathe."

I flung the mirror away and heard it shatter. Tore free of their hands and jumped out of bed, staggering on legs that hadn't walked in days. *"Put it back!"* I screamed. I backed up against the wall. *"Put it back! Put it back! Put it back!"* I wanted to claw at my new face, shred it and split it and pray I was still there, underneath.

"I'm going to give you a sedative," Doctor Franklin told me, sounding panicked. Then, to Calahan, "Hold her!"

Calahan's strong hands gripping me. A scratch in my arm.

And then nothing.

13

HAILEY

THE NEXT DAY, when I'd slept off the sedative, I asked to be allowed home, saying that I felt much calmer. Calahan wasn't fooled and wound up having another screaming match with Carrie in the hallway outside my room, but she and Doctor Franklin overruled him and discharged me. They wanted to believe I was okay.

At first, when I got home, I was jumping every time I caught my reflection in a computer monitor or a glass door. The sickening, violent *wrongness* of it surged up inside me and I'd almost have a meltdown. But the human brain is scarily adaptable. After just a few hours, the reactions started to taper off. When I went to bed that night and saw my new face in my water glass, it was barely a jolt at all.

That was almost scarier than freaking out.

The next morning, I groped for my glasses and couldn't find them. I opened my eyes to search for them...but everything was already sharp. That's when I remembered I didn't need them, anymore. It should have felt liberating but, as I put them away in a drawer, I couldn't help feeling a pang of loss.

Carrie had sent over Christina's luggage from her trip to Italy. There were four cases and every one was filled with eye-wateringly expensive clothes from top designers: dresses and blouses, sweaters and skirts...God, even her underwear was gorgeous. I tried on a dress as a test. With a bit of wiggling, it slid on fine over my lower half. But... *crap.* I'd been right. My breasts were bigger than hers. Everything was going to be a little tight, and some of the low-necked stuff would be a no-no unless I wanted to pop out of it. It wasn't Doctor Franklin's fault: I could imagine Christina posing like a model, expertly thrusting out her boobs to make them seem bigger than they were, while he flushed and mumbled. And meanwhile, I did my best to hide my bust under shapeless clothes. No wonder he'd overestimated her and underestimated me. But what if Konstantin noticed?

One whole case was full of shoes, most of them towering heels I was going to need practice to walk in. I picked up a pair at random and—

Oh, no....

I tried another pair, but they were no better. Christina was a full shoe size smaller than me.

No one had thought to measure our feet. *Shit!* How could all of us have missed something so obvious? I could buy a few replacement pairs for now, but when I got to the mansion, none of Christina's shoes were going to fit. I slumped down on the couch, my heart hammering in my chest. *What else haven't we thought of?* If I messed this up, if I was even a little off in my portrayal of Christina, Konstantin would know.

On my way to work, I had my hair dyed black and cut and styled just like Christina's. With my newly-blue eyes, the effect was uncanny.

When I arrived at Calahan's desk, he glanced up and then jumped to his feet. It was the first time he'd seen the full effect and he actually reached for his gun, thinking Christina had somehow escaped. Then he just stared at me sadly.

"Not bad, right?" I quipped. "Now I can find out what it's like to be a ten."

His mouth tightened. "You were—"

I frowned, curious.

He looked away and shook his head. "Nothing." He waved his hand at the dress, the hair, the whole thing. "It's good. You look just like her." And he turned and stalked away.

For the next two weeks, I practiced moving like her, laughing like her, tossing my hair like her. I immersed myself in Christina and wouldn't let myself surface, like an actor who won't come out of character. It was the only way I could do it in time. We called in a hair and makeup expert and she coached me on how to use the high-end products Christina used. The upkeep was going to be a nightmare, but I had to get used to it. A tattoo artist came in, his jeans and t-shirt incongruous in the FBI offices, and I knelt astride a chair, wincing, while he tattooed a bird on my lower back. My freckles were removed to give me Christina's flawless complexion.

I worked on my posture, trying to walk upright and proud, with my head held high. I made my movements languid and seductive, instead of awkward and jerky. As I moved around the building, men from other departments—men who'd seen me a hundred times as Hailey and ignored me—tried to chat me up. *Is this what it's like to be beautiful?* But that wasn't all that was going on. I was holding myself differently, making eye contact....

I wasn't hiding, anymore.

It felt *wrong.* I was in a constant state of panic. How dare I be the center of attention? Any second, everyone would realize I was faking it, they'd see I was no one and laugh at me. But I forced myself to keep going.

On the morning I was due to enter Konstantin's life, my phone rang.

"Hello?" I said.

Silence from the other end. Then, tentatively, "Hailey?"

Oh, shit! It was my mom, and I was still doing my Christina voice. I switched back to Hailey and—

For a sickening moment, I couldn't find Hailey's voice. After weeks of that polished, precise voice, I'd forgotten what I sounded like. Then it clicked into place. "Mom!"

"Are you alright? You sounded different."

I couldn't tell her. I couldn't even hint at what I was doing. Losing my dad had torn her apart. If she thought I was in danger, too.... "I'm fine. Getting over a cold. Listen, I have to go on a training course. A few weeks, maybe a month...."

I told her I'd make sure to put enough money into her bank account to cover any medical bills while I was away. Things were tight: the bills were brutal and my FBI salary wasn't high. It made Christina's lavish lifestyle seem sickening. I was going to be living like a billionaire, but at the same time, I could barely take care of my mom.

Calahan arrived with my plane tickets. Konstantin was expecting to see me get off a flight from Italy so I had to fly there, then fly back to New York and meet him at the airport.

He passed me a tiny earpiece, no bigger than a grain of rice, and helped me glue it out of sight inside my ear. "There'll be someone at the other end of this twenty-four seven," he told me. "And most of the time it'll be me." I nodded gratefully.

He showed me Christina's luggage and then the secret compartment he'd fitted into one of the cases. Inside was my FBI ID and a gun. "Just in case things go south," he told me.

I blanched. I'd never even fired a gun. Calahan patiently took me through how to handle it and aim it, while I watched and nodded and tried not to sound terrified. If Konstantin found me out, would I even have time to grab it?

Being Calahan, he insisted on driving me to the airport. We took the elevator down to the lobby, started across it and—

"*Shit!*" He tried to push me back into the elevator, but the doors had already closed. *What? What had he seen?*

And then an ear-splitting scream broke the air. I spun around and—

Another of those horrifying reality shifts. The floor seemed to lurch, the room spun. I was looking at *myself, but* it wasn't a mirror—

Christina. The real Christina. She was being led across the lobby in handcuffs, one agent holding each arm. And she was staring at me just as I was staring at her.

"*What are you doing?*" bellowed Calahan at the agents. "Take her out the back, assholes!"

But the damage was done. Christina had paled for a second, but now her face was coloring with anger. "*No!*" She sprang towards me and the two agents had to fight to haul her back. "*You can't do this!*"

"Get her out of here," yelled Calahan. "Now!"

The two agents dragged her away but they couldn't stop her screaming over her shoulder, her eyes locked on me. "You think just because you look like me, he'll think you're me? He'll *know,* you bitch! He'll *know!*"

And then she passed through the doors and was gone. Calahan and I stood there panting, shaking with adrenaline. "They must be moving her into protective custody," Calahan said. "We can't put her in jail until we arrest Konstantin: she might talk to someone and word could get back to him. I'm sorry. I had no idea they'd bring her out this way." He put a gentle arm on my shoulder. "It doesn't matter that she knows. There's nothing she can do about it. She's going to be in a safe house with a couple of guys watching her until you're safely home."

I nodded, but I couldn't speak. I wanted to throw up. What if she was right? What if Konstantin *could* tell?

Outside, we found Carrie leaning against Calahan's car. She motioned for him to give us a moment and he moved a short distance away.

Carrie looked downtown, towards the swathe of territory Konstantin controlled. Then she turned a slow circle: all the territory he *would* control. "We need to stop him," she murmured. "To save this city, we need to stop him. And I want this guy, Hailey, I want to bring him down *so much....*"

I nodded.

She took a deep breath and turned to me. "But."

She left it at that one word, but I understood what she was saying. She was giving me one last chance to step back from the brink.

But it was too late. I reached up and stroked my new face. "I already...."

She shook her head and took my chin between thumb and finger, her grip surprisingly firm. "You've got her face, but you haven't *done* anything, yet." She stared into my eyes. "Hailey... are you sure?"

I drew in a deep, shuddering breath and thought of all the innocents who'd die if Konstantin went unchecked. I looked Carrie in the eye and nodded.

She pressed her lips tightly together, looking for a second like a tearful, proud mother. "Just don't forget who you are, okay?" And she turned away, wiping at her eyes.

At the airport, Calahan pulled up outside the doors and we sat for a second, looking at each other. I'd be able to talk to him through my earpiece, but this was the last time I'd see his face until I was extracted and that might be weeks—maybe months. We nodded to each other, both of us too worked up to risk a proper goodbye. I climbed out of the car and—

"Hailey!"

I turned around. He'd lunged across the passenger seat and thrown open the door. For long seconds he just stared into my eyes, knuckles white where he gripped the door.

"Just... be careful, okay?" he muttered.

I nodded. And walked away.

Two hours later, I was on an economy flight to Italy. When we landed in Rome, I booked a first class ticket back to New York on Christina's credit card. Then I took out Christina's phone and texted Konstantin with my flight details. A text came back within seconds. *I'll meet you at the airport.*

The flight was a culture shock: artfully-presented food on real china plates, glasses of champagne, bags of high-end toiletries, all brought to my huge leather armchair of a seat. It felt so unfair: if I'd flown economy, the difference would have covered my mom's medical bills for months. But Konstantin would get suspicious if he looked at Christina's credit card bill and saw an economy flight, or the medical bills of some unknown woman.

I cleared customs, getting steadily more nervous with each step. *This will work,* I kept telling myself. I looked just like her. I walked just like her. None of *me* showed through the Christina shell I'd built, and even if it did, no one ever notices me.

I was walking into the arrivals hall when I saw him. He had four bodyguards with him, all of them tall and heavily muscled. But somehow, all that protection didn't make him look small, or weak. He was bigger than any of them, both in size and in presence. A slate-gray suit set off the light gray of his eyes, the expensive fabric stretched tight over that broad, hard chest. He looked *amazing.*

And then he saw me. And instead of waiting for me to get to him, he marched straight towards me, against the flow of passengers. The crowd broke either side of him like a river hitting a rock. Then he reached me and when I saw the raw hunger and need in his eyes, I went weak. I only just had time to let go of the luggage trolley as those big hands closed around my waist and he lifted me off the ground—

And froze.

He stood there holding me, our faces less than a foot apart, and the sea of people around us forgotten. He studied my face, my eyes... and frowned.

He knows.

14

HAILEY

I T WAS TOO LATE to run. He had me, those big hands holding me in the air like a toy. He could snap my neck in a heartbeat or bundle me into a car and take me off to interrogate me. The mission was over before it had begun. I stared back into those cold gray eyes, unable to breathe—

And then his eyes changed. That hard, glittering heat I'd seen in his hotel room. He *did* know something was different.

And he liked it.

His eyes narrowed. He dipped his head. *Oh God! He's going to—*

And then the lips I'd been dreaming about for two years were coming down on mine.

The first kiss was quick... or it was meant to be. Just a taste, a teaser for the main event. But as soon as that hard upper lip brushed against my softness, something happened. It was as if a million pink butterflies took flight in my chest, diving and wheeling through my body. I *melted.* Then that soft lower lip was dragging across mine and a low moan escaped my throat. I clutched at his arms, my whole body thrashing in his hands.

He drew back and I opened my eyes. I felt *drunk.* I'd been expecting hard, brutal lust, not...*that.*

Those gorgeous gray eyes regarded me from six inches away. His head tilted suspiciously and he brushed a finger across his lips. *Neither had he.* His hands hardened on my hips. He glowered at me with sudden doubt and confusion....

... and then lust.

He made a sound I'll never forget, a growl that came right from his chest like a beast who's caught the scent of its prey. One hand shot up between my shoulder blades. The other slid round to my ass. Suddenly I was tipped backwards, my hair flying out and my dress flaring up. I came to rest almost lying across his thigh, looking up at him. I'd been *swept off my feet,* like some Russian countess in a historical romance, just before the hero—

I drew in my breath just as his lips found mine again.

This time, it was different. It was urgent, almost violent. He needed me, *now,* his lips searching and pressing, spreading me open. I melted in a whole different way, opening and responding, lost. The hand on my back roved up through my hair and held the back of my head, silken strands tangling in his fingers as we twisted and moved. His tongue traced the edge of my lips and then plunged inside, finding mine and leading it into a dance. I'd never been kissed like this before: he was so knowing and confident. And the more I weakened, the more I gave myself up to it, the more turned on he got. I could feel it in the way his hand kneaded my ass, the way he pulled me against his chest. I was his without question. He was utterly in control. And yet somehow, at the same time... I was making him *lose* control.

My hand slid up over his stubbled cheek, exploring him. My fingers slid into his hair, pushing it back from his forehead—

And I felt something there. The raised line of a scar, slashing diagonally across his forehead, hidden by his hair—

He grabbed my wrist and pulled my hand away. *Something he doesn't want to be reminded of.* I explored his body, instead, running my hands over his back, his shoulders....

He finally broke the kiss and stood there panting, staring down at me. His eyes were hooded with lust, but there was anger there, too.

Shock, at how he'd lost control. For a second, I thought he was going to hurl me aside, that I'd displeased him.

Then he pulled me upright and put an arm around my waist. "We're leaving," he told his bodyguards, and they fell smoothly into formation around us, two in front and two behind.

The kiss had brought the arrivals hall to a standstill and now we were surrounded by gawping onlookers. I was hotly aware of the hundreds of eyes on me. I'd never felt so on display and all I wanted to do was run and hide. But what made it bearable, what made me feel safe, wasn't the four hulking bodyguards around us. It was Konstantin's arm around my waist. As we started to walk, he held me so close to his side that our hips rubbed, as if he couldn't bear to be separated from me by even a millimeter of air. And one glower from him was enough to make the crowd fall away in front of us.

He marched me to a black Mercedes that was parked right outside the door. As I slid across the soft leather seat, it hit me that I'd done it. I'd met him and he'd accepted me as Christina. I was in.

And I realized I'd completely forgotten about the mission as soon as his lips touched mine. *Jesus, what's wrong with me?*

We pulled away and joined the freeway. We were so cocooned in heavy steel and thick glass that there was barely any road noise and it was easy to think that we weren't moving at all. But when I looked up, the landscape was whipping past outside. As the high of the kiss faded, reality started to set in. I was alone with a man everyone feared, and every second took me further and further from my friends, the FBI, and everything I knew.

A noise that was familiar. An important sound, but I was so distracted it just bounced off my perception because it didn't apply to me. It came again. Again.

He touched my arm and I turned to look. "*Christina!*" he said, insistent.

Shit! That's what I'd been hearing. My new name! My brain had just tuned it out. My heart jumped up into my mouth and I felt my face go pale. How could I have made such a basic mistake? *I can't pull this off! He's going to find out!*

"Sorry," I said. "I—Just—" I searched my brain for an explanation and thought of the only time I'd been in hospital, when I'd had a bad kidney infection, age six. "Whenever I heard my name, in hospital, it meant someone was coming to jab me with a needle."

His arm immediately scooped behind my back and hooked around me. His eyes lit up with a protective gleam and my fear melted away into a warm glow. Then I saw him frown, and he glanced at his arm as if surprised at what he'd done.

A moment later, we turned onto a private road. Trees had been used to cleverly hide the fence but I caught a glimpse of it, eight feet tall and topped with razor wire. Men in suits with that somber, no-nonsense look of former military patrolled its length, huge Rottweilers padding alongside them. My stomach flipped over. I knew they were there to keep enemies out, but they'd be just as effective at keeping me in. If Konstantin found out I wasn't Christina, there'd be no hope of making a run for it.

The car swung around a sweeping driveway and as we broke through the trees, there it was. My breath caught in my throat and I tried not to stare. *I'm meant to be used to this.*

The mansion was a lot like him: imposingly big and unashamedly grand: three stories and two wings, doors that must have been twelve feet high framed by pillars too thick for me to wrap my arms around. It was outwardly cold, built from dark gray stone, but warm light from chandeliers spilled out through the windows and I could see the gleam of polished wood floors and the flicker of open fires. The place must have been at least a hundred years old and I wondered why he'd chosen it: he could have bought a huge, modern penthouse in the city for the same money.

Even as the car crunched to a halt on the gravel, a guard was already stepping forward to open my door. Konstantin seemed to be in a hurry to get inside, one of his big hands pressing on the small of my back to gently guide me. Two more guards were holding the massive front doors open for us... God, how many guards did he *have?* There were so many of them, all with the same heavy muscle, expensive suit, and the bulge of a gun, that their faces started to blend into one. It brought home just how serious the cold war between the different mafia families was.

There was one guard, though, who didn't look like the others. He was a little older than the rest, with a few streaks of silver in his short, black hair. He wasn't as heavily built as Konstantin but he was tall, lean, and good-looking in a craggy, old-fashioned kind of a way. I knew him from years of watching Konstantin: Grigory was the head bodyguard and also handled all of Konstantin's arms deals.

As Grigory fell into step beside us, he was looking directly at me. At first, I ignored it and focused on Konstantin as he hustled me along. Why *was* he in such a hurry? But every time I glanced at Grigory, he was still staring. *Shit!* Could he sense something different about me?

We swept inside and into a tiled, double-height hall. A grand staircase rose in front of us, storybook-huge, its polished wooden banisters as thick as my thigh. I had a crazy urge to slide down them. Flanking the stairs were a pair of antique vases, each as big as me and probably worth hundreds of thousands of dollars. I did my best not to stare at everything.

The doors closed behind us. Konstantin swung me around to face him. I looked up at him... and gulped. That look was back, diamond-hard but scorching, sending waves of raw heat thrumming down through my body to my groin until I wanted to twist and writhe and melt into a puddle on the floor. Now I knew why he'd been in a hurry to get inside. He'd needed to know I was safe within this fortress of a house... because then, he could enjoy me.

He put his hands on my shoulders, the heat of him throbbing into me through my dress. Then he slid his hands under my arms and smoothed down my body in one slow, continuous movement. His fingers hooked around my back and the heels of his hands brushed the soft sides of my breasts as they passed. The room went so quiet, I could hear my intake of breath. He followed the curve of me *in* at the waist, thumbs brushing either side of my navel, then *out,* over my hips, the warmth of his hands soaking into me and making me squirm as he passed my groin. He went as far as he could reach, right down to the hem of my dress, his fingers toying with the backs of my stockinged thighs, and only then, reluctantly, did he stop.

As he brought his hands back up, I felt them twitch and his breathing went tight. I glanced down. Christina's dress was tight on my bust and I was showing a lot of cleavage. He was staring right at it and—his hands twitched again, squeezing my shoulders. *And he's having to resist the urge to just fill his hands with my breasts.* I went weak inside.

He used a knuckle under my chin to gently tip my head back and looked me in the eye. His gaze was clouded with lust. "You've changed," he muttered thickly.

Oh God. A chill rippled through me. It didn't reduce the heat, just made me more aware of it: peaks of scalding lust alternating with troughs of icy fear.

Konstantin frowned. He gripped my chin and slowly turned my head from side to side, studying me. "There's something different about you."

Shit!

The squeak of a shoe sole on tiles, off to one side. I whipped my head around, startled. I'd forgotten there was anyone else in the room. Grigory and two other guards were still there and Grigory was glaring right at me. *He knows!*

My eyes snapped back to Konstantin, my heart hammering. His frown grew deeper and the fear slammed through me, like being dropped into ice water. But then he slid his hand through my hair, every brush of his fingertips sending pleasure fluttering through my body. Just like at the airport, I felt drunk, my brain bathed in adrenaline one second, endorphins the next. Was he about to kiss me or kill me?

He gave a sort of dismissive *hmph,* a quick shake of his head...and pushed me away. I went staggering back across the tiles, eyes screwed shut in fear, waiting for a bullet to rip through me—

My back whumped against the thick wooden post at the bottom of one of the banisters. And when I opened my eyes in shock, I saw Konstantin marching towards me, his eyes narrowed with need.

He hadn't been pushing me away. He just wanted me up against something solid.

I didn't even have time to draw a breath before his lips were on me, pressing, searching, drawing me up onto tiptoes to meet him. My head was tipped right back, my hair cushioning my head from the hard wood. He grabbed my hips and then slid his palms up my body, bringing the hem of my dress with them. I could feel the expensive fabric sliding higher and higher, the cool air of the room wafting against lacy stocking top and then bare skin. I felt my cheeks start to color: there were still three guards watching this. But the embarrassment evaporated as it met the greater heat of the kiss.

It was a dance. At first it was between two practiced partners, open-mouthed and hungry. Each brush of his tongue against my upper lip, each soft nip of his teeth against my lower was a beat in a rising rhythm. I followed him without even being aware of it, molding my body to his, grabbing his upper arms and exploring that gorgeous, hard upper lip with my softer ones.

But I didn't know the steps. I couldn't match him, couldn't *fight* him the way Christina must have. I realized too late that with her, this would have been a violent clash, a battle for dominance that he always won. I just *melted.* And that made him stop and break the kiss, frowning at me from just a few inches away. He ran his thumb over my lips, looking confused, and I was lost between *oh God, I've blown it* and *please please kiss me again.*

His lips came down on mine again and this time he was the teacher and I was the pupil. He led me, toyed with me, showed me what he liked and then rewarded me when I got it right. My hands found his shoulders and clung on, my legs weakening. *Oh God* it was amazing, that hard upper lip plundering me but the softness of the lower one stroking mine so gently. He was so confident, he knew so well how to pleasure me, how to hold me tight and kiss me deeply, how to tease my tongue with his. And yet each time I responded, however timidly, he gave a groan of lust that vibrated right to my core. I was different to Christina... and he liked it.

I was only dimly aware of his hand sliding up my thigh and

pushing the dress even higher. Then he squeezed my ass through my panties and I started wondering how much the guards could see. When his fingers hooked under the side of my panties, my eyes sprang open and I broke the kiss, panting hard. "I—"

My protest was cut off by him skimming his fingertips up over the lips of my sex. I could feel them swell under his touch, knew he could feel the slickness between them. "Konstantin—" I croaked.

He didn't answer, but with his other hand he grabbed the shoulder strap of my dress and wrenched it down over my arm. The neck stretched and, since the bra was built in, my breast was revealed, almost down to the nipple. I gave a strangled groan of horror: the hand between my thighs was sort of hidden by our bodies, but I was about to flash the guards. "They're watching," I panted.

His voice was a heavy rasp, his eyes hooded. "You never minded an audience before."

I opened my mouth to argue, but he chose that moment to plunge two fingers up into me and I arched my back and moaned—

Running footsteps, then an apologetic cough from behind him. Konstantin twisted around with a sound that was almost a snarl. But he didn't yell at the man who'd run into the room, just waited, his massive chest rising and falling as he panted.

The man said just three words. "It's Ralavich. *Here.*"

Konstantin just stared at him in disbelief. As he took it in, his face turned...*bleak.* Haunted in a way that made me want to wrap my arms around him.

Then his jaw tightened and his eyes went so mercilessly, bitterly cold I drew in my breath and pressed my back against the banister. I'd glimpsed a warmer side to him but this was the opposite. This was him filled with raw, jagged hate. *Ralavich.* I knew that name.

"I need to deal with this," muttered Konstantin. And he wheeled around and stalked out. I raced to pull my dress back into place before any of the guards got a good look at my bare breast and hiked-up skirt but I needn't have worried: when I looked around, every one of them had their eyes averted. They didn't *dare* look.

Except one. Grigory was muttering orders to the other guards but his eyes were still on me, his expression unreadable. I swallowed and hooked my shoulder strap back into place, then smoothed the hem down. I told the guards I was going upstairs to unpack and started to climb the staircase, but I could feel Grigory's eyes burning into my back. My stomach was in knots. *I must have made a mistake. Because somehow, he knows.*

15

KONSTANTIN

R alavich. I'd heard his name and suddenly I'd been twenty years in the past, watching everything I cared about being torn away from me.

And I'd frozen. *Weak. So weak.* I couldn't afford to freeze or hesitate, not even for an instant. Now the rage was thundering through me, the need to find him and destroy him making my hands clench into fists. I'd tried to have that bastard killed many times, over the last two decades. But he was as well-protected as I was. If he was really here in New York, maybe I'd have the chance to do it myself.

But he can't be here. It made no sense. Every scrap of New York was taken by me, Luka or Angelo. Soon, it would all be mine. Ralavich wouldn't be able to gain a toehold in this city... unless there was something I was missing.

I scowled. I don't like mysteries. I have enough to deal with, keeping everything running smoothly. And building, every day building, growing my empire a street at a time.

And meanwhile the FBI were always sniffing around, trying to find something they could use to bring me down. The woman they had running things, Carrie Blake, was like a dog with a bone. She made a point of coming on busts, just so she could glare at me as I watched one of my guys led away in cuffs. She was a straight arrow, impossible to bribe, which I had to grudgingly respect. She was good looking, too, in an elegant, older woman way, with silver hair that made me think of *beryozka* trees. I'd actually run into her at a party, once, by pure chance. She had her hair pinned up and was in a deep red evening gown. When we saw each other, she almost dropped her martini and I almost crushed my whiskey glass. But both of us rallied quickly.

She'd glared at me. *Mr. Gulyev. And I thought this was a civilized party.*

No, Ms. Blake. Apparently, they let just about anyone in.

The woman was a thorn in my side. I knew she had people watching me. I never saw them, but I could feel them, sometimes, like when I'd met that property developer at the construction site.

The only good news was that Christina was back. I'd sleep well tonight.

Christina. I licked my lips. She'd tasted different. Innocent in a way that didn't fit Christina at all. She almost reminded me of that woman in my hotel room, Hailey. Christina had always been eager and confident in bed, but ultimately she was... *glossy.* Like those magazines American women read, with the perfectly edited model on the front, alluring but somehow fake.

This new Christina was clumsy, tentative... almost shy. But she was real and that turned me on like nothing else. I'd only intended to kiss her, not go at her up against the banister like a couple of teenagers. But the accident had changed her, somehow... and I loved it.

I thought of the way she'd responded to me, her tongue urgent, almost desperate against mine, her walls satiny tight and slick, clutching at my fingers as I'd explored her. Even now, my cock was rock hard in my pants.

I'd find out what was happening with Ralavich. And then, tonight, I had to fuck her.

16

HAILEY

I WAS SO BUSY thinking about Grigory watching me, I'd reached the landing at the top of the stairs before I realized I had no idea where I was going. *I don't know where our bedroom is!*

I risked a glance over my shoulder. Grigory was still glaring up at me. He actually took a step towards the stairs as if he was going to follow, but then one of the other guards asked him a question and he cursed and turned to the man to answer him. While he was distracted, I raced up the remaining stairs and went right, picking a direction at random. I just wanted to get out of his sight and find our room before anyone—

"Well, that seemed to go okay."

The voice came out of nowhere and it was so sudden I literally jumped, then flattened myself into an alcove, eyes everywhere, trying to find the source.

And then it sunk in that the voice was familiar. Calahan, in my earpiece. I slumped in relief. Then, as I replayed what he'd said in my mind, my face went hot.

He'd been listening to everything.

I swallowed. The kissing at the airport, what had just happened downstairs...hearing wasn't the same as seeing, but...I remembered the moan I'd made, when Konstantin slid his fingers into me, and flushed harder. Had Calahan sounded jealous? Or was that just my imagination? "Yeah," I muttered at last. "Now I have to find our room. Any ideas?"

"Sorry," said Calahan. "We know zip about the inside of the mansion. You're going to have to do some exploring."

I started along the landing. The mansion was huge, but most of the doors I opened led to unused bedrooms, some completely empty and some with beds covered in dust sheets. The rooms were amazing: the ceilings were so high I had to squint to see all the intricate plasterwork and the chandeliers were iron octopuses the size of small cars, draped in glittering glass. You could have opened the place as a hotel for at least fifty guests. But it looked like Konstantin never had anyone to stay.

As I walked, I thought about the name I'd heard downstairs, the one that had enraged Konstantin. "Ralavich," I said to Calahan. "You don't think he means *Dmitri* Ralavich?"

Two years ago, in Alaska, my friend Kate had almost died when she'd come up against a Russian mob boss by that name. A truly evil man, notorious for trafficking women.

I could hear Calahan working a keyboard. "He started out in St. Petersburg, same as Konstantin. It would make sense for them to be rivals. But what the hell would Ralavich be doing in New York? There's no territory he could take here: Konstantin and the other two bosses have the city all sewn up."

By now, I'd made my way up to the top floor and right to the end of the west wing. I pushed open a big set of double doors... and gasped. I'd finally found the master bedroom, or rather the master bedroom *suite*. There was a massive bedroom complete with an Emperor-size bed, separate dressing rooms and bathrooms for Konstantin and me and a sort of lounge area. God, this place was fit for a king and queen. Or maybe a Tsar and his Tsarina.

I'd thought the clothes Christina had brought back from Milan were amazing, but her walk-in wardrobe was something else. One entire wall was devoted to shoes, from elegant, calfskin-leather knee boots to stilettos in every conceivable color. I picked up an amazing pair of midnight-blue kitten heels and sighed. I'm not big on fashion, but even I recognized this as shoe heaven... and none of them would fit. I was going to have to quietly buy some replacements in my size and use those. If Konstantin had a favorite pair he liked to see me in, I was in big trouble.

The clothes were less of a problem. They'd fit, if maybe a bit tightly on the bust. I'd just need to work up the courage to wear them. Christina seemed to like low necklines or high slits, or both. And then there was an entire section devoted to lingerie, each matching set neatly arranged on a hanger together with packs of expensive stockings. *Am I really going to wear this...for him?*

"How's it going?" asked Calahan in my ear. "Find anything useful?"

I quickly left the closet and started searching the room. "Got his laptop," I said. It was on a table next to a vase of flowers and I stared at the scene for a few seconds, my eye for detail kicking in and noting how the laptop was angled and where a few fallen petals had fallen onto it. I powered the machine on but just like Calahan, I was stymied when it asked for a hardware key. Without that, we weren't getting in.

There was a tiny crack on the landing outside the door. *Shit!* I powered off the laptop and angled it just how it had been, carefully replacing the fallen petals. I had time to take one step away from the table before—

The door crashed open and Grigory stood there, glaring at me. "What's going on?"

"Nothing!"

Grigory marched across the room and grabbed me by the upper arms. I felt my insides turn to water. "Stop playing games!" he snapped.

I'd been right: somehow, he knew I was an imposter. I screwed my eyes closed in fear. He was going to tell Konstantin and then the FBI would find my body floating in the harbor—

"Three weeks!" he snapped. "You call him, but not me. And then downstairs, you make me watch the two of you...."

My eyes flew open. *What?!*

He grabbed my face in both hands. "God, I've missed you."

And then his lips were on mine.

17

HAILEY

I WAS SO SHOCKED, I didn't try to struggle. I just stood there, my face tilted up to him, his thumbs rubbing gently along my cheekbones as he kissed me hard and deep.

Christina was having an affair with him! It exploded in my brain like a firework, lighting up everything else. *That's* why he'd been glaring at me, ever since I arrived. He thought I'd been ignoring him.

I was coming to my senses now, but I didn't dare stop the kiss because I had no idea what I was going to say to him when it ended. Now that I was over the shock, I wanted to strangle Christina. I'd known she was evil, but what sort of psycho bitch sleeps with a notorious crime boss... and then cheats on him, right under his nose? Konstantin would kill both of them, if he found out. And now I'd inherited the problem. *He could walk through the door right now and catch us kissing and—*

I broke the kiss and stood there panting and wide-eyed. "We can't! It's too dangerous!"

He put his hands on my waist. "*You* started this!" he growled.

I stared at him, incredulous. Christina had only been with Konstantin for four months and she'd already seduced another guy?

It made me furious... and weirdly, it wasn't just because I was going to have to deal with it. It felt *wrong.* Unfair on Konstantin.

God, was I starting to get protective of him?

I put a hand on Grigory's chest and pushed him back, trying to ignore how hard his pecs were under his shirt. He was good looking, if you went for slightly older guys. But I had to try to cool this down...without making him suspicious. "It's too risky, with me just back," I told him. "Give me time."

I walked him slowly back across the room, all the way to the door. And despite his size and his frustration, he let me do it. I thought back to the kiss: he'd been desperate, but... tender.

This was about more than just sex. He was in love with Christina.

I stared at him, amazed. But it was true: the way his eyes kept going to my lips, the way he alternated between glaring in frustration and looking totally helpless. This big, tough, older guy, the one I'd been so intimidated by downstairs... he was as lovesick as a teenager.

And I knew in my gut that Christina hadn't loved him in return.

She'd just strung him along, using him for sex, wrapping him around her little finger. And now I'd inherited that power. I'd never had that before, never had a man crazy for me. It made me awed...and humbled. However risky this was, I had to let the poor guy down gently. I couldn't just break his heart.

"Just be patient," I whispered, as I guided him out of the room. "We'll be together soon."

Before I could stop him, he lunged forward and kissed me sweet and quick on the lips. Then I managed to get the door shut and leaned back against it, sighing in relief. But as I gazed around the room, the relief didn't last long. I'd had no idea about Christina and Grigory. What else didn't she tell me?

All I wanted to do was to stay in the bedroom, where I couldn't run into anyone else and blow my cover. But I had a job to do and I wasn't going to get evidence on Konstantin here.

I felt ridiculous creeping around the house in a fancy dress so I changed. Most of Christina's skirts were more like belts, but I managed to find a slate gray pencil skirt that actually came down almost to my knees, although the soft, stretchy fabric did hug my ass and hips a lot. And after a lot of digging, I managed to find a sweater that didn't have a plunging neckline, a beautiful angora wool turtleneck in rust red.

I took some time to touch up my make-up: Christina always looked perfect and I had to maintain that, even though it took me twice as long as it probably took her. Then I crept slowly downstairs.

I thought Konstantin would be down on the first floor, but by homing in on the deep rumble of his voice, I finally found him on the second, in a room whose door was ajar. I pushed it quietly open....

Everything about Konstantin's study was old-fashioned. He sat in a big, high-backed, swivel chair, the green leather faded until it was the color of money. The desk looked like something Lincoln might have sat behind, the mahogany so dark with years of polish, it was almost black. In one corner of the room was a black-painted safe the size of a refrigerator, like something that would have held the payroll in the Old West. Konstantin hadn't seen me yet. He was leaning forward, his elbows on the desk, one hand holding a phone and the other cradling his head. "*Da*," he said, nodding. "*Da svidania.*" *Goodbye.* He ended the call and sighed, then rubbed the back of his neck with both hands. Only then did he open his eyes. But when he saw me, he didn't look pleased. He looked shocked.

I pushed on with the plan: I'd comfort him, just like Christina would have, and let him vent all his troubles to me. I started across the room, trying to swing my hips like she did. "What's the matter?" I asked. "Is Ralavich really in New York?"

But he just stared at me as if I'd gone crazy and then gave me a quick, frustrated shake of his head. Reminding me of some rule they'd established long ago.

I froze. Something was horribly wrong. This whole plan relied on the assumption that all criminals confide in their girlfriends. But what if Konstantin was the exception?

I stared into those cold gray eyes and I knew I was right. It wasn't just that he didn't love Christina, she wasn't even his confidante. He was so ruthless, he didn't share a damn thing with her.

"Sorry," I muttered, and backed out of the room. Just as I left, I thought I caught something else in his face...and then I pulled the heavy door closed and stood there staring at my hazy reflection in the polished surface. My mission had just become a thousand times harder...and more dangerous. But there was something else.

It bothered me that he wouldn't share his secrets with me. Even though I was living proof that his secrecy was right, that he *should* be paranoid...it bothered me. Because I wanted to help him. Sitting at his desk, his head in his hands, he'd looked so alone. And then there was what I'd glimpsed on his face, just as I'd left. He'd been angry but...regretful. As if it was himself he was angry at, not me. As if he wanted to share everything with me but couldn't.

I pushed the thought away. *He's the enemy!* And if he wouldn't share stuff with me, I'd just have to get the evidence some other way.

I went back to the stairs and carried on down to the first floor. I found a massive ballroom at the back of the house, which must be where Konstantin held his famed parties. There were several lounges, the smallest of which seemed to be permanently set up for poker, a gym and a sauna: I'd heard about how Russians liked their saunas.

I passed through a set of double doors and the whole mood of the house seemed to change. The furnishings were less lavish and more practical, and where the rest of the house felt quiet and echoey, this part was a hive of activity. I realized I'd strayed into the part that I wasn't supposed to see: the staff area. I saw women wheeling laundry carts around and others carrying trays of food. There was a huge pantry and an even bigger kitchen, where a man in a chef's hat seemed to be briefing the cooks for the evening meal. When he saw me, he jumped to his feet. "Miss Rogan! Can I get you something to eat?"

He was smiling and seemed friendly enough. But he'd gone pale and his smile was too wide, too forced. *Does Konstantin keep them all living in fear?*

I shook my head. "No. Sorry. I'll leave you in peace."

I passed through a hallway lined with closely-spaced doors. A few were ajar and I could see people lounging on beds, reading or listening to music, like a college dorm. *This is where the staff live. God, what must all this cost?*

At that moment, a pretty blonde in a maid's uniform who couldn't have been more than twenty rounded a corner and saw me. Her face went snow white. "*Miss Rogan!* Did you ring? I'm sorry! I didn't hear! What do you need?" She literally ran the rest of the distance to where I stood. "*I'm sorry!*" she said again.

She was shaking. She was actually shaking.

And I realized I knew her face. She was Christina's personal maid, the one I'd seen mistreated on the airport security footage. And suddenly I knew why the chef had seemed weird.

The staff weren't scared of Konstantin. They were scared of *me.*

"It's okay," I said gently. "I didn't ring. I don't need anything."

She blinked and searched my face, confused. *Then what are you doing here?*

And I realized that what I was doing was wrong. I was meant to be Christina and if Christina kept these people in mortal fear then I had to, as well. I had to snap at her, berate her for nothing at all, and make her cry. I steeled myself—

The maid looked at me, hopeful but scared. A puppy waiting to be kicked.

I couldn't do it. Not even if it meant arousing suspicion. "I came down here to thank you," I said. "I don't do that enough."

The maid looked doubtful, as if it might be a trick. "You—You're very welcome, Miss."

I realized I had no idea what her name was. "Um. Look, I'm really sorry but you're going to have to remind me...."

"Victoria, Miss." Weirdly, asking her name didn't seem to surprise her. Knowing Christina, she'd just called her *girl* or *bitch* or something.

"Victoria." I smiled at her. And she gave me a nervous smile back.

I retraced my steps back to the main part of the mansion and found a staircase that led down. The mansion extended deep underground. The first basement held the guard's quarters and the armory. Deeper down, I found an underground garage. And below that....

The first warning was the stairs. They changed from smooth concrete flights to a rough stone spiral and the walls went from brick to rock. The electric lights ended and were replaced with candles that barely lit the way. I slowly descended, now deep below the earth. "What the hell is *this?*" I muttered, just to break the eerie silence. But there was no reply from my earpiece. "Calahan?"

Nothing. I realized that I was so deep, the rock was probably blocking the radio signal. I nearly turned back...but if I wanted to find out Konstantin's secrets, this seemed like the perfect place to look. I carried on down.

When I finally reached the bottom of the stairs, I was in a room walled in solid rock. There was a door of dark oak, banded with iron, and I hauled it a little way open. *God, it must be a foot thick!*

As soon as the gap was wide enough, I slipped through.

Oh no.

18

HAILEY

I STOOD JUST BEYOND the doorway, not wanting to believe what I was seeing.

The room was roughly rectangular and about the size of one of the big bedrooms upstairs. But the walls weren't quite straight: they curved in and out like a frozen sea. The room had been carved out of the rock, the walls chiseled smooth with millions of individual hammer blows. Then the walls had been painstakingly polished so that all those tiny flat surfaces shone like the facets of a diamond, the dark rock reflecting the light from a fireplace until it looked like the walls themselves were on fire. The floor was tiled with white marble, the firelight turning it creamy and warm.

There was a beautiful four poster bed with cream sheets and a crimson comforter, hung with matching crimson drapes. The wood of the frame was so old that there were no square corners left.

But what had stopped me in my tracks wasn't the amazing room, or the bed. It was the rest of the furniture.

It was in the same style as the bed. Maybe it had even come from the same European palace, hundreds of years ago. It was all handmade, with elaborately carved wood, cold cast iron, and soft scarlet leather. It was beautiful. But terrifying.

On shaking legs, I started across the room, looking at each piece in turn. A bench that you would kneel on, your lower legs bound and your upper body pressed against the leather. An X-shaped thing you would stand against, your wrists and ankles held by straps. A thing like a gymnastics horse that you would bend over, your ass in the air, legs spread....

I came to a stop at the end of the room, next to a wooden rack holding whips and riding crops.

A dungeon. This was a dungeon.

Which meant Konstantin was into this stuff. I had a sudden vision of Christina bound to one of the benches and Konstantin hulking over her, teasing her and taking her over and over again as she wriggled and begged.

Except it wasn't him and Christina, anymore. It was him and *me*.

But I'm not into this stuff! I'd tried BDSM once, with a boyfriend. He'd tried to tie my wrists to the bed but the plastic clothesline he'd used wouldn't hold a knot and kept slipping apart, and he was too timid to be convincingly menacing.

Konstantin, though...he was plenty menacing. I looked down at the thing I was next to, the one I thought of as the "kneeling bench." With those big hands, he could absolutely push me onto that thing, *naked,* my breasts pressed just *there,* and pin me there while he bound me....

A drumbeat started inside me, slow but insistent, resonating up into my head and down into my groin. I pushed my hand experimentally against the leather padding. Soft but firm. It was cool against my palm but it warmed to my body in just a few heartbeats. I kept my hand there, transfixed, and the room was so quiet, I could hear that my breathing had gone tight. The drumbeat inside me was building in power, each crash of it radiating out in slow motion, shattering everything in its path.

I fingered the thick leather straps and buckles. Once he fixed me in place, I'd be helpless. That word felt weirdly powerful, echoing again and again in my head, blending with the rising drumbeat and making me crush my thighs together. *Helpless.* Tied tight, all I'd be able to do was thrash and plead, and he'd just take me, just *utterly, utterly, take me*—

I snatched my hand away, shocked at what was in my head. *I have to get out of here. Right now.*

I spun around...and froze. The door was wide open and Konstantin's huge form was silhouetted in the doorway. He stepped into the light.

"I should have known I'd find you here," he told me.

And he kicked the door closed behind him.

19

HAILEY

A S SOON AS the door closed, the atmosphere in the room changed. There was so much rock above us and the door was so thick, we were completely isolated from the rest of the mansion. *I could scream and no one would hear me.* That should have terrified me but instead I felt the crash of that drum inside me again, just a single loud *boom* that resonated right to my fingertips and made me ache between my thighs. *What the hell is happening to me?*

Konstantin started towards me, each heavy footstep vibrating through the marble floor and up into my body, making me twitch and quiver like a tuning fork. I'd never known anyone to have such a physical effect on me, just by their presence. The effect got stronger the closer he got: before one footstep could die away, the next hit me, setting up harmonics that made my breathing tighten and my heart race. By the time he stood in front of me, I was a panting mess.

"Look at me," he ordered.

And that was when I realized I *wasn't* looking at him, I was focused on his polished black shoes. I *wanted* to look at him, wanted to see that gorgeous face, fill my senses with his pecs, his shoulders. But for some reason I'd cast my eyes down as soon as he'd approached. It was something about this room.

Or...was it something about *me?*

I lifted my head and looked up at him. Instantly, I was pinned by that glittering, ferociously hot gaze. But there was something else going on, too, something I couldn't put a name to, something that made the breathless heat inside me tighten and coil all the way down to my groin, where it became slick wetness. Konstantin is big, but I'd never felt so *small.*

"Never ask about my work again," he ordered. "You know better."

I nodded quickly. *I'll have to fake this.* Because obviously Christina was into this whole BDSM thing, she was some sort of...*submissive.* So I had to pretend to be, too.

He leaned down, bringing his lips within a half inch of my ear. "Undress," he ordered. And it *was* an order. He'd done nothing *but* order me around since he walked in. Each word loaded with weight and power because of who he was, but made slippery silver by that Russian accent, so smooth and beautiful that obeying them was a pleasure. The *ss* of *undress* was like silk brushing over my mind.

I could hear the blood rushing in my ears. *I'm pretending. Just pretending. For the mission. That's what this is.*

So why was the heat thrashing inside me, twisting into a spiral and grinding down between my legs? Why was I wetter than I'd ever been?

I began to take off my clothes.

20

KONSTANTIN

SOMETHING was different.

I'm what the Americans call a dominant, but I don't dress it up in fancy terms or over-analyze it like they do. I command. She obeys. Simple.

I love normal sex, too. The feel of a woman's body as she thrashes in ecstasy beneath you, breasts stroking your chest. The changes that you can feel come over her as you drive your cock into her. I love the give and take of sex. I don't *need* to tie her up.

But sex like that is the sex of people in love. And love is a weakness. If I had sex like that, with the intimacy and the cuddling afterwards...I might start to feel something.

So ever since my life was torn apart, I've made sure sex is just physical. A release. And the best way to separate it from anything more intimate is with these games. I tie her, I pleasure her, and I take her. I maintain absolute control at all times.

But now, something had changed.

Christina was always happy to be tied up. Enthusiastic, even. She played along. But it was just that: *playing*. Her orgasms were real enough but I could tell she wasn't getting off on the idea of being restrained.

But *now*...where the old Christina would have boldly thrown off her clothes, sticking out her breasts and posing like a stripper, this new Christina was hesitant and nervous. Almost shy. Instead of faking enthusiasm, she acted like she'd never done it before. And yet underneath, in the way her hands trembled, in the flush I could see at her neck, in the tightness of her breathing...she needed it. She had that instinctual urge for this, just as I had the matching, dominant one. And the idea of *that*, combined with this strange new innocence she had, made my cock harder than it had ever been.

She pulled her sweater over her head. Her pale breasts strained at the bra...I swore they seemed bigger. And then, as my eyes tracked down her body, I saw the scar. A burn of some kind, low down on her side. I felt a sudden, unexpected surge of protective anger that something had hurt her. But she saw me looking and she...*shrunk.* Her eyes went to the floor, her hair hanging down to cover her face. She was embarrassed by it. She thought it made her not beautiful. As if such a thing was possible. Her hand went down to cover it and I got even angrier, that she'd been hurt in that way, too.

I took her wrist and gently pried her hand away.

Then I leaned in and, very softly, touched my lips to the scar. Her head jerked up in surprise...and then she relaxed a little, her confidence restored.

I stepped back and the slow strip resumed. She unbuttoned the skirt and wriggled it down over her hips where the old Christina would have expertly twisted like a dancer and made it fall down on its own. I let my eyes roam up and down those beautiful, shapely legs, even found myself trying to get a glimpse of her ass, despite having seen it a hundred times before. It was almost as if I was seeing her for the first time.

I was so turned on, I didn't realize at first that she was unbuckling her high heels. She normally always left them on to make her legs look longer. But before I could think to stop her, she'd stepped out of them, and then stripped off her stockings, too, gasping a little as her bare soles hit the cold marble. It was weirdly endearing.

I caught myself. *Don't think like that.*

She looked up at me, now just in bra and panties.

I waited.

She waited.

I smirked. Of course, it was deliberate. She knew I meant for her to take everything off, but she was trying to turn me on by being a little disobedient. She was cunning, like that. "*All* of your clothes," I told her.

She gave a tiny intake of breath and her eyes went wide. I frowned. Christina's acting had suddenly gotten a lot better. She really did seem shocked and nervous...and turned on. I didn't know how she'd done it, but I loved it.

I watched as her bra slipped free, her breasts bobbing and swaying. They *did* seem bigger, or maybe I'd just forgotten how beautiful they were. Full and heavy and creamily pale...I couldn't wait to fill my hands with them.

Only one little scrap of clothing remained. My eyes locked on that triangle of fabric between her thighs. I couldn't remember ever having been this turned on, watching her undress. Or watching *any* woman undress. Since she got back, she had some hold over me....

I clenched my jaw. Those sorts of feelings could be the end of everything. *Maybe I should just tell her to leave.* It would be fatal to become attached: our "relationship" was never meant to be that. But...as the fabric started to move down her body, pushed a few millimeters at a time by her shaking hands, I knew there was no way I could do that. I *needed* to see her, needed to touch her.

She'd stopped moving the panties. "Go on," I told her. "Unless you want me to rip them off you."

21

HAILEY

O H GOD. I couldn't believe I was stripping in front of him. I'd got naked for sex, of course, but that was clothes coming off in a hurried tangle at the last minute, not stripping while being watched.

The moment when I'd unhooked my bra had been terrifying. *What if he doesn't like me?* And yet as soon as it was off and my bare breasts were throbbing in the air, the heat of his gaze just bathed me, washing over the valley of my cleavage and the sides of my breasts, stroking over my nipples. It was a rush like nothing I'd ever experienced. And the way he'd kissed my scar: that had been like a weight lifting from me. I'd been self-conscious about it for my whole adult life.

Now he wanted my panties gone, too, and I knew it wasn't an idle threat. He really would rip them off me if I didn't do it myself. And a little part of me almost wanted to shake my head and refuse so that he'd have to reach down with one big hand and gather them and tug—

What the hell is wrong with me? I pushed my panties down my thighs and let them fall to the floor, then stepped out of them. I looked up into his eyes....

He glanced down between my legs and gave a little shake of his head. But he didn't look angry, like he had in his study. He was smirking. I looked down—

I hadn't even been aware of it, but I was holding my hand over my groin to cover myself. And he was telling me that was *unacceptable*.

I moved my hand slowly aside and felt the heat of his gaze *there*. It soaked into me and became a deep, needful ache.

"You let it grow back," he murmured, sounding fascinated.

Oh crap. I'd never even considered that. I keep everything neat, but from the sound of it, Christina must have been waxed completely smooth. I nodded.

"I like it." I could hear the growing lust in his voice. He stepped right up to me, until one polished shoe was between my bare feet and the soft fabric of his pant leg was just brushing my pussy lips. He bent to whisper in my ear. "Now," he said. "Get on the bench. You're going to show me that you're still my dirty *shlyukha*."

I didn't speak Russian but I could have a pretty good guess what *shlyukha* meant. I followed his gaze to the kneeling bench. As soon as I looked at it, my breathing sped up. A hot rush swept through my body and in its wake I felt a *tug*. An ache, deep inside me, a need. Maybe it had been there ever since I started watching Konstantin, but I'd never allowed myself to feel it until now. *He's going to tie me up, fuck me, make me his plaything and—*

And I want him to.

I felt as if the floor had dropped out from under me and I was plunging down into scary, wonderful blackness. *How could I not know this about myself?!*

"Get on the bench," he repeated. He ran his hand down my back, cupped my ass, and pushed me forward.

The air was suddenly thick and heavy. I could hear my pulse crashing in my ears. I put one knee on the padded leather....

The door flew open and crashed against the wall.

22

KONSTANTIN

I WHIRLED AROUND and my glare made the guard take a step back. Normally, I wouldn't be angry at them for interrupting sex. For them to disturb me down here, it had to be an emergency. But I wasn't thinking clearly...thanks to her.

"Fire," said the guard. "Three different places, some injuries at one of them."

I turned back to Christina. She was flushing, trying to cover her nakedness with her hands. I pulled off my suit jacket and put it round her. "Get the car," I told the guard. "We're going out." He ran off.

Christina dressed and it was like a reverse strip-tease: little glimpses of bare thigh and curling dark hair as she pulled on her panties, a flash of nipple and soft flesh as she put on her bra. It had me even harder in my pants than when she'd *undressed* because it was as if her nakedness was being taken from me. By the time she put on her sweater, I was almost panting. *What the hell is wrong with me?* I like sex, I especially like sex with Christina, but this was something else. I *needed* her.

Standing on one leg to put on her heels, she overbalanced. Her hand went to my arm to steady herself and... something happened to me. The sight of her small hand there, the feel of her touching me...it made something swell in my chest. I put my hand on hers, unable to speak.

She looked up at me, blushing and confused, and I stared down into her eyes. She seemed so *light,* so *good. Innocent,* not like Christina at all. I didn't understand it.

I shook my head. "You're still my *shlyukha,"* I muttered. "But now...." I ran my other hand over her cheek, pushing her hair back, and frowned. "You're my *golub,* too."

She frowned.

"My dove," I told her. Then I shook my head. "Come on."

She quickly slipped her other shoe on. "I don't have to come. I mean...I understand, if it's business."

I felt myself soften again. She was trying to make it right, after asking me about Ralavich in my study. As if we were a real couple who'd had a fight. And she was right: she didn't need to come with me, she *shouldn't* come with me. But.... "No," I said firmly. "You're coming."

She nodded, but cocked her head to one side. *Why?*

And suddenly it just burst out of me, before I could stop it. "Because I don't want to let you out of my sight."

We both stared at each other, me twice as shocked as her. Then I turned and marched towards the door. *What's going on?* I'd allowed this relationship to happen because I knew I'd never feel anything for Christina, because she was as cold as I was. But now....

Now, she made me weak.

23

HAILEY

L ESS THAN TEN MINUTES later, we were in the back of the black Mercedes, speeding into the city. My body was still throbbing and shaky, my mind whirling.

He'd called me his dove. My chest went light, when I thought of that. I tried to crush it back down. *This is Konstantin Gulyev. He doesn't have a soft side.*

We were driving in convoy, with a big black SUV full of guards in front of us and another behind. As we passed through neighborhoods Konstantin didn't control, I saw criminals start to flee. A pimp suddenly darted into an alley, leaving the women he'd been talking to behind. A dealer turned and sprinted, dropping a packet of drugs behind him and not stopping to pick it up. They must think Konstantin was arriving to take over, but why were they so scared of him? Weren't criminals all ultimately on the same side?

Then we reached one of the neighborhoods he *did* control. And instead of fear, I saw...relief. The people out at night here weren't criminals, they were people out walking their dogs or on their way to and from bars. They nodded respectfully as we passed. A young couple were walking together and I saw the woman squeeze her partner's hand as she saw us. *It's okay now.* That seemed to be the mood. *It's okay, now. He's here.*

Half a block further on, the street had been closed off. Three separate buildings were ablaze and the fronts were so badly damaged, it took me a while to figure out that one of them used to be a restaurant, one a bar and one a nightclub.

We pulled up behind the fire department's barricade and climbed out. A crowd of people had gathered to watch, but they parted immediately to let us pass. The fire department were doing their best but all three places were infernos, the heat so intense that I could feel it on my skin, even from all the way back here. The interiors looked to already be completely gutted. *How could a fire take hold that fast? In three different buildings?*

And then I saw the fury on Konstantin's face and kicked myself for being so naive. These fires weren't accidental.

A man raced up to Konstantin. His expensive suit was singed on the cuffs and his shirt was smudged with soot. "We got everyone out," he said breathlessly. His accent was a thicker, heavier version of Konstantin's. Then he started coughing and couldn't stop.

"Injuries?" demanded Konstantin. I could see the emotions battling on his face. He wanted to wait for the poor guy to stop coughing, but he needed to know, *now,* because....

I looked around at the crowd, at the way they were looking at Konstantin. *Because these were his people.* They were in awe of him, respectful of him, but they weren't living in fear of him. They lived under his protection.

"Three," the guy managed at last. "The family who live above the restaurant." He pointed to where white smoke was pouring out of a second story window. "It spread so fast... I got them out, but the man and woman have smoke inhalation. And one of the kids has burns on his arm."

I saw Konstantin's chest swell as he sucked in his breath. His huge shoulders drew back and he had to turn and stare at the fire for a moment just to control his rage. It was the angriest I'd ever seen him. He reached out and silently squeezed the guy's shoulder: *you did good.*

When he was finally able to speak, he started snapping out orders. "Take care of the family's medical bills and move them to a hotel— the best. Make sure their insurance pays out for the fire and give them whatever extra they need to rebuild. Cover up any signs that it was arson. We don't want the FBI sniffing around. And have some of your men patrol the neighborhood for the next few weeks. We can't let this happen again." He nodded towards Grigory. "Talk to Grigory here if you need more guns for your men, he can get you anything you need."

The guy nodded and hurried off.

Konstantin turned to his guards, his voice low but vicious. "And *bring me who did this!*"

The guards scattered, with just four staying to protect us. Konstantin started to walk the crowd and, timidly, people began to approach him, shaking his hand, and telling him what had happened. Some, he gave money. Others just needed reassurance.

I trailed after him, stunned. This wasn't the Konstantin I'd imagined. In the year I'd watched him, I'd focused on his meetings with politicians and other criminals, and he was ruthless with them. But when it came to civilians.... I took another look at the streets around us. This neighborhood was *safe*. There were no dealers or pimps here. Now I understood why street criminals were scared of him. He cleared them out, in the neighborhoods he took over.

Konstantin was terrifyingly powerful, but he ruled as a benevolent king. He was *liked*.

The fire started to spread and the fire department wanted to move their barricade back. The guards helped them clear the crowd and then we left, leaving a handful of guards searching for the arsonist.

As the Mercedes pulled away, Konstantin sat slumped in the back seat, rubbing his stubbled jaw. He was furious...and the person he seemed angriest at was himself. He glanced at me and saw I was watching him. "It's not right," he muttered at last. "A child getting hurt."

I knew I shouldn't say anything. Christina would be nothing but loyal. But I needed to understand. "If there's a war between you and the other bosses, more civilians will get hurt. More children."

He scowled and shook his head. "War is inevitable."

I blinked at him. "Only if you keep expanding. Can't you just...*stop?*"

He turned and stared at me. And those gray eyes gave me my answer, one that made my heart sink. He'd never stop. He *couldn't* stop. And that meant Carrie was right: we had to stop him.

And yet...when he turned and looked through the rear window at the orange glow behind us...he looked like the loneliest man alive. As if he really didn't want a war, didn't want innocent blood spilled...and yet he had no choice.

Without thinking, I reached out and took his hand.

He looked at me again, this time in shock, then stared down at our joined hands. *Christina never did that,* I realized. I remembered looking at the photo of the two of them, about to board his private jet. *That* was what had been wrong with it: they hadn't been holding hands. I'd *never* seen them hold hands. It was true: they really weren't in love.

Konstantin kept staring at our hands and I thought he was going to pull away, or tell me off. But after a few seconds, I felt his hand slowly start to curl around mine, enveloping it in warmth.

I gave his hand a tiny, tentative squeeze.

He looked at me and there was confusion in his eyes. Not *what are you doing?* This was helpless confusion: *what's happening?*

And then he slowly squeezed back.

We sat like that in silence for nearly an hour as the convoy circled the neighborhood. And then a phone call came in and the driver turned to Konstantin. "They've found the guy who set the fires," he said.

Konstantin's grip tightened. "Take me to him."

24

HAILEY

W E CLIMBED OUT of the car and I wrapped my arms around me against the sudden chill. A fierce wind was blowing down the street, scattering trash like leaves. When I looked up, I saw we were at the foot of an enormous skyscraper but...there was something wrong with it. The thing was so *black,* it just seemed to soak up light. And its sides seemed to be moving.

I squinted and, as my eyes adjusted to the dark, I drew in my breath. The skyscraper was still being built. There was no glass in the windows, that's why it didn't reflect. And lots of the floors didn't have walls, yet, just sheets of plastic, flapping in the wind. *We're going in there?*

There was an elevator for the construction workers, but it was just a yellow-painted cage, completely open above waist height. Konstantin and I climbed in and I gulped as the ground dropped away. I don't like heights. I'm okay when I'm looking through my camera because I feel like I'm down on the ground with my target, but I don't like being reminded that I'm up high...and with the wind tugging at my clothes and the way the cage swayed and creaked, it was impossible to forget. When we passed the tenth floor, I couldn't look anymore. I closed my eyes and clung onto the handrail and prayed for it to be over.

But we kept climbing, higher and higher. The wind grew steadily worse and soon I was hugging myself to keep warm: it was October and I'd run out of the mansion in my thin sweater and skirt.

After what felt like forever, we stopped. I opened my eyes....

We were on the roof. And from how small the lights below us looked, we must have been at least thirty stories up. The roof was huge but we were in one corner of it so the edges were far too close for comfort. And the parapet hadn't been built yet: there was nothing to stop you falling off.

We started to move and, before I knew what I was doing, I pressed close to Konstantin, my arm hooking around his and our bodies pushed together from shoulder to hip. That made me feel better. We took several steps before I caught myself. This was *Konstantin.* How could a man like that make me feel safe?

But he did.

In the center of the roof, the rest of the guards waited, holding a struggling man in place. He had long, greasy black hair and his stained t-shirt was stretched over his gut. But he looked strong, too: his biceps were huge and it was taking three of the guards to hold him still. There was something unsettling about the way he stared at us, a kind of arrogance. *He's not afraid.* I'd never seen anyone not be scared of Konstantin.

The guy spoke up as we approached. His Russian accent was heavy and rough, the syllables like splintering slabs of lead. "This is why you bring me here?" He nodded at the guards. "So you can watch your trained dogs beat me?"

I looked around and realized why we'd come here. We were the tallest structure for miles: no one could see us, up on the roof. I was guessing Konstantin owned the building, so no need to worry about security cameras, either.

Whatever happened here, the authorities would never know.

"My guards won't be needed," said Konstantin, his voice dangerously quiet, and he started across the roof towards the men. As soon as he was gone, my vertigo came back. The wind was getting worse: I swore the whole building was swaying slightly, each time a gust hit. I backed up against the elevator and grabbed hold of it, trying not to look at the tiny lights far below.

Konstantin slipped off his suit jacket as he walked and tossed it to one of his men. He unfastened his tie, then took off his shirt.

It was the first time I'd seen him topless and he was breathtaking, his back a wide vee of hard, tan muscle, his shoulders hulking and powerful, as if they could bear the weight of the world.

Near his collarbone, two ten-pointed star tattoos marked him as a leader. Then came those huge, hard pecs. If I'd put both my hands on just one of them, fingers spread as wide as they could go, I still wouldn't have been able to cover it all. He narrowed down to a tight core, the ridges of his abs bisected by a deep line, and then the diagonal slash of his adonis belt, disappearing down into his pants. He was ripped, but it wasn't the jacked up, veiny look of bodybuilders. It was a hardened look that made me think of a soldier. He'd got this way by fighting, by building his empire one battle at a time.

"Let him go," Konstantin told the guards.

Oh God, he's going to deal with this guy himself?! Konstantin was strong, but the other guy looked mean as hell. There was real muscle under the fat and both of his hands were covered in big, ugly-looking rings. I imagined those fists slamming into Konstantin and—

I was worried about him. This man I'd come to betray, the one who'd kill me if he found out who I really was... I didn't want to see him get hurt.

The guards released the man and he charged at Konstantin, lowering his head at the last minute. They slammed together and I drew in a panicked breath as Konstantin slid backward. *What if he goes off the edge?!*

But Konstantin regained his footing and the fight began. I winced as the other guy started throwing punches at Konstantin's face and ribs...and Konstantin just took it. He stood his ground, barely moving, and when a punch snapped his head to the side, he turned it back for more. *Why isn't he hitting back? He's going to get killed!* I wanted to look away, but I forced myself to watch.

And then I saw what was happening.

Konstantin's teeth were gritted and he was panting in pain, but with each punch he absorbed, his face set a little more, becoming a mask of fury. *He's punishing himself,* I realized. *He thinks he deserves this, because those people got hurt.* That's why he was fighting the man himself instead of letting one of his men do it. This was his responsibility.

And when his rage had built to a peak, he exploded. His first punch sent the guy staggering back across the roof. His second knocked him almost off his feet. Then Konstantin grabbed him by the throat and, despite his size, hefted him into the air. "*Who do you work for?*" he bellowed.

The guy spat out a tooth. "I answer to Dmitri Ralavich," he said with pride.

I caught my breath. Then my stomach lurched as the whole roof shifted under my feet. It wasn't my imagination: the building *was* swaying in the wind.

Konstantin scowled. "You're lying. Ralavich is in St. Petersburg."

"Ralavich is here in New York, with a hundred men like me." The arsonist lifted his chin. "We're going to take this city from you."

I listened, stunned. No one was looking at me, so I risked whispering to Calahan. "Are you getting this?"

Calahan answered immediately. "I'm getting it." He sounded as worried as me. Konstantin was the most notorious crime boss, but Ralavich was pure, undiluted evil.

"Ralavich will never take over here," Konstantin snarled.

But Ralavich's guy wouldn't back down, even though Konstantin had him by the throat. He was nothing like one of Konstantin's men, with their calm order and military discipline. He reminded me more of the dealer who'd killed Rufus, just a street thug but with an ego swollen with power. "The people you protect will be ours," he said. "The women will be our whores and the men our slaves and the ones who won't obey will burn in their beds. And you and your family will be forgotten."

For a second, Konstantin's eyes went colder than I'd ever seen them. A merciless cold, a cold without hope. There was so much pain there, so much loss, it made my chest ache. This was the root of all the cold I'd seen in him, I was sure of it. This was what those brief glimpses of warmth were fighting against.

Then he roared in fury and strode towards the corner of the roof, the guy still dangling from his fist. "Oh Jesus, he's going to kill him," I whispered.

"Don't interfere!" said Calahan quickly. "Remember, you're Christina!"

I knew he was right. Christina wouldn't care if Konstantin killed the guy. And I knew that Konstantin must have killed before: he couldn't have gotten this far without taking a life. But I couldn't just stand by and watch him kill someone. Not even when it was an arsonist who'd nearly killed a whole family. "Stop!" I yelled. But the wind had risen to a howl and it snatched my voice away.

"Hailey, don't!" warned Calahan.

I had to get closer and that meant.... I gulped and started running towards Konstantin. He was on my side of the building, but at the opposite end, so my path took me right along the edge of the roof. I was terrifyingly close to that sickening black drop and the wind was coming in fierce, unpredictable gusts, ready to send me over. "Stop!" I yelled again. This time, some of the guards heard and looked around in amazement. But Konstantin didn't react.

I was halfway along the roof when the gust of wind hit me. I went staggering sideways, awkward and unstable in my heels, and came to a skittering stop—

I looked down. My feet were six inches from the edge of the roof.

Two of the guards were running towards me but I ignored them, took a deep breath, and ran on. Konstantin was dangling the arsonist over the edge, now, his feet kicking in the air. All he had to do was open his hand.

I stopped just a few feet from Konstantin, which was as close to the corner of the roof as I dared get. The drop filled my whole vision and I went woozy with fear, rocking on my heels, my stomach trying to climb into my mouth. If the wind blew me now, there was nothing I could do except scream all the way to the bottom. "*Stop!*" I yelled over the wind.

This time, Konstantin must have heard me. But he still didn't react. His eyes were wild and he was breathing in huge, rasping pants.

So I did the only thing I could think of: I lunged forward, my toes right on the edge, and grabbed hold of his outstretched arm.

25

KONSTANTIN

T HE MAN WAS HEAVY, but I could have stood there holding him all night. The pain was thundering through my veins, stronger than it had been in years. I could see the faces of the people Ralavich had taken from me. I could feel the bite of the icy water. It made me strong, made me sure of what I had to do.

And then *she* was there, her arms wrapped around my bicep, tugging my arm down, trying to bring the guy back onto the roof. "*Stop!*" she was yelling. "*Please!*"

I blinked at her. Just for a second, I didn't recognize her. It was Christina's face, but the horror in her eyes at what I was about to do... that wasn't Christina at all. Christina would have understood me killing him, maybe even urged me on. But this woman....

She thought I was better than that.

I scowled. I had to kill him. Anything else would be weak. If she'd forgotten what I was, in her time in hospital, she'd soon remember. As soon as I opened my hand and—

"*Please!*" she begged again.

My hand twitched. The man's sweaty neck slipped in my fingers and Christina caught her breath....

...but I couldn't seem to open my hand all the way. I could see the pain in Christina's eyes. The hurt I'd cause if I did it. And I couldn't bring myself to hurt her. *Weak. Weak, weak, weak....*

I turned and hurled the guy back onto the roof. He rolled to a stop, bruised and battered...but alive.

My guards were well disciplined. They surrounded the man and looked to me for orders as if nothing had happened. But I could see a few of them casting furtive glances at Christina, and at each other. *Did she really just...?*

I had to re-establish control. "Take him!" I snapped. "Put him out of commission but don't kill him. Wait for us downstairs."

They grabbed the man and ran off. When the rooftop was empty except for Christina and me, I marched over to her, furious. "What's the matter with you? You can *never* go against me in front of my men!"

She nodded meekly, her eyes on the floor. God, she suddenly looked so small, so scared. And yet she'd stood up to me when I was in a blind rage. Even my guards wouldn't dare do that. I had to admire her bravery... and that made me start to soften.

I tried to coax the anger back. "You never cared what I did before!"

She looked up at me, eyes huge. "I—I know, but...." She flung her arms out, helpless. *I can't explain.*

And I couldn't explain what was happening to me. The more I looked down into those big, innocent eyes, the more I felt my control slipping away. Down in the dungeon, her goodness had fired my lust. But now, up here, it was triggering something else in me, something that *lifted* in my chest. I *couldn't* feel that. Not since that day all hope died. But it was real, just as real as the pain. And then I saw that she was shivering. God, she must be freezing. And I couldn't give her my jacket, it was thirty stories down, with one of my men. I gave one last sigh, furious with myself for being weak... and then I grabbed her and pulled her against my chest, wrapping my arms around her. Her breasts squashed against my chest, but for once, it wasn't about wanting to fuck her. I felt protective. Tender. *Weak.*

I shook my head. "Damn you, *golub*," I muttered.

26

HAILEY

W HEN WE GOT HOME, Konstantin headed straight up the stairs to our bedroom. My heart started thumping in my chest, speeding up with each stair we climbed. This was it: he'd want to continue what we'd started down in the dungeon.

The bedroom had an adjoining bathroom for each of us. He disappeared into his and I heard the shower turn on. I raced into mine and did the same, washing the smell of smoke from my hair. Then I rushed into the closet in a towel and tried to figure out what to wear. What the hell did Christina wear for bed? Lingerie? Just panties? Nothing at all? In the end, I went for panties, but kept the towel wrapped around myself, too self-conscious to be topless straight away.

When I walked back into the bedroom, Konstantin was sitting on the bed, booting up his laptop, a towel wrapped around his waist. God, he looked incredible, the tan of his skin standing out against the soft white towel, droplets of water falling from his wet hair and leaving wet trails as they slid down his chest and abs. As I watched, he made a fist and pressed his ring to a metal plate on the edge of the laptop. I saw the screen change as it finished booting and his email appeared. *His ring is the hardware key!*

I sat awkwardly on the corner of the bed while he dealt with his work. What was their normal routine? Did Christina just wait for him? Did she do her own thing? He kept throwing glances my way and each time he looked, his gaze was a little more heated. I felt the warmth start to ripple down my body and my breathing went tight.

He suddenly snapped the laptop shut and strode over to a bureau. I jumped up and met him there, breathless and expectant, but still uncertain of the routine. Would he grab me? Kiss me? Just hurl me on the bed?

He opened the bureau and took out a bottle of vodka and two glasses, then poured us both a shot. *What?* They drank before sex? I looked uncertainly at my glass: I've never been much of a drinker. But he knocked his back and I did the same, feeling it burn all the way down my throat and then slam into my brain, making me reel.

He took the glass from my fingers and put it down. I saw his gaze track down over my face, my neck...down to my breasts. I looked down. The towel must have slipped a little when I jumped up from the bed because the top of it was dangerously low: another inch and you'd be able to see my nipples. When I looked up again, he was glaring at me. I was completely confused. Downstairs in the dungeon, he'd had me strip naked. Why would seeing some cleavage annoy him now?

He stepped closer. One big hand grabbed the towel at the front and twisted, bunching it, as if about to pull it off. He drew in a shuddering breath, every muscle in that magnificent chest going hard. *What's the matter? Why is he hesitating?*

And then he closed his eyes and said, "Goodnight, Christina."

And he turned and stalked off towards the bed. I was left standing there, hurt. *Doesn't he want me?* Part of me was shocked by how fast things had changed: just hours ago, I'd been worried that he'd want to sleep with me. Now, I was worried that he didn't.

He climbed into the huge bed...and lay down on his side, right at the very edge, his back turned to me.

And suddenly I understood.

Sex was for the dungeon. All that lust was carefully contained and locked in a box and he only let it out down there, where he could be in absolute control. Because if he had sex with me here, in a bedroom, if we acted like a normal couple....

Then he might start to feel something for me.

That's why he was annoyed when my towel started to slip. He'd thought I was tempting him, and he'd had to fight with himself not to whip the towel off me and fuck me. It wasn't that he didn't want me. He wanted me *too much*.

I slowly climbed into bed and lay down on the edge furthest from him, just as Christina would have done. But I faced towards him so that I was staring at his muscled back. It was the saddest thing I'd ever seen. To sleep alone is horrible. But to deliberately sleep alone *when you're with someone,* to deny yourself not just sex but closeness.... All I wanted was to press myself against his back and cuddle him, to ease the pain I'd seen on the rooftop.

It wasn't just me. I could see the tension in his back, feel the need rolling off him in waves. He wanted to turn around and hold me. And I wanted him to because... being held by him would make me feel safe. I knew it made no sense: I knew how dangerous he was and what he'd do to me if he found out I was FBI. But when he'd wrapped me in his arms on the rooftop, I'd felt like nothing bad could touch me and I needed to feel that again.

But he stayed there, an immovable rock. And so I stayed where I was, four feet and a thousand miles away.

When I was sure he was asleep, I slid across the bed and sat looking down at him. Even in sleep, his face was tense. I brushed the hair back from his forehead and gazed at his scar: a nasty, jagged thing that led up under his hairline. What the hell had happened to him? What could make anyone shut themselves off so completely from anything that might make him feel?

One thing I knew without any doubt: Christina had been telling the truth about not loving him, and he hadn't loved her, either. Because if they'd had any feelings for each other at all, the arrangement wouldn't have worked. They would have snapped within days and grabbed each other.

Konstantin had found the one person in the world who could handle a relationship without emotions. Christina had been perfect for him.

The problem was... I wasn't Christina.

27

KONSTANTIN

I THRASHED UPWARDS through black water, my hands clawing at ice that wouldn't give... and woke disoriented and panting, sucking in the warm, dry air of the bedroom until the ache in my chest went away.

The dreams were back. That made no sense. They should have gone again, now that Christina was back.

I turned to look at her. She was still asleep, lying sprawled on her back, her arms up beside her head, open and trusting as a child. That was different, too. Before the accident, she'd always gone to sleep curled up on her side, like me, and stayed turned away from me until morning.

I allowed myself a moment to stare at her, knowing it was weak. God, she was beautiful. More beautiful, since she came back to me. The face was the same but there was an openness to her. As if she no longer had any secrets from me.

I slid out of bed. It was still early and I didn't want to fire up the shower and wake her so I threw on a robe and marched out into the hallway, heading for my study. I almost walked into Victoria, Christina's young, blonde maid, carrying an armful of dresses. "All

Miss Rogan's clothes from Milan are pressed and ready, Sir," she told me. "Is she awake? Can I go and hang them for her?"

She was smiling. Victoria never smiled, not when she was anywhere near our bedroom. Christina had always been viciously cruel to her: nothing was ever good enough or quick enough and she'd reduced the poor girl to tears many times. I think it was jealousy, because Victoria was pretty.

And yet now Victoria actually seemed happy. I took the dresses from her and said I'd pass them on, then slipped quietly back inside our room and stared at Christina again.

She'd changed. She'd become gentler, kinder, more innocent.

And what was unsettling was how much I liked it.

28

HAILEY

I WOKE, rolled onto my side, and groped around blindly. *Where are my glasses?*

"What are you looking for?" asked a Russian voice that vibrated right down my spine.

I sat bolt upright, the memories landsliding down on top of me. The mission. The mansion. My new face. *Konstantin.*

He was standing next to the bed, wrapped in a soft white robe that set off his tan. The inner edges of that strong chest were visible through the vee in the front and all I wanted to do was run over to him and push up against him like a cat, sliding my head inside his robe and resting it against that hard, warm muscle. *God, what's happening to me?*

There was a robe for me, too, and we wore them down to the dining room for breakfast. I stared at the flawless white tablecloth and gleaming silver cutlery, at the waiter who stood ready to take our orders. *We can order anything we like?!* My usual breakfast was coffee and an energy bar, eaten at my desk.

Konstantin ordered eggs, bacon, sausage and toast. I was about to do the same when I realized I had no idea what Christina normally ate.

To my relief, the chef asked, "Your usual, Miss Rogan?" I nodded in relief. "Yes, please."

He blinked and cocked his head, as if me saying *please* was a surprise, and then hurried away.

A waiter brought Konstantin *The New York Times* and he shook it out and disappeared behind it. Papers at breakfast: *awesome*. I'm a news junkie and I hadn't caught up in days—

The waiter handed me a glossy fashion magazine. *Oh.*

Konstantin's breakfast arrived: a groaning plate loaded with at least four eggs, a teetering stack of bacon, a pile of thick sausages and half a loaf of toast. My mouth started to water.

Then the waiter set a smoothie in front of me. Not above my place setting, where a drink would go. Right where the plate would be. That *was* my breakfast.

And it was green. Not the bright, cheerful green of apples and kiwi fruit and other tasty things. An ominous gray-green halfway between avocado and kale.

I looked up at the waiter, thinking maybe he was messing with me. But he wasn't smiling: in fact, he looked scared. "It's just how you like it, miss," he reassured me. When I just stared at him, he started to go pale and I had to quickly smile to make him relax. God, were *all* the staff terrified of me?

I took a sip. God, it was disgusting, thick and gloopy and I could taste broccoli and fish oil and something bitter and pungent that could have been Brussel sprouts. I looked up at the waiter. "It's perfect, thank you," I managed.

"I don't know how you drink that stuff," muttered Konstantin from behind his paper.

I wanted to get it over with as quickly as possible so I gulped it down and was finished long before him. I climbed the stairs towards our bedroom, full of vitamins, but in desperate need of something to wash the taste away.

But on the second floor, I stopped. Konstantin's study was right there. I bit my lip. I still had a mission. And I knew he'd be safely downstairs for at least a few minutes.

I sneaked inside. The room must have been a bedroom originally because a door led off it to a small bathroom. The map on the wall was of New York, with neighborhoods color-coded to show who controlled them. Right in the middle of Konstantin's territory were three red spots, like drops of blood, showing where Ralavich had set fires the night before. I frowned at them. Why had Ralavich done it? He couldn't possibly hope to take over those neighborhoods, let alone hold them: Konstantin was far too powerful. So what did Ralavich hope to gain by scaring the people who lived there?

I searched the drawers of Konstantin's desk, but they were empty and the desk itself was clear. He must lock everything in the safe every night.

I crept over and took a look at it. The thing was ancient—why were so many things in the house so old? But it was still sturdy enough: there was no way of getting it open without the combination. I had my phone in the pocket of my robe so I snapped a quick photo of the door and sent it to Calahan: maybe he could help.

Then I heard the stairs creak. *Shit!* I raced out onto the landing and turned towards the next flight of stairs...but it was too late. Konstantin rounded the corner and saw me.

His mood changed in a heartbeat. "What are you doing?" he snapped.

I took a faltering step back. "Nothing! Going upstairs!"

He stalked over to me and frowned suspiciously at the door to his study. "Were you in there?"

I backed up again. "No! Of course not!"

He took a step towards me. I shrank back against what I thought was the wall. But my ass hit something smooth and polished and when I put my hand behind me to steady myself, it hit only air. I screamed and flailed as I tipped over the banister—

He grabbed the front of my robe and jerked me forward to safety. I slammed into his chest and he wrapped his arms around me, holding me close. I could feel my heart pounding at how close I'd come...and I could feel his heart hammering as well, at the shock of nearly losing me.

When he gently pushed me back, all the anger had gone out of him. He didn't say *sorry, but* I could see the guilt on his face. His eyes had a protective gleam that made me go weak inside and he gripped my wrists like he didn't ever want to let me go. "Don't go in my study," he said gently. "Okay?"

I nodded quickly, too awash with adrenaline to speak.

He disappeared into his study and closed the door and I climbed the stairs to our bedroom on shaking legs. If he'd finished breakfast a few seconds earlier... if he'd seen me taking a photo of the safe....

In the bedroom, I drank a tall glass of water and leaned against the wall while I tried to slow my breathing.

"You okay?" said Calahan's voice in my ear.

I sat down heavily at the dressing table, staring at my reflection in the mirror. "Yes," I lied.

What I didn't want to say was, in that moment when he'd nearly caught me, I hadn't just been scared. I'd felt...*bad.* Just for a fleeting second, I'd felt disloyal for betraying him.

"Tell me about Ralavich," I said. I started to do my make-up as we talked.

"He's *very. Bad. News.* Lots of drugs. Some guns. But his specialty is brothels in St. Petersburg that...they aren't normal brothels. The women are all trafficked and the men, they pay to...." Calahan's seen a lot of evil, in his time. I knew this must be something awful, for it to be so difficult for him to say. "They call them *rape clubs,*" he managed at last, his voice shaking with anger and disgust.

"And now he's trying to expand into America," I said, my voice tight. "He wants to bring that *here.* But how could he possibly hope to take on Konstantin?"

Carrie came on the line. "Hailey, the mission is Konstantin."

I bit my lip. "But if you'd seen what Ralavich did...he was happy to burn families in their homes, just to make a statement. I feel like *he's* the real danger. Konstantin...people *respect* him. He protects them. They're not the same—"

"*All* these men are the same," said Carrie sharply. Then, more gently. "Hailey, it's important not to get drawn in."

I flushed. Was that what was happening? Was my judgment sliding, because I was attracted to him? "Yes ma'am," I said, chastened. But it still felt wrong.

I told them about the safe and they said they'd show the photo to the FBI's technical team. Then I finished off my make-up and did my hair. I was gradually getting faster at it, but I was also realizing it's a lot easier to look glamorous when you don't have a job to rush off to each morning.

The weather had changed. The freezing winds of the night before had dropped away and it was a bright, clear day. I pulled on a green jersey dress and a soft pink cardigan to keep my shoulders warm. I wasn't going to risk any more sneaking around, not right now. So I figured I'd explore the rest of the mansion. But when I opened the bedroom door to step out, Grigory was there, his hand raised to knock.

Before I could stop him, he'd pushed me inside and kicked the door closed behind him. "Konstantin's in his study," he panted, his hands already on my waist and sliding upwards. "We have at least an hour."

My eyes went wide. *This* is how they'd done it? Right here in our bedroom, while Konstantin was downstairs?! It was a miracle they'd never been caught!

Grigory walked me backwards towards the bed, our bodies pressed together. His hands pulled my dress up over my ass and I could feel his cock hardening against my thigh. "No," I said into his shoulder, but he ignored me. "*No!*" I said, more loudly.

He stopped and I twisted away from him, breathing hard. I staggered away, tugging my dress back into place.

He ran a hand through his hair, angry and hurt. "What's the matter with you? You normally...."—he shook his head—"you *enjoy* the risk."

I swallowed. "Not anymore."

He shook his head. "Then let's get out of here. Leave him and let's *go!* You keep saying it'll be soon. *When?!*"

I stared at him. It was worse than I thought: Christina hadn't just been having an affair with him, she'd been planning to run away with him. "Things are different, now," I croaked. "Konstantin—"

"He doesn't love you! But I do!"

And I could see in his eyes that it was true. I felt awful for him and I could see exactly how it had happened. Of all the guards, he was the one who was closest to Konstantin and Christina. He'd been with them every day, for months. He'd seen his boss's sexy girlfriend, seen how she was trapped in a loveless relationship, and he'd wanted to rescue her. I actually started to feel a little sorry for Christina. Maybe I'd been too hard on her. Maybe, starved of warmth and affection, she *had* fallen in love with Grigory, and planned to run off with him as soon as she'd accrued enough money from Konstantin.

I took a deep breath. "I need to think," I told him. "Just be patient."

I started to back away, but he grabbed my shoulder and drew me back to him. And then he leaned down and—

I drew in my breath as he kissed me. He was very different to Konstantin: there was no heady rush of pleasure, no dominant, commanding intensity that sent a spike of heat straight down to my groin. But each press of his lips was full of love: it was a slow, sweet, lover's kiss, light as a butterfly but loaded with the weight of how he felt for me. He buried his hands in my hair and it felt so good, for a second I lost myself in it....

And then I gently pushed him away. "I have to go," I told him. And ran.

I raced down the stairs, lips still throbbing. As I passed the door to Konstantin's study, my cheeks exploded into heat and my chest contracted. *Guilt?* I told myself it made no sense. I was lying to Konstantin, plotting to betray him. What did it matter if I let some other guy kiss me?

But that's how I felt. I knew I couldn't let Grigory kiss me again.

I didn't want to run into him again so I hurried out of the back of the mansion, somewhere I hadn't been yet. When I saw what was in front of me, my run slowed to a jog and then a walk. And then I just stopped and gazed around in wonder.

Many years ago, someone had planted a garden to match the mansion. There were flower beds full of color, tree-lined paths where lovers could stroll and red-brick walls that divided the garden up and created secret, shady spots where you could sit on a bench with a book.

But while the mansion had been maintained and modernized, the garden hadn't had any attention in decades. The grass was knee high and wildflowers fought with roses in the flower beds. The trees had grown out of control, some of them twisting together until you couldn't see where one stopped and another began. Ivy had engulfed one of the oaks, transforming it into a rearing dragon with shining green scales, while three more trees had fallen in storms and lay on their sides, gathering moss. Some of the walls were crumbling and the wooden benches had been bleached almost white by the sun.

It was insanely beautiful. The sun filtered through the trees casting dappled light on the ground and throwing shafts of gold onto old sundials and other abandoned treasures. The leaves had just finished their transition to the red and copper of fall and a gentle wind turned them into a rolling sea of vivid color. I could hear birdsong from high above and brightly-colored butterflies fluttered through the flower beds. And then, just as I started forward, a rabbit hopped out of the undergrowth and onto the path, looked at me, and hopped off into the grass.

I felt something inside me *lift*...and tears prickled at the corners of my eyes because I was suddenly aware of a deep, crushing ache that had been there ever since I left Wisconsin, a need I'd been pushing out of my mind all these years.

I ran into the garden and started exploring. I felt twigs catch and pull at my dress as I pushed through bushes. A stocking tore, scraped on rough bark as I climbed over logs. The heels of my shoes sank deep into the earth, the shining leather ruined forever. And I didn't care about any of it. I was drunk on nature: there were birds and rabbits and hedgehogs and field mice...I wished I had my camera. It was the happiest I'd been in a long time.

Hours flew by. Then I heard something huge crashing through the undergrowth behind me. "Christina?"

I was getting used to the name, now. And hearing it in *that* accent...the silvery hiss of the *is* like a soft breath against my neck, *then* the hard *t* that was almost a kiss. It made me go shaky every single time. I turned to see him clamber over a fallen, mossy tree trunk.

"What are you doing?" He sounded genuinely bemused. "One of the guards said he saw you come out here hours ago."

I looked around in wonder. "It's *amazing!*"

He gazed around, bewildered. *What is?*

I was so blown away by the place that I forgot to be Christina. "Look around you! It's *wild,* it's like nature's taken over!"

He shook his head. "It's a mess." He rubbed at his stubble. "We should get it all cut back. An assassin could use the undergrowth to sneak close to the house."

I stared at him. "Do you have to see *everything* as a threat?"

He frowned at me, astonished. *Everything is!*

I sighed and moved closer. "*Look!* Just look at...." I turned a slow circle. There was so much to see, I couldn't pick just one thing. "*Everything!*"

He frowned deeper, exasperated, and picked a leaf out of my hair. But he gamely turned his head and looked at the trees, the flowers, the butterflies...and nothing happened. His eyes didn't light up. He didn't *see*. Whatever had happened to him, it had made him narrow his worldview down to his empire: money and allies and enemies and threats.

"Can't you see the beauty in *anything?*" I asked, looking up at him in desperation.

He slowly turned his head towards me. Then he looked down into my eyes. And that's when I saw the gray flicker and soften, that tiny trace of blue slipping through. I swallowed, feeling my chest go light, feeling that helpless flutter. And the longer we held each other's gaze, the more the battle in his eyes grew.

My breathing hitched. He took a step forward, awkward and

halting. I saw his hands twitch. The mood was totally different to the airport, or at the bottom of the stairs. This was soft and romantic, everything he denied he could be. He was going to—

He leaned down. His finger lifted my chin, tilting my head back to meet him. His lips brushed mine....

And then he tore himself away, straightening up and cursing in Russian. For a moment, he wouldn't look at me and I was left there stunned. *I wanted him to. God, I really wanted him to.* There was no way I could deny it, now. I was starting to have feelings for him...and I wanted him to have them for me. *Am I falling for him? For someone I know is pure evil? Someone I know I'm going to betray?*

I had to get out of there. I turned and stumbled off into the undergrowth, heading for a building I'd seen earlier but hadn't explored yet.

It was a glasshouse that must have been built at the same time as the mansion. The bricks came only to knee height and then it was all ironwork and panes of glass. The green paint was flaking off the metal and the glass was so old and cloudy, it distorted the outside world like a funhouse mirror. Inside, I paced up and down past tables laden with ancient, crumbling flowerpots. *Remember who he is! He'd kill you if he found out who you really are!*

And then I saw him coming after me. The cloudy glass made him just a huge, dark shape, a monster approaching.

He opened the door and for a second he just stared at me. He was breathing fast with anger but it didn't feel directed at me. He was mad at himself. *Because he nearly let himself feel something?*

"You must come out of there," he told me. "It's not safe." He glanced up at the ceiling. "It's very old. The glass could fall from the frames."

I looked around. The metal had baked and frozen through so many New York summers and winters that it had deformed, and most of the putty that held the glass in place had crumbled away. Probably everything *was* pretty precarious. I looked up at him and there was a sudden swell of warmth in my chest. He'd followed me in here because he was worried about me.

I nodded and he held the door for me as I walked out. He followed me back to the mansion, but his heavy footsteps never came closer than ten feet. I could feel his eyes on my back the whole way and it wasn't just lust, anymore, it was something deeper. A longing that was so dangerous, he had to hang back so it didn't overwhelm him completely. *Oh God, what am I going to do?* I could feel myself rushing towards a precipice I wouldn't come back from.

Back inside the mansion, I headed upstairs and heard Konstantin break off behind me and enter his study. Just as I reached our bedroom, the pocket of my cardigan started to buzz. I pulled out Christina's phone, confused. I hadn't set any alarms.

But she had. A reminder was on the screen. *Meet Mom to give her birthday gift.*

My eyes widened. *Shit!* I'd been so focused on Christina's relationship with Konstantin, I hadn't thought about her having family or friends. I'd fooled Konstantin and Grigory...but how the hell was I going to fool Christina's mother?

29

HAILEY

T HE REMINDER came with a time: noon, which was in forty minutes, and a place: the food court of a fancy shopping mall in Manhattan. The problem was, I couldn't leave without the gift, and I had no idea where Christina had left it. I filled Calahan in as I searched. First I went through the walk-in closet. Then the drawers. Then it occurred to me that the gift might be something small, and Christina might be carrying it around in her purse. But all I found in there was money, make-up and a parking permit for an apartment complex called Barlow Heights.

"The shopping mall's a half hour drive away," said Calahan in my ear. "You need to be leaving *now.*"

"Not helping!" I told him. I went through Christina's drawers a second time. Checked under the bed. Went through the drawers *again*, this time emptying them out onto the floor. Nothing. *Where is it?!* I ran to check under the bed again and cracked my ankle against an open drawer.

"Have you tried the closet?" asked Calahan helpfully.

"*Yes,* I've tried the closet!" I snapped, clutching my ankle in pain. But I ran back in there again and—

On the floor in one corner, there were some piles of neatly-folded winter clothes. Which was weird because there was plenty of hanger space for them. I lifted a coat off the top of the pile....

There was a box wrapped in lurid red metallic paper and tied with a silver bow. The card taped to the top read *Mom*. Christina had wedged it into the corner and then piled clothes all around it and on top of it. *Why hide a birthday gift?* But it didn't matter now. I grabbed it and ran.

When I asked one of the guards if he'd drive me into the city, he didn't even bat an eyelid: apparently shopping trips were how Christina spent most of her time. Within minutes, I was in the back of the big black Mercedes, speeding towards Manhattan.

I arrived at the mall with five minutes to spare and found the food court. But then I had a new problem. "How am I going to recognize her?" I asked Calahan.

"I'm working on it," he said. "Trying to find a photo."

I paced back and forth, clutching the gift, my heart racing, desperately looking for someone who looked like an older version of Christina. *How am I going to do this?* What if she started talking about family gossip, or stuff from my childhood I had no idea about?

"Get out of there!" yelled Calahan, so loud it hurt my ear.

I started moving. "What? What's going on?" I reached the edge of the food court and merged into a crowd of shoppers. "Talk to me!"

"I found Christina's mother," said Calahan breathlessly. "She died four years ago."

30

HAILEY

I RACED into the restrooms and shut myself in a cubicle. "What the hell is going on?" I asked Calahan.

"Well, clearly Christina wasn't coming here to meet her mom. It must be an errand for Konstantin. A delivery."

I stared at the gift for a second. Then I sat down on the toilet and opened it up.

The whole thing was filled with stacks of $100 bills. I ran some rough math in my head. "There must be a quarter of a million here," I croaked.

I could hear Calahan rubbing at his stubble. "Makes sense. Konstantin knows the FBI are watching him so he gets Christina to deliver it for him."

"But why did Christina have it in her calendar as meeting her mom?"

Despite everything, I heard Calahan chuckle. "You're adorable. You think she's going to carry around a phone full of stuff like, 'Meet arms dealer for lunch,' and 'Pay bribe to politician'?"

I flushed. I wasn't cut out to be a criminal. Then I checked the time. "It's noon," I told Calahan. "I need to go to the meet."

"What?! No!" I could hear the fear in his voice. "A quarter of a million dollars? This is something big. It could be dangerous!"

I stood up, trying not to let my legs shake. "That's why I'm here, right? To find the *something big*. This could be what we need to bring down Konstantin."

"You don't even know who you're meeting or what they look like!"

"We'll just have to hope they recognize me."

Before he could argue, I walked out of the restroom and back into the food court. I started threading my way between the tables, looking at every face. Could he be a criminal? Her? *Them?*

I felt a hand grab my wrist and tug. Before I knew what was happening, my ass was on a seat and I was staring at a slender, dark-haired guy across a table.

"Jesus, he said it would be gift-wrapped," said the guy, nodding at the garish package. "I didn't expect *that.*"

He grabbed the gift from me. And then, before I could speak, he was up and walking, pushing his way through the crowd. "He's getting away!" I whispered to Calahan. "I have to follow him!"

"No! He'll know there's something wrong. I'll try to get him on the mall security cameras." I could hear him frantically pressing buttons and calling for help. "Shit! We don't have agents in place in the parking lot. We thought you were just meeting your mom!" I waited, holding my breath. Then, "We lost him."

I slumped in my seat. We had no idea who the guy was or what Konstantin had just paid him to do. We just knew that something big was happening and that meant the mission would take on a new edge. It wouldn't be enough for me to passively observe, anymore. I'd have to find out what Konstantin was planning so we could use it to bring him down.

Just as I was developing feelings for him, I was going to have to betray him.

31

HAILEY

C ARRIE WANTED a conference call so I'd gone to the one place I knew I could be alone: the garden. I was sitting on the moss-covered tree trunk where Konstantin had found me and I'd found a new friend. Moments after I'd sat down, the biggest, fluffiest ginger cat I'd ever seen had emerged from the long grass like a miniature tiger. After just a few moments of cautiously nuzzling my hand, it had sprung into my lap. It was good cover: if a guard saw me mumbling from a distance, he'd assume I was talking to the cat. Plus, stroking it helped keep me calm and I needed that because the more I talked to my friends at the FBI, the more stressed I felt.

"Do you think you can ask Konstantin what the money was for?" asked Carrie in my earpiece.

I shook my head before I remembered she couldn't see that. "No, that would make him suspicious. He doesn't tell me anything. I was never meant to know what was in that box, I was just meant to hand it over."

"We asked Christina," said Calahan. "Unsurprisingly, she wouldn't talk."

That threw me for a second. Then it clicked that he was talking about the real Christina, the one in FBI custody. God, I'd started thinking of *me* as Christina.

"You'll have to go digging," said Carrie. "His laptop: there must be something in there."

I froze and the cat scowled at me. I resumed my stroking. "The laptop's impossible. It's locked with his ring." But it wasn't just the risk that had made me tense.

Calahan spoke up. "I trust Hailey's opinion. If she says it's impossible, it is."

Carrie went silent. I could feel her brooding on it: she didn't want to put me in danger but.... "This is the best chance we've ever had," she said at last. "Maybe the best chance we'll *ever* have. Something big is going down. If we can find out what that money was for, find out when it's happening, we can catch Konstantin in the act. If you can't get into his laptop, you'll have to get into his safe."

This time, my whole body tensed. "The safe is impossible, too. He's in and out of the study all the time, if he sees me in there...." I remembered how he'd snapped at me, when he'd caught me on the landing—

And how he'd grabbed hold of me, to stop me falling. The guilt in his eyes, the fear at nearly losing me.

I was terrified of getting caught. But more than that: some stubborn, stupid part of me didn't want to betray him.

Carrie sighed. "Then we're back to the laptop. You'll just have to figure out a way to—"

"Christina?"

The cat felt me freeze and sprang off my lap. I jumped up and spun around to see Konstantin striding towards me. He was too far away to have heard anything but that didn't stop my insides twisting with guilt.

"Where did *that* come from?" he asked, looking at the cat.

"I think he lives in the garden. He's really friendly, look." I squatted and reached out to the cat, who eyed me suspiciously, still annoyed at me for jumping up, and then began to nuzzle my hand.

Every few seconds, though, it would break off and look up at Konstantin. "You're scaring it," I told him. "Come down here."

Konstantin blinked, unsure if I was joking. Then he slowly squatted down next to me. He stared around, as if he'd never looked at the world from so low down, before. Then he looked at the cat, utterly bemused.

Fortunately, the cat knew what to do. It rubbed its furry cheek against his knuckles...and approved. It gave them a lick and started to rub against them in earnest. Konstantin stared at it....

I held my breath....

And the corners of his mouth twitched, just a little. It was almost as if he was remembering *how* to smile. For a second, he looked happy—*free.*

Then he turned and looked at me and...I don't know what it was I was doing, I was just enjoying being there, doing something so normal and fun with him. But it triggered something in him. The heat flared in his eyes: that glittering, molten look I was getting to know so well.

He suddenly grabbed my wrist and stood, pulling me to my feet so fast I wobbled on my heels and had to cling onto his arm. "What?" I asked, looking up at him. I could feel myself reacting to his gaze, the heat of it melting me inside. "*What?*" I asked again, hearing my voice go tight with excitement.

He just shook his head and wouldn't explain. He marched towards the house, eating up the distance in huge strides, and I think he would have dragged me along if I hadn't hurried to keep up. When we reached the hallway, he pulled me close. His eyes were glazed with lust and his eyes tracked up and down my body. *What is it? What did he suddenly see, out there?*

He leaned in and put his lips to my ear. He almost breathed the words into me, the dark heat of them twisting around my mind and drawing tight, sending shockwaves down between my thighs. "Go upstairs and put on something...." He paused, considering, and took another look down the length of my body. "Put on something *for me.* Then come downstairs."

And he glanced down, towards the dungeon.

32

KONSTANTIN

I T HAPPENED so fast.

That damn cat was licking my hand and, just for a second, I'd felt like a different person. Maybe the person I could have been, if my life hadn't been torn apart. The sort of man who would have fallen in love, got married, had kids. And then I glanced at her and....

I wasn't looking at Christina. Not the Christina I knew. The Christina I knew was like me, cold-hearted and controlling, incapable of love. This woman was....

This woman was the other one that I would have found. A normal, innocent, *good* woman.

I didn't know how it was possible. Part of me screamed that it was dangerous, that something was wrong. But the lust took over: all I knew was that *I had to have her.* She was the light to my dark and the thought of her writhing under me as I plunged into her...I almost ran her to the house, I was so hard for her.

Now I waited impatiently for her in the dungeon. I'd lit a fire to warm the room. She was going to be naked for a good, long time....

The door creaked open and then her head appeared around it, her eyes going wide as she glanced around. She seemed so nervous...

she normally strutted in here, full of confidence. *Is she playing the innocent to turn me on?* If she was, it was working.

She slipped inside and closed the door behind her. She was wearing an ivory satin robe that covered her down to her knees: why so shy, all of a sudden? Christina normally loved to run through the house in just her underwear, teasing the guards into looking.

That warning bell at the back of my mind again. She'd changed, somehow, since the accident. But: *it's okay. It's Christina, after all.* "Take it off," I ordered, the lust making my voice thick and slow as honey.

She unbelted the robe. Hesitated. And then, in a little show of courage that made my heart ache, she suddenly flung the robe back off her shoulders and let it slither to the floor.

I'd said to wear something *for me* and she couldn't have chosen better. Her creamy breasts—I *swore* they looked bigger—looked amazing in silky bra cups the color of a lush forest, edged with gold thread. What really drove me crazy was the delicate gold ribbon that joined the cups. It was tied together in a bow, the ends hanging tantalizingly down. One little tug and she'd be revealed. The panties matched: a simple triangle of green fabric that concealed her, but that could be stripped away by pulling on the golden bows at her hips.

I'd seen her in lingerie a hundred times but she'd never looked like *this*. Alluring and yet innocent. Seductive and yet *good*. I realized that she wasn't wearing heels or stockings, like she usually did, and it made her seem not just smaller but more naive. As if she wasn't Christina, the vampish sex partner, but some civilian who'd wandered in here by mistake. The idea made my cock almost painfully hard in my pants.

I beckoned her over to me.

33

HAILEY

THE TILES were freezing beneath my bare feet. But with each slow step I took towards him, with each second his gaze soaked into me, I could feel the heat strumming and building, melting me from the inside out. By the time I reached him, I felt like I was on fire and the tiles felt pleasantly cool.

I glanced around and my breathing went tight. *I'm really here.* Deep underground, where no one could hear me scream. This time, there'd be no interruption, no rescue....

And this time, I hadn't wandered down here by accident. He'd told me to come down here and I'd obeyed. Willingly.

I had to, I told myself. *For the mission.* But as the broad sweep of his chest filled my vision, as my fingertips tingled with the need to touch him, to smooth my hands over the soft cotton of his shirt and feel the hot muscle underneath... I knew that wasn't the reason.

He slid a hand over my bare back, making me gasp, and then buried his fingers in my hair. He tugged gently, just enough to make me tilt my head back to look up at him.

I swallowed. God, the raw heat in his eyes, like he wanted to devour me whole. *What had he seen, out there in the garden?*

He moved his head down and I closed my eyes. But he didn't kiss me: not quite. He stopped when our lips were just barely touching and *stroked*, drawing my lower lip down and opening me, and then letting it go, again and again.

The intimacy of it was amazing: our breathing fell in time and my lips became so sensitive that it felt like I could feel his whole body, all of his size and strength, in that one tiny contact. With each brush of his lips, the pleasure rose and spun, making me heady...but what made me go weak was the way I could feel him struggling with himself. He wanted to just full-on kiss me, to bury his tongue in me and *ravish* me, but he was forcing himself to keep everything locked down and controlled, to make it a choreographed dance with exact steps.

And he was losing the fight. First one big hand grabbed mine, then the other. He stood there, his muscled body trembling, his hands kneading my smaller ones as his lips stroked and stroked....

... and *paused*....

He suddenly whirled around and flung me onto the four poster bed. I landed on my back, legs kicking. Before I could speak, he was marching towards me, using his foot to pull something out from under the bed. I leaned over and looked. A wooden box, filled with everything from colored ropes to brutal-looking black leather straps. *He's going to tie me up.* And before I'd even finished thinking it, he took out what looked like a long, black satin ribbon. Then he grabbed my wrist and pulled me.

Something was happening inside me, a thrashing, urgent heat that went straight down to my groin. It had started when he'd thrown me onto the bed, but when that hard grip closed on my wrist and he pulled me, my ass sliding across the covers, it doubled, trebled. It was the way he manhandled me so easily, the way he didn't *ask*.

And then he started to wrap the ribbon around my arm, starting right up near my elbow and spiraling it all the way to my wrist. Just a thin slice of pale skin showed between each loop of glossy blackness. I watched, transfixed. It almost looked as if I was wearing black opera gloves.

Then he made some clever, looping knot at my wrist and tied the rest of the ribbon to one post on the four poster bed. I was trapped. The heat coiled and twisted, lashing inside me, the blood pounding in my ears. When I pulled, the ribbon spread the load all the way up my arm: I wasn't just trapped, I was *imprisoned,* and that idea gave me a strange, fluttery feeling in my chest. I pulled again and felt the tightness all the way up to my elbow. It wasn't painful, but it was firm. *I can't get free.* The heat thrashed even faster inside me. It was like that moment on a roller coaster where the safety bar comes down and you realize you're not getting off. I started to pant.

Then Konstantin was moving around the bed and that hard grip was on my *other* wrist—

Why am I letting him do this?

I knew the answer as soon as I'd asked. Because, against all reason, I trusted him. I knew he wouldn't hurt me.

He bound my left wrist to the other post, so that my upper body made a wide Y on the bed. I was gulping down air, now, trembling. *Oh God...what's happening to me?*

He walked around to the foot of the bed and just... *glowered* at me. Almost as if he was saying this was my fault, that this was the punishment I deserved for tempting him, somehow. *All I did was play with a cat!*

He lunged forward and grabbed my ankle. My heart started crashing against my ribs. *Oh God* that was even better than a wrist. A strong man gripping your wrist might want to kiss you or arrest you but a strong man grabbing your ankle—*Did I really just think that?* And yet my face didn't go red. I didn't have to lie about what I liked, not with him.

He pulled me down the bed until my body was taut. God, he moved me so easily! And that gorgeous face, those merciless gray eyes glaring down at me as he tied me and spread me, making me ready for him. This was every secret fantasy I'd never admitted to, since I started watching him.

He started to draw my left ankle to the left, opening me—

I quickly crossed my legs, right over left, cinching them tight. I can't explain why I did it, I just had to.

He scowled at me, but I could see the glittering heat in his eyes burn hotter, darker. He took one ankle in each hand and—

His forearms bulged and suddenly my legs were forced apart. I actually went a little dizzy with how good it felt: my inner thighs quivering, weakening...and then my muscles giving up and my legs flopping open on the covers, only for my ankles to be quickly bound in place with more ribbons. By the time I was a spread X on the bed, the heat inside me was spiraling out of control. I'd never felt so utterly helpless.

Konstantin moved around the bed, staring down at me, and every heavy footfall sent a shockwave of heat reverberating through me. I bucked and wriggled in response, and that made my wrists and ankles tug at the ribbons, and the feel of being bound turned me on even more.

The bed creaked and sank as he put one knee on it, then the other. He knelt there, the top of his head almost reaching the bed's canopy, hulking between my pale, straining thighs. We watched each other for a second, his massive chest rising and falling under his shirt and jacket. I knew what was underneath it, now, could visualize every hard ridge of tan muscle, every dark swirl of ink. God, I'd watched this man for so long. I just couldn't believe he was staring back at me.

He leaned forward and plucked at the ribbon that tied my bra together between my breasts. It slipped loose with a silken whisper and he knocked the cups aside with two impatient swipes of his hand. Suddenly, my breasts were throbbing in the cool air of the room, my nipples puckering and tightening as his gaze roved over them.

He grabbed the bows at the sides of my panties in both hands and pulled. My panties fell away. I writhed and ground my hips, feeling his gaze like a touch as it ran over every secret fold. I knew he'd be able to see how wet I was.

He'd been silent for so long that when he spoke, it was a shock. "You're just...*so*...." He shook his head. "I'll never get tired of looking at you."

I flushed, but then my chest contracted. It wasn't *me* he was talking about. I'd stolen someone else's face.

He reached down and touched my naked hip, then followed my leg all the way down to my ankle. His touch was almost reverent. "Since you got back, there's something...." he pressed his lips together and shook his head in confusion. " I don't know what it is. But I can't take my eyes off you. I want you *all the time.*"

A big, warm wave rose in my chest and broke through me.

He lifted one hand towards my breast...and then pulled it back and gripped the bedpost, knuckles white, denying himself. He got up and walked to the rack of implements. I arched my back off the bed and craned my neck but I couldn't see what he was choosing...and I knew that he'd designed this room like that deliberately. *What if it's a whip? Or a cane? Something that'll really hurt? Maybe Christina was into that. Or what if—*

My stomach twisted. *What if he knows?* What if he'd just been toying with me, all this time, and now that he had me naked and bound, he was going to interrogate me?

He crossed back to the bed, one hand hidden behind his back, and—

As soon as I saw the lust in his eyes, I knew: he still thought I was Christina. The mission was still on. *Everything's fine.*

Except...a shockingly strong part of me wanted to just stop all the deception. Not to drop the Christina act and tell him I was Hailey. To forget I was Hailey and just *be* Christina.

He brought his hand down and there was a musical hiss....

A second later, my body exploded into heat. Not pain, exactly, more like the aftershock of pain, when the adrenaline thumps through you and you catch your breath. Warmth radiated out across my stomach, turning to a twisting, darker heat as it sunk into my body and slid down to my groin. *What* was *that?*

It flashed down again, too fast to follow, and this time I was anticipating it. A flash of heat, like a pinch or a slap, but much subtler than either, crackling across my skin and leaving me panting and glowing. I stared at his hand and for the first time I got a look at it.

He gripped a carved wooden handle in his fist. Immediately above that, it became a thick bunch of soft, flat strands as long as my forearm. A flogger? Was that what it was called?

His eyes met mine and there was a wicked gleam in them. He glanced down at a particular spot on my body—

I followed his gaze and saw my naked breasts. Then it clicked. *What? No! Not there!*

But part of me burrowed my ass down into the covers and hissed, *yes, there!*

The flogger came down again and there was a *flash*, white-hot but so quick it didn't register as pain, and then the heat and pleasure rumbled through me like thunder, leaving my breasts throbbing and sensitive, and my nipples straining and pebble-hard. I let out a breath I didn't realize I'd been holding and it came out as a low, throaty groan.

He knew exactly how to use it. He could land the lashes just where he wanted them and he could twist and flick his wrist to come at me from different angles so I never knew what to expect. One second, heat was exploding across my inner thighs, melting up into my groin and making me moan and grind against the bed. The next, it would be a light touch on my breasts, the strands brushing over my nipples as gently as palm fronds, and I'd be clawing at the air with my hands, arching my back to get *more, more!*

He kept going until every inch of me was ablaze, until I was a straining, panting, thrashing mess...and then he dropped the flogger and climbed onto the bed.....

The first time his tongue bathed my nipple, I almost came. I hadn't realized how super-sensitive the flogging had left me. Everything was throbbing and tingling with heat and suddenly the wetness of his tongue, swirling around the base of my nipple and then flicking over the top—I gave a short, hard yell of shock, the pleasure expanding and turning silver-edged and scarlet.

He went to work on me with his hands and his mouth and every touch of his fingers, every press of his lips, was magnified a thousand-fold. All I wanted to do was grab him and rub my body against him, press my breasts against his mouth and hump my groin towards his hands to show him where I needed it. But I couldn't do any of that. The ribbons held me fast and all I could do was gasp and plead and arch my back and trust that he knew where to go next. And he did. He knew better than I knew myself, and he showed me sensitive spots I'd never discovered.

But instead of making me come, he drew out the pleasure for as long as I could bear, toying with me. He drew blistering paths of heat with his lips that wound from my mouth to my breasts to my groin. He pushed two fingers deep inside me and found that hidden spot that made my brain explode into silvery trails, the heel of his hand grinding down on me while I rocked helplessly against him. He let me feel the edges of his teeth on my nipples while his tongue darted over their tops. I lost track of how many times I came.

By the end of it I was a limp, red-faced wreck, drunk on endorphins. All I could do was beg him. "*Please,*" I moaned, beyond shame. "Please f—fuck me."

He pushed himself effortlessly back so that he could look at me and I saw the victory in his eyes. But not victory over *me.* Victory over himself, that he hadn't lost control, hadn't gotten...involved. He *would* fuck me, he'd allow himself this release, but it would still be on his terms. It was so *sad*...but I couldn't stop myself. I needed him more than I'd ever needed anything in my life.

"*Please,*" I said again.

He froze. His look of victory faded. It was the same look he'd given me in the garden. I thought I saw a flicker of blue in all that merciless gray, a softening...and then his eyes lit up, hotter and harder than I'd ever seen them. He suddenly grabbed for his belt buckle, shoving the heavy leather through the loops. He tore at his suit pants, but a button on the fly caught, foiling him—

There was a clatter as the button went skittering across the tiles. Then he rammed his pants and shorts down his thighs and—

I drew in my breath. It was the first time I'd seen it. Not just long but *thick,* with a beautiful, purple-pink head and a tan shaft. I remembered what he'd said on the phone, about Christina's first time with him: *You weren't sure you could take me, but you did....* I gulped. I suddenly knew exactly how she'd felt. "Go slow," I said, and it came out in a kind of throaty whisper, half nervous and half lusty.

The sound of that excited him even more. I swore I saw his cock twitch and strain. But he gave a tiny nod as he brandished it in his hand, bringing the head of it between my spread thighs and *ah!* just nuzzling it against my folds. God, I was soaking...

A ripple of raw need ran through me. I'd closed my eyes for a second but now I opened them and stared up at him. He was glaring down at me and not with that masterful, dominant glare of power. This was fury. Outrage, at being out of control. *How have you made me do this?*

I had no answer.

His eyes hardened. *You asked for this.* And his hips pushed forward....

Despite his anger, he *did* go slow. The silken head of him spread me, spread me, *stretched me*—and then he was plunging deep into me and both of us cried out together at how good it felt. I panted and looked down at the spot where we joined. He was still fully dressed, save for the pants shoved down around his thighs, and I was not just naked but *stripped,* my lingerie untied and strewn around me, and tied to the bed with black ribbons.... There was something about the imbalance of that that was *wrong* and yet so very *right.* It set off a depth-charge of heat right in my core.

He began to thrust: slow, powerful strokes that drove him a little further into me each time. My breathing tightened and I moaned as I felt myself slowly filled.

He lowered himself onto his forearms, hulking over me, but careful not to hurt me, staring into my eyes for any sign of pain. My moans became low, guttural groans as he slid deeper, deeper, hot and hard and throbbing against my satiny walls....

He groaned as he finally rooted himself inside me and our groins kissed together. Each throb of his cock sent a new wave of pleasure rippling through me. He cursed in Russian and then, *"God...* my *shlyukha,* you feel amazing." He leaned down and kissed me once, tenderly.

Then he shook his head and his face darkened. He kissed me again, open-mouthed and aggressive, a kiss that plunged deep and took what it wanted. He wanted this to be a battle so that he could win. He wanted this to be just fucking, so that it meant nothing.

He began to fuck me, fast and hard, and it was amazing: the silken stretch of him, the hot, steely plunge of him and the ache as he withdrew. He was brutal and hard, his hips slamming into me, but it felt so good, each thrust compressing the pleasure and making it brighter and hotter. God, wasn't this every guilty fantasy I'd ever had about him, even if I hadn't admitted it at the time? Naked and tied, helpless under him as he had his way with me?

I gazed up at him, my eyes hooded and heavy with pleasure. God, the wonderful size of him, the power of that chest and those huge shoulders, those cold gray eyes glowering down at me.... And then it got even better. I saw something moving in the gloom behind him and made out a gold-framed mirror, over by the door. I could see his reflection, the tan globes of his ass pounding between my thighs. *Oh God....*

He took his weight on his elbows so that he could fill his hands with my breasts, his thumbs rubbing over my slickened nipples. I cried out, the pleasure arcing down to my groin and making it twist and coil. His hips were a blur, now, pounding me. He was determined to fuck me into submission, to make me come long before he did, so *he* stayed in control.

And I knew he'd win. Because what could I do? I couldn't wrap my arms around him and draw him close, or hook my legs around him, or even run my fingers through his hair. I suddenly understood why he'd tied me up.

All I could do, as the pleasure tightened and tightened and became a glowing bomb that I couldn't contain was...look up at him. Look up into those cold, gray eyes as he pounded and pounded and *know* what I'd seen there, know that somewhere inside there was another man....

He glared down at me, furious. He pumped me harder, faster, but I felt his strokes falter as he struggled for control—

I cried out as the orgasm ripped through me, my whole body jerking in its bonds. And as I spasmed and clenched around him, I heard him growl. I looked up and for a second I saw that tiny hint of blue in his eyes....

He slammed forward and buried himself in me just before he erupted in long, hot jets.

We lay there for long seconds, riding out the storm we'd created. When I managed to focus on his face, he was staring down at me with utter shock. *How did you do that?*

I just stared back at him. I couldn't answer. Because the truth was, right at the moment he'd lost control, I'd forgotten all about being Christina...and I was just being me.

34

HAILEY

I LAY IN THE DARKNESS, watching the silhouette of his body as he breathed. I had to be sure he was asleep.

My body was still warm and pleasantly achy from the sex. It should have been a happy time, a time for cuddling and closeness. But closeness wasn't allowed, with Konstantin: just as before, once we'd finished downstairs, he'd brought me up here, we'd shared a vodka nightcap, and he'd laid down on the opposite side of the bed.

What the hell had happened down in the dungeon? I'd glimpsed that other man, the one he tried so hard to hide. A man I really liked.

And now—my stomach knotted—I was going to betray him.

I counted thirty minutes in my head and then very carefully slid out of the bed and crept around the room. He didn't snore so there was no way to be certain he was out. As I picked up his laptop and walked over to him, I held my breath. I was half-expecting to see him staring right at me.

But as my eyes adjusted to the darkness, I could see his eyes were closed. The covers were around his waist, one arm on top of them, the moonlight making him into a silent, marble statue.

I knelt down on the floor next to him, carefully opened the laptop and—

Shit! The glow from the screen lit up the room like I'd turned on a lamp. It blasted directly into Konstantin's face and he muttered something.

I slammed the lid almost closed and turned it away, heart racing. I knelt there staring at him, praying....

He didn't wake. I opened the laptop again, this time facing away from him, cranked the screen brightness right down, and then turned it back. It asked for his hardware key.

I reached for his hand, my own hand shaking. This part seemed like more of a violation than actually looking at his secrets, somehow. The ring was scratched and even chipped in places, as if it had been through at least one war. Glued to the top of the ring, like a high-tech jewel, was the strip of coded electronics he used to unlock the laptop. It was tiny, maybe half the size of a grain of rice. He could have kept it on a card in his wallet or had it made into a shiny, new ring. Why had he chosen to put it on this thing that looked like it came from an antique store?

I just stared at him for a moment in the glow of the screen. In sleep, he was strangely vulnerable: that hard upper lip relaxed just a little and his frown disappeared. *How can I do this? This is wrong!*

Wrong?! He's the enemy! If I didn't find the evidence to bring him down, he would trigger a gang war. All those innocent lives, lost....

I reached for his hand. As soon as my fingertips brushed him, I caught my breath. Every time he'd touched me ran through my head on fast-forward, each one searing hot in my chest before sinking down, heavy and fluttery, to my groin.

I gently lifted his hand and brought the ring to the laptop. As soon as metal touched metal, the laptop unlocked and I was looking at his email.

I carefully put his hand back down and got back into bed, throwing nervous glances at him the whole time. If he woke and saw me with his laptop there'd be no way to explain, no excuse I could come up with. Whatever his feelings for me, he'd kill me.

I hunkered there in the darkness for a half hour, sifting through his emails and....

Nothing. Not a damn thing about any big new deal, or paying someone a quarter of a million in cash. My shoulders slumped and I let a long, silent sigh.

Then the guilt hit me. Was I *relieved?* I thought of what Carrie had said, just before I went undercover. Had I forgotten who I was? My mission was to bring him down.

I searched harder, digging through archived mail, and finally found a hidden folder where everything between Konstantin and one anonymous person had been filtered. I knew straight away I'd found it. This was the man I'd met at the mall.

The conversation started a month ago. Konstantin told the man he had a job that needed doing. There were no details, just a link to a picture hosted on some website, and when I clicked on it the picture had long since been deleted.

The man said he'd take the job for $250,000. *I can do it any week day. 1pm seems to be the best time. But it will need a particular tool - perhaps with your contacts, you could help me acquire it?* Again, there was a link to a picture and again, it had been deleted. *Dammit!* But I had to give them credit, it was a clever system - even if their emails were intercepted, the really important stuff was still hidden.

Konstantin replied saying yes, he could get the "tool." And that he'd send a woman to deliver the money. "It'll be in a box wrapped in red gift wrap. Don't discuss things with her, she's just the courier."

Thank God I hadn't asked Konstantin about the money. I'd been right, he'd kept Christina strictly need-to-know.

The exchange ended with the date for the job being set as the 18th October, with Konstantin agreeing to send the "tool" the guy needed on the night of the 15th. I shut the laptop down, slipped out of bed and put it back where I'd found it, then got back between the covers.

And it was over. I'd done it! I'd got a lot more information on when this thing was happening, even if we still didn't know what the job was. Carrie would be happy. And I'd gotten away with it: Konstantin hadn't woken up. I knew I should be elated or at least relieved.

But all I felt was bad.

I stared at Konstantin's back and thought of him living here in the mansion by himself, with the appearance of a relationship but no actual warmth or love. Making these plans alone, not trusting even Christina enough to share them with her. If I didn't bring him down, he'd take over the entire city..., and when that day came, he'd have no one to share the victory with. It was heartbreaking. I'd never met anyone so utterly isolated. *What the hell happened to him?*

I fought the urge to reach out and touch him.

He's evil. He's the enemy.

So why did betraying him feel so wrong?

35

HAILEY

OVER THE NEXT WEEK, life in the mansion became...*normal.* The expensive dresses and even the fancy lingerie started to feel routine. I got faster at doing my hair and make-up, too. And I managed to solve the problem of Christina's heels not fitting.

"Don't you already have a pair just like that?" muttered Konstantin as I returned from a shopping trip and he saw the shoes I'd bought.

I gave a theatrical sigh. "Men *always* say that. They're completely different!"

He grabbed my hand, pulled me close and gave me a long, deep kiss, one hand roving down my back to grab my ass. When he drew back, he stared at me, one big finger combing through my hair as his eyes searched mine. I thought I could see...a *yearning.* A wish that we had a real relationship, that we could banter like that all the time. And then he shook his head and stomped off downstairs to his study.

And I went to my closet and carefully replaced a pair of black heels with the identical pair I'd just bought in my size.

There was a full week to go until the night of the 15th, when Konstantin would deliver the "tool" for the job, so in the meantime Carrie told me to go back to watching, listening, and gaining his trust.

Every night, I'd dress in lingerie for him and meet him down in the dungeon. The sex was like nothing I'd ever experienced. He fucked me standing up, my wrists manacled to the wall above my head. He fucked me bent over a bench, his hands filled with my breasts. He fucked me on my knees on the bed with my hands tied behind me and my cheek pressed to the sheets, grunting and cursing and whispering that I was his *slutskya*. I was discovering a side of myself I hadn't known existed and he was enjoying teaching me.

Afterwards, there was never any cuddling or intimacy. But each night, I could see him having to work a little harder to maintain the distance, to shut me out and turn away from me in the bed. Soon, it started to feel like every look, every touch outside of the dungeon was charged, that any of them could be the final straw. And every time it happened, my chest tightened because...I wanted it. I wanted things to be deeper, to be real.

Even though I knew that was wrong, that I shouldn't want a man like him to feel something for me.

Even though I knew it would complicate things, that it was best for the mission if things stayed clinical and distant.

Even though I knew it was crazy to want it to be real when *real* was the one thing I couldn't give him.

I was shopping for dresses when Calahan called on the earpiece. "Your mom left a message." He hesitated and I could hear the embarrassment in his voice. "Her medical bills are higher than she figured, this month," said Calahan. "She's short."

I cursed under my breath. I didn't ever have to worry about money, with Konstantin. As well as the bottomless credit card, he'd press a wad of bills into my hand every time I went shopping. I didn't even need the money and meanwhile, my mom was struggling to stay afloat and Hailey's account was empty. I pulled today's wad from my purse flicked through it. *There must be a thousand dollars here.*

"Just in case you're thinking what I think you're thinking," said

Calahan, "*don't*. I'm serious." He lowered his voice. "You think the FBI wouldn't find out? Taking criminal assets and using them to pay your family's bills? That could be jail time for you *and* your mom."

I wanted to scream. I knew he was right but—

"I'll see what I can scrape together," said Calahan. "I'm sure we can figure something out."

God, he was so great. But I knew he didn't have any more money than I did, and this was my responsibility, and instead of looking after my mom I was living this fantasy, luxury life buying *dresses*—

"Wait," I said. "There's no rule saying I can't choose *where to shop,* right?"

The guard who was driving me looked around at the shabby storefronts. "You sure you want to go shopping *here,* Miss Rogan? I can have you back in Manhattan in no time."

"This is a *very very bad idea,"* said Calahan in my ear.

"I'm sure," I said firmly, and climbed out of the car, cinching my coat tight against the cold wind. And then I was pushing open the door to my mom's store and—

Oh God, she looked so *thin!* It had only been a few weeks...no, God, longer than that, I hadn't been able to see her since the surgery. *She must think I've abandoned her!* I took two running steps forward, ready to wrap her into my arms.

My mom looked up, startled. "Can I help you?"

I came to a faltering stop. I'd known she wouldn't recognize me, but the reality was nothing like I'd imagined. The reality was *horrible.* When I'd seen her, I'd had that warm glow you always get when you see family...but now I could feel it sputtering and dying, going black and cold.

I *wasn't* family. Not anymore.

"I'm looking for a dress," I managed.

My mom blinked. I *did* look as if I'd walked into the wrong store. Christina's clothes were about three times the price of anything in my mom's store and were a lot more revealing. But my mom didn't let it throw her. "Well, alright then. For an occasion? For every day?"

And then she broke off and coughed. A nasty, rib-shaking cough that she hadn't had, the last time I'd spoken to her.

"*Both*," I said, my voice strained. "Like, five or six dresses for parties. And at least that many for every day."

My mom stared at me. "Well, okay! Let's get you sorted out." And she led me into the depths of the racks.

An hour later, I'd filled the trunk of the car with seventeen dresses. As I finished paying with Konstantin's credit card, I was feeling victorious.

Then my mom doubled over, coughing, and couldn't stop.

I ran forward, but she waved me back, embarrassed. "*I'll be fine*," she wheezed between coughing fits. But she wasn't.

"I think you should call someone," I said desperately. "Have them drive you to the emergency room, get your chest looked at."

She shook her head. "My daughter's away on some training course." She leaned forward conspiratorially and the pride in her voice made my chest hurt. "She's in the FBI."

"Hailey," said Calahan in my ear, "I'm going to go over there right now and tell her I work with you and that you asked me to look in on her. *I'll* drive her to the emergency room, okay?"

It was the hardest thing I'd ever done. "If you're *sure* you're okay...." I ground out.

My mom nodded quickly and waved me towards the door, still wheezing. All I wanted to do was run up to her and give her a hug....

I forced myself to turn around and walk out. Just as the door closed, I heard her start coughing again. I climbed back into the car, tears in my eyes.

I carried on as normal. I went back to the mansion, I picked out some lingerie, and I went down to the dungeon to meet Konstantin. But just as I started to shrug off my robe, he suddenly clapped a hand down on my shoulder, stopping the fabric from falling. "What's wrong?" he asked.

But there was nothing I could say. I shook my head.

He frowned, stepping closer, and I saw that protective gleam in his eye. "Christina?"

But I just looked at the floor.

He started to speak again...and then shook his head. Remembering that we didn't have that sort of relationship. But maybe —just like me—wishing we did.

That night, Calahan told me that he'd taken my mom to the ER and that it was just a chest infection. They'd started her on some meds and she was sounding much better. And she now had more than enough money to pay her medical bills. But I still lay awake all night worrying about her, and feeling like the worst daughter in the world.

The next morning, at breakfast, I slumped exhausted into my seat. The chef beamed at me—like the rest of the staff, he seemed to be getting less scared of me. "Your usual, Miss Rogan?" He was already turning away to go and prepare it.

I opened my mouth to say *yes, please* but...I just couldn't face another glass of that gloopy gray-green sludge. "Actually...maybe something different, today?"

The chef's head whipped round. Konstantin looked up.

"Maybe...waffles?" I asked hopefully.

The chef straightened up, his chest rounding in pride. "May I suggest....with some fresh blueberries and raspberries, some whipped cream and a jug of maple syrup?"

"...and maybe a large cup of coffee?" I said. "That would be wonderful, thank you!"

When the chef returned and laid the plate in front of me, his grin told me exactly how much he'd hated preparing that smoothie every morning. And the waffles were amazing, crispy on the outside, and buttery-soft inside, and drenched in maple syrup.

"It's good to see you eating proper food," muttered Konstantin.

I smiled at him.

"It's good to see you smile again, too."

I froze, the fork halfway to my mouth. I couldn't believe he'd said something so sweet.

He looked away, as if he was going to pretend he hadn't said it. Then he looked back at me with such a fierce, smoldering glare, such a, *yes, I did damn well say it* look, that I just melted in my seat.

And then the chef brought my coffee and when I looked at Konstantin again, he was back behind his newspaper. But even so, just that brief glimpse of the man I knew was in there, felt amazing.

The good feeling lasted all day. Right up until we got the phone call.

36

KONSTANTIN

I SHOULD have seen it coming.

Maybe having Christina back had distracted me. Maybe it was the dreams disturbing my sleep—they still hadn't gone away. But that night, when I got the call to say there'd been more fires, not in restaurants and bars, this time, but in people's homes, I grabbed Christina and raced over there to help. I never considered that I might be taking her into danger.

A few years before, I'd bought up some slum areas just before the city announced a big redevelopment scheme that made them triple in value. A typical backroom deal, for me: my contact in the planning office got a bag of cash and I made about eighty million. But when the redevelopment was done, there were still a lot of people living in crumbling tower blocks, trying to raise kids in a place with syringes on the landings and urine on the stairs. The mayor shrugged: those people weren't likely to vote for him, so why spend money on them? I wasn't happy about that. No one deserves to live like an animal.

So I used my own money and built new, safe apartment buildings for them, with a playground for the kids, and I had my people make sure no dealers came near it. It turned into a nice neighborhood.

And now someone had tried to burn it down.

When we arrived, the streets were slick with water from the firefighters' hoses, and they reflected so many roaring tongues of flame, it looked as if the streets themselves were on fire. My heart sank. Four different buildings were ablaze and it wasn't just a few apartments: flames poured from entire floors.

I checked in with the firefighters. No one was hurt: I'd insisted on the best fire alarms and everyone had gotten out in time. But the arsonists had spread gasoline up and down the hallways to ensure the fire spread fast: we'd likely lose all four buildings. Hundreds of people lined the street, shivering in their nightclothes as they watched their homes burn. Cinders started to drift down out of the sky: little fragments of what were once wedding photos and favorite toys.

I sent guards to organize hotels for them and then walked through the crowd, checking what people needed and reassuring them it was going to be okay. I turned to check Christina was alright and—

Before the accident, she'd always been sort of reserved, when it came to meeting the people who lived on my streets. I used to gloss over it and tell myself she was just shy, but she never seemed shy when she was at some party surrounded by celebrities.

Now... I watched as she helped to distribute blankets and organize hot food. The old Christina had thought she was above these people. This new one was... humble. *How? How has she changed so much?*

I was still thinking on it when the squeal of tires split the night. People scattered as three huge black SUVs roared up the street and skidded to a stop right next to me.

I knew who it was.

People think that bonds are formed of love but they can be formed of hate just as easily. You can't do what he did without creating something permanent, something that'll link us like a thread, across miles or continents, until one of us kills the other. I could feel him in that car, the raw evil of him throbbing out of it in waves, shaking loose the memories I work so hard to lock away inside me. And the memories unleashed the pain, jagged and violent, clawing its way up into my chest. By the time he finally stepped from the car, I was standing there with fists bunched and my breath shaking, fighting for control.

"Hello, Konstantin," said Dmitri Ralavich.

I took a step forward without consciously willing it. The blood was roaring in my ears. I wanted—*needed*—to kill him and I needed to do it myself, to punch and crush and gouge until there was nothing left.

Eight men leveled guns at me. I froze. While I'd been focused on Ralavich, the other two SUVs full of his guards had emptied. I'd sent most of my guards off to help the victims of the fire and only three were close by. We were completely outnumbered.

This whole thing had been an ambush.

And the talk about Ralavich bringing lots of his men to New York was true. *Why? Why bring an army here when he has no hope of winning?*

Then a sudden, unexpected stab of fear cut through me. *Christina! Where is Christina?* I spun around and found her a few steps away, staring at Ralavich, her face pale.

Ralavich is an ugly man, in every sense. He's strong, but he's too fond of beer and gorging himself on platters of meat and cheese. His gut stretches out his shirt and the waistband of his suit pants and this thick, nicotine-stained fingers look like pale, uncooked sausages. But it's his face that sticks in everyone's mind.

He hadn't been a handsome man even before Luka Malakov caught him running one of his "rape clubs" in Moscow. Luka had beaten him so badly the surgeons couldn't fix it, and he'd healed with one side of his face sickeningly misshapen. No woman would willingly be close to him. But then—my stomach twisted in disgust—Ralavich never liked them to be willing.

Even as I had that last thought, I knew something was different. I was facing off against Ralavich like I'd done a hundred times before, the two of us glaring at each other, both refusing to move an inch. But even the soul-deep hatred for him was being overshadowed by something. *Christina.* I didn't want Ralavich anywhere near her.

And so, even though I knew it looked weak, I took a step back. And then another. And then I could put myself protectively between Ralavich and Christina, and I felt immediately better.

Ralavich threw back his head and laughed. "The rumors were true, Konstantin. Your American's made you soft."

I looked at the burning buildings. "Why did you do this?"

"To send you a message. Change is coming." He raised his voice for the benefit of the crowd and I realized this was an ambush on another level, too. He was making me look weak, saying to the people, *Look! I'm the one who burned your homes and your protector stands here and does nothing!*

One of my guards glanced at me. A few more of them had returned and it was five of them now versus eight of Ralavich's men. Mine were better trained and more loyal. We could probably take them, kill Ralavich once and for all. God knows he deserved it. But—

Ralavich grinned. "What's the matter, Konstantin?"

The whole street was lined with people. There were children there. If bullets started flying it would be a bloodbath. I gave my guards a tight shake of my head.

"That's why you'll lose," Ralavich told me. "Your fucking morals."

"Go back to St. Petersburg," I snapped. "New York is mine."

"You've done a good job preparing it for me." Ralavich grinned. "Now I'll take it from you. I'll finish what my father started. Soon, the Gulyev name will be a memory." He shuffled closer and peered around me to leer at Christina. "And when you're gone, I might just try my cock in your American and see how loud I can make her scream."

The rage burned through me, lit by his words, fueled by twenty years of hate. But then, as Ralavich came closer still, something else happened. I realized—

He's close enough.

Fuck, he's actually close enough.

In his arrogance, Ralavich had swaggered within grabbing range:

I could break his neck before his men could stop me. It was the best chance I'd ever had, probably the best chance I'd *ever* have. Every muscle went tense, ready to spring. They'd kill me, but I wasn't afraid to die, not as long as I took him with me.

And then, at the last second, I stopped.

Christina was right there. If I killed Ralavich, his men would be sure to kill her—or worse—in revenge.

He was *so close. The best chance I've had in twenty years....*

No. I couldn't let them hurt Christina.

So I stood there, trembling, fighting to control myself, and watched my one chance for vengeance melt away. It felt like someone was slowly pulling my heart out of my chest.

Ralavich walked right up to me and grinned in victory. Then he climbed back into his SUV, gave me a mocking wave through the window, and they drove away.

I stood there panting. The loss was physical. I couldn't believe what I'd done. And yet I knew I'd do the exact same thing again, if I had the choice.

My mind was whirling. I should have been worried about how Ralavich had humiliated me, how he'd made it look as if I couldn't protect my people. I should have been trying to figure out his plan: it made no sense, he couldn't hope to defeat the empire I'd built in New York. And why not just shoot me when he'd had the chance? But I didn't think about any of those things.

I just turned, grabbed hold of Christina and pulled her close. My hands slid from her hips all the way up her sides until I held her cheeks. Then, without words, I leaned down and kissed her. Exactly the sort of kiss I never allow myself. The smell of smoke and the heat of the flames and the chill of the night all dropped away and she was all that mattered, soft and feminine and *good*.

She'd cost me everything I'd been dreaming of for two decades. And she was worth it. Being with her gave me an electric thrill I didn't understand. Deeper than just lust. Like I was a teenager again.

We surfaced for air. Christina looked down the street towards

Ralavich's departing convoy. "What did all that mean? Why is he here?"

I scowled at Ralavich's tail lights as they faded into the distance. And I said something I'd never say in front of my men. "I don't know," I admitted. "But now that he is...from now on, you don't go anywhere on your own."

37

HAILEY

T HE NEXT DAY was the 15th October: the day Konstantin had agreed to deliver the "tool" for whatever criminal job he'd hired the guy at the mall to do. I watched him closely all day, but he never left his study.

Meanwhile, the staff were scurrying around getting the mansion ready for a party. Konstantin was known for his parties and anyone who was anyone in New York wanted an invite: models, business moguls, even politicians. Konstantin didn't care about socializing, of course. For him, the parties were a chance to do deals in a quiet corner, or in the poker room, without having to worry about the FBI watching.

This party was different, though. This was Konstantin's annual ball. The men would be in dinner jackets, the women would be in big, elaborate dresses and there'd be formal dances. It all sounded amazing, and very traditional and Russian, the sort of thing where some young Tsarina would meet her future husband. What I couldn't work out was why Konstantin was doing it. A normal party would have worked just as well as a way to do deals. And that's all Konstantin cared about...right?

Whatever the explanation, the preparations left me at a loose end.

I'd started to hang out in the staff areas during the day, chatting to the cooks and maids while I lent a hand folding sheets or setting the table. Today, though, there was no time for chat. Everyone was rushing back and forth with trays of food, boxes of glasses and stacks of chairs, and a team of four men were maneuvering an ice sculpture through the middle of it all. I was just in the way so I made myself scarce.

I didn't give much thought to actually going to the ball, or what to wear. I usually have to be dragged to parties and then spend the evening in the corner looking at my feet. But, a few hours before it was due to start, Konstantin marched into the bedroom carrying a box so big, he had to turn sideways to get through the door. He set it down on the bed and then gestured towards me.

I stared at him, startled. *For me?!*

He nodded.

I approached the box. It was cream and the cardboard was as solid and stiff as wood. There was a name embossed in gold in the center: *Beringham and Chase,* done in that particular, curly font that suggested Beringham and Chase were British, old-fashioned, and quite possibly on good terms with the Queen. I hinged open the top....

That was the moment I first saw the dress. Just the bodice and a lot of folded skirt, at first, but that was enough to clue me in to what it was and I gave a kind of squeak of disbelief.

It was exactly what a princess would wear in some animated fairytale. It was made of thick, glossy satin the pale blue of the sky on a perfect spring day. There was a tight bodice with a square neckline, short sleeves and a big skirt. Everything was done with ribbons and buttons: I couldn't see anything as modern as a zipper anywhere.

I lifted it gently up from the box, surprised by how heavy it was. That's when the skirt unfolded...and then unfolded *again*. I'd completely underestimated it. It was a full-on, bell-shaped, floor-length extravaganza. It had only fit in the box because all the frilly stuff that filled out the skirt was missing—that must be somewhere else.

I looked at it in awe. "I can't wear this. I mean, it's lovely but...." I turned to him to explain that this was a dress for a princess, and I wasn't—

But the words died in my throat. Those gray eyes were smoldering down at me and telling me, very firmly, that I *was*. And that he'd damn well dress me appropriately.

I flushed and nodded, my heart suddenly pounding.

"I'll send in Victoria," he told me, and left.

Victoria? Why would I want my maid in here? But within thirty seconds of picking up the dress, I saw why. The back was a confusing mass of buttons, none of which seemed to line up with each other, and I had no idea what to wear underneath or how the skirts worked. When Victoria knocked on the door, I let out a sigh of relief.

I let her take charge and just did what she told me. First of all, she showed me what I should be wearing underneath: a silky, cream-colored corset with an embroidered pattern of silver roses winding around it and real metal ribs. It wrapped around my waist and then curved up just barely high enough to cover my nipples. I looked like a sexy princess, or an old-fashioned superheroine.

Then Victoria pulled on the laces. *Hard.* All the air hissed out of me as the thing cinched tight. "*What are you doing?!*" I croaked.

"Corseting you," she said, as if this was the most normal thing in the world. Then she tugged again and I had to grab hold of the end of the bed so that I didn't stagger backwards. I could feel my waist shrinking each time she heaved on the laces. My eyes bulged. "Okay," I managed. "I think that's enough."

"Yep," she agreed. But then pulled the laces tighter and I realized she was just humoring me. "Just about done." *Tighter.* "Really not much more—" *Tighter* "—to go." She was having to grunt with effort, now and I wondered if this was revenge for all the times Christina had been cruel to her. "You're really—*unh! Just—nngg—about...there!*" She gave a last, sudden jerk and then tied them and stepped back. "How's that?"

I was squeezed so tight, I could barely answer. I had to breathe one small mouthful at a time. I turned to tell her that I couldn't possibly stay like this.

Then I saw myself in the mirror. My waist had shrunk down smaller than I would have thought possible—hell, with Konstantin's big hands, he'd practically be able to span it. And my ass and boobs now flared out into an hourglass. "Oh wow," I croaked.

Victoria grinned and pulled the dress up around me, buttoning it up the back and adjusting the ribbons. Then she went into my closet and unpacked a huge box of frilly underskirts and attached them, filling the skirt out to its full, four-foot-wide magnificence. She helped me with my make-up and managed to get my hair to lie in one long black waterfall, cascading over one shoulder and down my front. She'd only just finished when an impatient Konstantin knocked on the door. She scurried out. He strode in and—

It was the first time I'd seen him in a tuxedo since Boston, what felt like a lifetime ago. I'd forgotten just how good all that black looked on him, how it emphasized the size of those broad shoulders and strong chest, how the soft white dress shirt hugged his pecs and revealed the muscled flatness of his abs. It wasn't just the clothes, it was the way he wore them, as if he'd been born to this world. Those brooding good looks, the confidence...he looked *royal.*

Then he saw me and—

He was always unshakeable. But for once, he just *stopped.*

"Is it..." I swallowed, suddenly nervous. "Do you—"

He marched across the room and grabbed my hands, lifting them. His lungs filled as he gazed down at me, his thumbs brushing over the backs of my fingers. "You—" His voice was tight with emotion and he fought to control it. "You look...exquisite."

I felt something lift and soar inside my chest. My hands squeezed his and we stared at each other.

"Here," he said, digging in his pocket. "I want you to wear this."

He could have draped me in some huge, garish, diamond-encrusted thing worth hundreds of thousands of dollars—that's what most rich Russian men would do. But instead, he opened a simple black jewelry box and handed me something much more valuable.

It was very old, the silver lovingly polished. A single, thin chain held a pendant in the shape of a ten-pointed star. The gem at the center was the same pale blue as Konstantin's eyes, when he had one of those rare moments of softness.

Like now.

My heart was thumping. I knew there must be a story behind it, one that went deep into his past, but I didn't dare ask. He came around me and started to fasten it on me. I dipped my head forward obediently and the slow dance of his warm fingers on the back of my neck as he pushed my hair out of the way and then fastened the necklace was the best thing I'd ever felt in my life.

"There," he said, and pressed lightly on my shoulders to tell me to turn around. I turned to him, glancing down. The pendant was resting just above my breasts. I looked up and—

All the moments when he'd smoldered at me, all those times when it had nearly bubbled over into something real, something more than just sex...all of those moments paled into insignificance next to *this*. His eyes blazed blue, as if they were reflecting the gem. Then his gaze slid down to my lips and I could feel them throbbing and tingling, and then *my* gaze was sliding inexorably down to *his* lips and—

He tore his gaze away, dropped my hands, and shook his head savagely as if telling himself not to be silly. *No*, I thought desperately. *Don't! Keep going!* Then I caught myself. *It's better, like this.* Things were complicated enough, without us falling for each other. If that could even happen. I couldn't have feelings for a man like him...could I? And according to Christina, he was incapable of feeling anything.

But if that was true, what was going on? Organizing this super-traditional ball, buying me the dress, giving me the necklace...that felt the opposite of cold and heartless. This whole thing...it meant something to him.

He took a deep breath, gathering his self-control, still not looking at me. "There are shoes in the box," he told me.

Shoes. My mind was still whirling from the nearly-kiss so I didn't pick up on it. I dug in the tissue paper in the box and found heels in the exact blue to match the dress. It was only when I bent over to slip them on that I remembered that he'd have bought them in Christina's size. *Crap!* I wriggled my toes in. Yep: they were a full size too small. And I had nothing in my size that was remotely similar and anyway, he was standing right there. *I'll tell him it must be a mistake in the manufacturing. They say five, but they're really a four.* I looked up at him and opened my mouth to speak—

He was looking down at me with a look of almost childish anticipation. He really wanted to see me in the full outfit.

We hadn't talked about the ambush the night before. But it had shaken both of us: the way Ralavich had looked at me had given me nightmares and Konstantin had been grim-faced and silent all morning. I knew now not to ask about his work, or try to ask about his past and what Ralavich had done that made him hate him so much. But there was one thing I could do to make him feel better. For some reason, he cared about this ball. Well, fine. If it was important to him, I'd make it perfect.

Taking a deep breath, I crammed my left foot into its shoe. I had to lever the unyielding leather with both hands to force it over my heel, but I did it. The right one felt even tighter. I had to cross my toes over each other and arch my foot, hook the heel in and then try to flatten things out, careful to keep smiling. *Owww!* Walking was going to be agony.

But when I saw the look on his face, it was worth it. Just for a second, he looked happy and warm. He could have been any normal guy who'd bought his girlfriend a dress and loved how she looked in it.

Then he pouted and looked away, brooding, trying to shut that happiness down. I was beginning to understand that happiness was weakness, in his eyes. My chest went tight. *Konstantin....*

I put my hand decisively on my hip, forming a crook he could hook his hand through. "Let's go to the ball," I said.

He glowered, eyeing my arm suspiciously.

And then he nodded, threaded his arm through it, and led me downstairs.

38

HAILEY

A S WE DESCENDED the stairs, I started to wake up to the scale of this thing. As we passed one of the rear windows, I saw a Lamborghini cruise past, engine throbbing and snorting, to park next to a long line of other exotic sports cars. A sea of limousines were parked out front. The grounds had been transformed: tens of thousands of tiny white fairy lights had been strung from the trees, giving them a frosty, magical glow, and flaming torches lit the way to the door.

Instead of going down to the main hall, we veered off on the second floor and went down a back staircase, emerging from the big double doors that led into the ballroom. Grigory was there, and he nodded to us. "Everyone's here," he told Konstantin. And he put his hand on the doorknobs, ready to open them wide.

I suddenly realized what was about to happen. "Wait!" I said desperately.

Konstantin and Grigory looked round at me in confusion.

"I—" *It's probably not as bad as I think,* I told myself. But I had to be sure. I let go of Konstantin's arm, stooped and put my eye to the keyhole.

It was much worse than I thought.

The enormous ballroom had been lined with tables of food and a life-size ice sculpture of an angel stood at one end. A string quartet was sitting in one corner, instruments poised. And something like two hundred people were arranged in two thick crowds on either side of the room, the women all in huge, elaborate dresses like mine. That left an aisle down the center for...*us.*

We were the guests of honor. We were going to make a grand entrance.

I felt myself go pale. I was used to hiding. This was my worst nightmare.

"Christina?" asked Konstantin in puzzlement.

Now my face went red. I was scared and I was ashamed of being scared. I knew I should just fake the confidence: Christina would have lapped up the attention. But the idea of all those eyes on me made me want to curl up into a ball. And now Konstantin and Grigory were staring at me and wondering what was going on and—

"Sorry," I mumbled. "I just—" I glanced helplessly up at Konstantin, trying to find a way to explain. *They're expecting someone glamorous, but they're going to get* me—

I saw him frown and I quickly looked away. *I'm not surprised he's annoyed, I'm ruining everything.* I saw him nod to Grigory and the guard quickly made himself scarce. *He's going to tell me off, like on the rooftop.*

But instead, one knuckle pressed gently under my chin and lifted my head to look at him. He was frowning even harder but, when I saw the glint of blue in his eyes, my fear melted away. He wasn't annoyed because I was scared; he was *furious* because I doubted myself.

He spoke with the same quiet intensity that he used to strike fear into mob bosses and mayors. But for once, he was using that power for good. "You listen to me," he ordered. "There isn't a woman in that room, not one of them, who compares to you." He took my hand and squeezed it. "Do you hear me?"

I nodded dumbly and my heart gave a huge, hot, *thump-thump.*

He squeezed my hand again. "Then let's go in there." And he threw open the doors.

Cheers and applause rose into a deafening roar, engulfing us. Konstantin led me gently forward and I managed to stumble along beside him, trying to remember to nod and smile and wave. What he'd said to me kept spinning around my head, giving me the confidence to walk down the length of that massive room, and the feel of his arm hooked through mine did the rest.

At last, we reached the far end and the applause died down. The string quartet started to play and everyone relaxed and started to mingle. I let out a silent sigh of relief. It felt like something had shifted inside me. I felt...different.

For the next hour, we moved around the floor. There were politicians and celebrities. There were industry leaders I recognized from *Time* magazine and notorious underworld figures I recognized from FBI files. And yet, whoever they were, however important meeting them was to expanding his empire, Konstantin never let me feel that they were more important than me. Even as he talked to them, his gaze kept flicking my way, as if he couldn't take his eyes off me. My feet were in agony after the first twenty minutes, but I didn't care, not when he looked at me like *that.*

He finished the conversation he was having and then led me decisively off across the room. My eyes widened when I saw what was in front of us. An area had been set aside for dancing, right next to the string quartet, and a handful of couples were gliding elegantly around in some sort of waltz. My first thought was *God, no:* I had no idea how to do it, and my feet felt like they were on fire. But then I thought about dancing with Konstantin. Being swept around the floor in his arms, that muscled body guiding me. That was worth any amount of pain and embarrassment. So as we stepped onto the floor, I turned to him with a nervous smile, lifting my hand to take his like the other couples were doing....

He looked at me blankly. My face fell. Then he realized what I'd been trying to do and *his* face fell. "I'm sorry, *golub.* I wasn't—" He nodded towards the far side of the room. Through a set of open doors and across the hallway, I could see the poker room. Of course: he'd just been cutting across the dance floor on his way to make some deals. Even at a ball, he had to build his empire. He looked at the dancing couples around us. "I don't...dance."

I went scarlet. *Of course he wasn't taking you to dance! You idiot! Have you forgotten what he is?* I nodded frantically. "I don't dance either," I told him. I didn't want him to think I was disappointed. Because I wasn't...right? Of course I wasn't. I was relieved. "Go do some business," I told him. And I gave him a quick kiss on the cheek, the way Christina would have, and turned and hurried away as fast as my aching feet would allow.

As soon as they saw I was on my own, a gaggle of women surrounded me. They were all desperate to know about Konstantin: did he really kill any man who looked at me? Did he really sleep in a coffin? One of them grabbed my arm, her eyes huge. "*Did he brand you with his mark?*"

They reminded me of me, back when I used to watch him from a distance. I wanted to tell them that he was more than just a bunch of myths, that he was complex... *damaged.* That sometimes, I could see a whole different man underneath all the coldness. Or I thought I could.

"Excuse me," said Konstantin from behind me. "I need to borrow her."

I slowly turned around.

He held his hand out: *would you like to dance?*

I looked around us. Everyone was pretending not to look, but I could hear the amazed murmurs spreading through the room. *Is Konstantin going to dance?*

But he ignored the crowd. He ignored the group of whispering women and the men waiting for him in the poker room. There was only one thing that was important to him. That made my heart fill and lift, tugging me up so hard that my throbbing feet didn't seem to even touch the floor. I took his hand and he led me past the other couples and over to the string quartet, just as they finished the current piece. He spoke to the cellist, a tiny woman with glasses who wasn't much bigger than her instrument. "Can you play the slow movement of Elgar's Cello Concerto?" he asked her.

The cellist blinked. The rest of the quartet stared at her, worried. Whatever that piece was, apparently it was a serious ask. Then the cellist nodded, sat up very straight, wriggled her shoulders, and flipped through her music with the air of someone refusing to back down from a challenge.

She began to play and it was beautiful, a haunting tune that made me think of the might of an army and loss...unspeakable loss. But it also lifted and carried you, lending you hope. Konstantin allowed me only a bar or two to get used to it and then we were off.

I'd barely ever danced with a partner before. My memory of dancing with men is awkwardly shuffling around a dance floor with one of the ushers at a friend's wedding, trying not to step on each other's toes. This was not like that. This was amazing.

He *led*. Head up, back ramrod straight, sweeping me around the room in great, bold arcs and looping swirls. The whole crowd had stopped to watch, but he wasn't self-conscious at all. His eyes never left mine. His only focus was on making me happy.

And somehow, even though I had no idea what I was doing and my feet were screaming in pain, I managed to stay with him. He was so strong and he hauled me around with such confidence, I just had to give up control and go with it. It helped that I always knew exactly what he was going to do: he communicated in the way he held me: a press of that big hand on my back meant we were going forwards, a gentle squeeze on my hand meant we were breaking left...I forgot to be shy and scared, I forgot about all the people watching, and I just enjoyed it.

God, he looked so *right,* dancing like this. The music suited his looks, bold and beautiful, strong yet graceful. *Noble,* which seemed like a crazy term to put on a criminal. But it fitted.

We finally glided to a stop and the room erupted into applause. The cellist put down her bow and slumped, panting but grinning. Konstantin took both my hands in his and looked down at me.

"Thank you," I said with feeling. "Where did you learn to dance like that?"

His eyes flickered blue for an instant, softening as he remembered. "My grandmother." He glanced away for a second as if pushing the momentary weakness away, but when he looked at me again, the blue was still there. He'd enjoyed the dancing, despite himself. We both had. He pulled on my hands just a little bit and I stepped closer, looking up at him, my body molding to his. His eyes fell to my lips again and I felt my heart tighten and lift in anticipation.

And then he seemed to remember who he was, what our relationship was. He squeezed my hands one last time and then dropped them. "I should...." He nodded towards the poker room.

I nodded quickly. "Go."

We walked off in opposite directions. I could feel the eyes of every woman there on me and heard a hundred whispered conversations. No one could believe what he'd just done, including me. How could he be so cold, so mercilessly evil, and yet do something so warm and romantic? I wanted to scream at them, *see? He's more than you think!*

Then I saw Grigory through the crowd. I ducked back behind a cluster of politicians. I didn't want to run into him on my own and have to talk my way out of another kiss. I'd managed to keep my distance over the last week, never letting myself be alone with him, but I could tell he was getting frustrated.

He wasn't looking for me now, though. He was talking to one of the guests, a man I didn't recognize. They were speaking in low tones, using the hubbub around them as cover. This was important, I could feel it.

I sidled closer, keeping my back towards Grigory. "You have it?" he asked the man. "I need to deliver it tonight."

The other man had a thick, wiry beard and a heavy Russian accent. "I have it. You have my money?"

"I'll get it. Meet me downstairs, in the parking garage, in five minutes," said Grigory.

They headed off in different directions. I thought fast. Today was the 15th, the day the "tool" was meant to be delivered to the man I'd met at the shopping mall. Konstantin must have asked Grigory to take care of it, just as he'd asked Christina to deliver the money. Grigory was about to buy the "tool" and then deliver it. This was my only chance to find out what it was.

I raced for the stairs...and staggered, cursing. I'd forgotten about my feet. After an hour of walking around and then a bout of dancing, they were in agony. I wasn't racing anywhere.

I limped up to our room, grabbed my phone, and then crept down the stairs to the basement, wincing with each step. The skirt of my dress was so wide, it almost touched the wall on both sides. *How the hell am I supposed to creep around in this?*

I made it to the garage before anyone else and quickly looked around. Fortunately, I'd had a lot of practice when it comes to hiding. A broken light had left a patch of deep shadow right at the back of the garage and I hunkered down there, peeking out around one of the big SUVs.

Grigory arrived first, a thick envelope in his hand that must have been packed with cash. A moment later, the man with the beard showed up, carrying some sort of suitcase. "I hope Konstantin knows what he's doing," he muttered as he handed it to Grigory. "Using this thing will bring a lot of attention."

Grigory looked suddenly grim. "He knows what he's doing." He handed the man the money and carried the case around to the back of a black Mercedes. He was going to load it into a car and deliver it right now! This was my only chance to find out what it was.

Trying to move silently, I pressed my back against the side of the SUV and shuffled sideways along its length, keeping it between me and Grigory. He was muttering to himself, moving things around in the Mercedes' trunk to make room for the case.

I reached the SUV's front fender, less than six feet from where Grigory stood. As he put the case in the trunk, his back to me, I craned my head out from behind the car and lifted my phone. Then, just as he swung the trunk closed, I took a photo.

My phone camera clicked, the trunk slammed and I dropped back behind the SUV, all at the same time. I heard Grigory whip around—he'd heard something. I sat there with my back pressed against the cold metal, heart hammering, trying not to breathe.

On the screen was the photo I'd taken, the suitcase clearly visible. It was one of those toughened flight cases with a vaguely military look. There was a number on the side that meant nothing to me, but maybe Calahan could decode it. I quickly sent him the photo: if Grigory caught me, at least all this wouldn't have been in vain. But the email just sat in my outbox. *Shit!* There was no signal because we were underground.

I heard Grigory take a step towards the SUV. I imagined his eyes searching the silent garage. I was paranoid that my phone was going to ring and give me away, so I powered it off.

Over a minute went by. Then I heard Grigory curse in Russian, climb into the Mercedes and speed off. I slumped against the SUV, panting. Then I levered myself up and began the long walk back up the stairs to the ball. Before, I'd been running on adrenaline but now I felt every hard, concrete stair under my soles, every jolt as my heel came down, and the shoes bit into my skin. By the time I reached the ballroom, I was a wreck. But I pasted a smile on my face, opened the door and slipped inside.

I walked the length of the room looking for Konstantin. *Maybe he's still playing poker.* It was only when I reached the far end that I felt a warm hand on my bare shoulder and spun around. That was a mistake: my right shoe dug into the side of my foot in a particularly vicious way and I staggered sideways.

Konstantin grabbed me under the arms, taking my weight like it was nothing. "What is it?"

I shook my head. "Nothing." But as I tried to straighten up, a bolt of pain shot up my leg and I couldn't disguise my wince.

Konstantin looked down at my feet, then frowned at me. "Why didn't you say something?" He shook his head. "We're leaving. I'll take you upstairs."

"You can't leave!" I said, horrified. "It's your party!"

"If it's my party," he said firmly, "then I can do what I like."

And he hooked one arm under my back and the other arm

behind my knees and suddenly I was scooped up in his arms, my huge skirt flowing down over his forearm, and he was carrying me through the room. Everyone turned to look and I would have curled up and died from embarrassment but—

But nobody else mattered because I was looking up into his eyes. And the deep concern I saw there, the tenderness, took my breath away. It was even more overwhelming because of who he was, because I knew it was coming through all those layers of coldness.

He carried me all the way up to our bedroom and kicked the door shut behind us. Then he dropped me gently onto the bed. Christina probably would have found a way to land gracefully, but I just sort of sprawled, arms and legs everywhere, and then I reached down and pried off my shoes. The relief was almost spiritual. I lay back with a contented groan.

And then I realized he was looking at me in a very particular way.

"What?" I asked.

He didn't answer, just stood at the foot of the bed, staring down at me.

I glanced down at myself. I wasn't doing anything sexy. I was just lying there untidily, my skirts all in a mess, barefoot and with my hair all disheveled but—

But his eyes...they were like I'd never seen them. Not just a faint flicker of blue but a steady gleam. Not just lust. Something deeper.

"What?" I asked again.

This wasn't the dungeon. This was our bedroom. Nothing was allowed to happen, here, but....

But his knuckles had gone white where they gripped the foot of the bed. The tension that had been building for a week rose up between us, the air going thick and heavy.

"Wha—"

But I never reached the *t* because he suddenly lunged forward, grabbed me, and kissed me.

39

HAILEY

I T ALL HAPPENED so fast. He almost dived onto the bed, his knee between my thighs, and then his hands were on my cheeks and his lips met mine—

And suddenly, he was *unleashed.*

I'd caught those tiny glimpses. I knew there was emotion buried under all that ice. But I hadn't realized just how long he'd been denying himself any real feelings. Years...*decades.* And I could feel every single second of it in how he kissed me. He needed me like a man twenty years in the desert needs water.

He was actually growling with the urgency of it, the sound coming from low in his throat and rolling up through our lips as he moved and pressed and spread me open, the tip of his tongue meeting mine. A crackling wave of energy rolled through me and I pushed up against him, needing to sit up so that I could kiss him back. We twisted, both of us frantic, never breaking the kiss. My hands found his shoulders, sliding under his jacket and over those thick, hard muscles, and we fell back onto the bed with me on top, straddling him. Then he flipped us over, my skirts rustling and fluffing between us, and *he* was on top, kissing down into me. We rolled and twisted, breathlessly kissing, until I had no idea which way we were facing anymore: I hadn't opened my eyes for what felt like an hour. We wound up on our knees in the center of the bed, our bodies pressed together and our fingers intermeshed, kissing just as desperately as when we started.

He started to run his hands over me and it was as if he was touching me for the very first time, his palms smoothing over my shoulders and sides and hips and then back up to my breasts, exploring me even though he knew me so well....

I realized with a jolt that I felt like *me*. Not like I was being someone else. Was that why it felt so different?

He was mumbling something between kisses, his lips so close to mine that they stroked me with each syllable. "*Ya khochu potselovat' tebya*" He was so out of control, he was talking in Russian.

"I have no idea what that means," I panted.

"I want to kiss you and never stop kissing you," he muttered. "I want to fuck you and never stop fucking you. You're *mine,* now and forever."

My chest filled and lifted, a warm glow flooding through me. "...*uh huh,*" I panted, and kissed him hard.

I was exploring the hard contours of his back through his shirt. I'd been longing to touch him all week, but he never let me: my hands were always tied. Now I was going crazy: the more I touched him, the more turned on I got.

His hands found my breasts through the layers of dress and corset, squeezing and lifting them, his thumbs rubbing in circles over my nipples. We twisted again, the dress flaring out around me as I tipped sideways and across him, winding up lying across his knees.

I managed to push his jacket off his shoulders. Then, as I ran my hands over the warm bulges of his biceps, he leaned me back and kissed me again, one big hand running up and down my body, squeezing my breast and smoothing over my hip and ass, and the other—

The other hand dived under the layers of skirt, searching me out. I gasped as his fingers found bare leg, then followed it upward...over my knee...up my thigh...I gripped his shoulder with both hands, but not to stop him.

His fingers glided over my upper thigh...my *inner* thigh. I drew in my breath, his stubbled cheeks burning my palms as I grabbed him and kissed him, open-mouthed and hungry. God, it hadn't felt like this since I was a teenager, fooling around with my boyfriend and from his breathing, he felt the same. My whole world narrowed down to the feel of his fingertips, scalding hot against my skin as they dared higher, higher...nudged up against the softness of my panties—

"God, I want you," he growled.

"D—Do it," I panted, light-headed and giddy with the thrill of it. After everything we'd done down in the dungeon, how could this feel like such a big deal? But it did, because...somehow, this was *me*.

His fingers traced my folds through the thin material, flattening my panties against my lips and *God* I could feel how wet I was. Then they hooked under the elastic at the side and... I drew in a shuddering gasp as he ran his fingers over me, rolling, and stroking my softness. I could feel myself opening. My eyes closed as our lips bumped again and his fingertips parted me—

"*Yes,*" I gasped.

And then the full, knobbly perfection of his fingers, sliding up into me, making me jerk and wriggle against him, my ass grinding against the top of his thigh. He kissed me and then pulled back a little, and when my eyes opened, he was staring deep into them, watching my reaction as he... *pushed* and then pulled back and *God, pushed,* the pleasure turning silvery and electric as he hooked his fingers and circled *just there.* I hooked my arm around his neck and dragged him down for another kiss, panting into his mouth as his thumb started on my clit. With my other hand, I fumbled for his belt, wrestling it open and then working at his fly. He shuffled his hips, helping me. This was so different from downstairs, when I'd had to be passive, when he'd always stayed dressed. When I wasn't allowed to....

Touch. We both groaned as my hand wrapped around his cock. I'd only ever felt it touch *me,* not the other way around, and it was glorious: the hot thickness of it, the way it filled my hand. I stroked my hand experimentally along its length and felt his whole body come to attention. Another slow stroke....

Suddenly, he was rolling on top of me and trying to tug my dress down, desperate to have me naked. But the thing was held at the back by buttons. He rolled me over so that I was straddling him and groped with both hands for them, working his way down my back, *pop pop pop.* I was bending forward over him and I felt the neckline sag as it loosened, more and more of my cleavage becoming visible. And then he was frantically pushing it down over my shoulders and over the corset, and I twisted and kicked it down my legs, and finally I was free of it.

I panted, straddling him again, the feel of his cock making me go weak as it rubbed along the front of my soaked panties. I could see him staring at my breasts, the top of the corset only barely keeping them contained. He reached for them, but it was my turn. I undid his bow tie and started working my way down his shirt buttons, more and more of that gorgeous chest becoming visible. For the first time, I could really see him: solid slabs of smooth muscle, broad and thick and loaded with power, so much that I couldn't resist sliding my palm across his pec, drunk on the feel of him. The blue-black of his ten-pointed star tattoos stood out bold and unapologetic against his tan skin. It was impossible to forget who he was, and I knew he'd never try to hide it.

I undid the last of the buttons and pushed back his shirt to reach his abs. God, I'd wanted to touch him here so many times. I rubbed over them in hungry circles, letting the heels of my hands ride the hard ridges and then lowering my head and kissing down the hard center line, nuzzling all the way up and between his pecs and meeting his lips as he bent down to meet me.

As we kissed, I could feel his hands on the back of the corset. During the party, the pain in my feet had made me forget how tightly I was laced and it was only now, as I felt him pulling at the bow, that I remembered. The laces went loose, his strong fingers wrenched the two sides apart and *oh,* the sudden rush of air as my lungs properly filled for the first time in hours. My breasts spilled free and he pressed his palms up against them, growling and cursing in Russian. "You feel so good," he told me.

The corset was tangled around my lower back so I shimmied it down and off. I knelt there for a second, straddling his legs, in just my panties. His eyes had taken on that molten look, but even that was different to how it was downstairs: I could still see the blue and that emotion, that humanity, made it even hotter. His eyes were locked on me: on my face, on my breasts, on the damp scrap of fabric that was all that covered me. It was like he was seeing me for the very first time. And I felt different. I wasn't being Christina, but I wasn't just the old Hailey, either. He'd restored the confidence I'd lost.

I wasn't hiding, anymore.

He reached for me but, for once, *I* was in control. I ducked back out of reach, hooked my fingers into his pants and drew them and his boxers down his legs, tugging off his shoes and socks at the same time. I dropped the whole tangle over the foot of the bed. Then I shuffled back up his legs...and wrapped my hand around his cock.

He drew in his breath and rose up on his elbows. Then, as I dipped my head, his eyes went wide in shock. "But—" he started.

I looked up at him and we stared at each other, the head of his cock inches from my lips.

He couldn't put it into words so he used just one. *"Golub!"* Dove! He was saying: *but you're so innocent!*

And I smiled wickedly, opened wide and engulfed the head of him, relishing the hot saltiness of him, the satiny touch of the head against my tongue. And he let out a stream of Russian curses and grew even harder in my mouth, his hips rising helplessly towards me. When I drew my mouth off him with a wet sucking sound, he was looking at me in utter amazement. Then his eyes narrowed and he stared at me with such blistering, unrestrained lust, I felt the reaction between my thighs. The thought that I was innocent, *good,* and yet also *like that*...apparently, that was the hottest thing ever.

With a yell, he grabbed my waist and twisted, flipping me onto my back and climbing on top. He stripped the shirt off his arms and tossed it away and then he was pushing my thighs apart, his cock hard and hot against my thigh. I could hear myself panting and I was shocked—and turned on—by just how much we both wanted it.

I was still wearing my panties. I hooked my thumbs in them to push them down but he just grabbed with one big hand, the fabric disappeared into his fist and—

There was a snapping sound as the elastic snapped and then I was naked. The tip of his cock, still shining from my mouth, brushed up against me and—

We both cried out as he filled me in one long thrust, the heat of him throbbing through me. It was so different, like this: I could feel his naked body against mine, could reach up and run my hands over him, could *kiss* him. I drew my knees up, soles sliding along the bed, and bit my lip in joy as he went deeper.

He began to thrust, his forearms either side of my head, that hard, tan ass rising and falling, driving him into me. At last, I could move, I could answer the building pleasure in my core, circling my hips and twisting around him as he plunged. He cursed and went faster, and every thrust, every silken stretch of him, notched the pleasure higher in my chest, until I was grabbing at his shoulders and back to urge him on. God, the size of him, the feel of those wide pecs stroking against my breasts, the way he crushed me into the bed just a little....

He sped up, his stomach slapping against mine, the base of his cock grinding against my clit at the apex of each thrust. The pleasure was starting to spin and compress inside me, building in energy like a hurricane. I drew him down to me and kissed him hard, lips bumping, teeth clacking in our urgency. My nipples were achingly hard as they dragged back and forth along his chest but I needed more—

I pushed up and twisted and he let me, rolling over with me so that I was on top. Both of us groaned as I leaned back a little, impaled on him, and his cock hit a new angle inside me. Then I began to rise and fall and he filled his hands with my breasts, stroking the nipples with his thumbs and then gently pinching them. I half-opened my eyes, my lips parted in a groan of pleasure. He was shaking his head in wonder. He'd forgotten how good it can be, when you let yourself feel.

I spread my hands on his chest, marveling at the hardness of him, the solid warmth of him. I used him to push against as I lifted and lowered myself, bouncing my ass against his thighs, filling myself with him again and again, the pleasure twisting and tightening, making me go faster and faster, until he suddenly grabbed me and rolled us, pinning me to the bed beneath him. He buried his cock in me and began to slam his hips into me, carrying me up to the edge. I could feel the climax thundering towards me. My legs wrapped around him, squeezing tight as he pounded and pounded—

He leaned down, his lips a half-inch from mine. "*Ya lyublyu tebya,*" he gasped.

The orgasm was right on me, my whole body trembling with it, about to release—

"*I love you,*" he translated.

And *oh God* as I realized.... "I love you, too."

And then the pleasure exploded through me, my hips circling and thrashing as he ground down into me. I bucked and trembled, crying out, and felt him shoot in long, hot streams deep inside me.

40

HAILEY

I WOKE to the firm, warm curve of Konstantin's pec under my cheek, the reassuring solidness of his bicep under my fingers. I was half on top of him and it was the best thing in the world, like cuddling up to an enormous, heated teddy bear. How could a man so terrifying also be so comforting? But maybe it made sense: all that scary power was turned outward, now, away from us. I knew that he'd never allow anyone to hurt me and that made me feel protected like nothing else.

I had no idea what time it was. The sun wasn't up yet and Konstantin was still asleep. In my post-sex fog of cuddle hormones, all I wanted to do was stay snuggled into his chest, sleepy and warm. But my throat was like a desert. I really, really needed a glass of water.

I slipped out of bed and padded to the bathroom, not bothering to turn the light on. There was just enough moonlight to see by as I filled the glass. As I lifted it and drank, I was smiling, already looking forward to sliding back into his arms.

"What's going on?" asked Carrie's voice in my ear.

The water turned to acid in my mouth. I couldn't swallow. I had to open my mouth and let the water spill into the sink, like being sick. I'd completely forgotten they were listening.

They'd heard everything. They'd heard *I love you*. Somehow, that was more of a violation than them hearing the sex.

"We need to pull you out," said Calahan. I'd never heard him so shaken.

I thought of being taken away from Konstantin and ice closed around my heart and crushed it, jagged and cruel. "No," I whispered quickly. "No. It's okay. Everything's okay."

Silence for a moment. Then Carrie's voice, worried but with a cautious note of hope. "You were just playing along?"

I reached forward and turned on the light on the bathroom mirror. My hair was tangled and stuck to my forehead. My lips were still tender from all the kissing. They silently formed the words we'd said to each other. *I love you.*

"Yes," I lied. "Just playing along."

They went silent for a moment. I imagined them looking at each other. Then, "We'll talk in the morning," said Carrie.

I reached out and touched hands with my reflection. *What the hell do I do now?*

41

KONSTANTIN

I WOKE UP and frowned. Something was different.

I was on my back, spread out across the bed, but it wasn't that. Christina lay half on top of me, her head on my chest. I had one arm protectively around her waist and one of her legs was tangled with mine. Her hair trailed across me and the sweet smell of it was in my nostrils. Instead of being on opposite sides, we were as closely together as it's possible for two people to be. But it wasn't that.

It was a *lack* of something. I searched through my half-awake mind, feeling for the black water, the ice in my chest...and I didn't find it.

I hadn't had the dream. And yet there wasn't the gray void and the aching head I was used to, either. There was something else there. A *good* dream.

The concept was alien to me. It had been so long, I'd forgotten what they were like. I had to tentatively probe my memories, and then I suddenly hit an image of her—*us*—somewhere away from the city, somewhere green and clear. And it made me frown and keep probing, trying to draw back more of the dream because...it felt good.

I looked down at her. She was still asleep, her lips pursed and a tiny frown on her face. I wondered what was troubling her. *It must be wonderful, to not have a care in the world....*

I thought about what I'd said. *I love you.* And it was true. I loved her and somehow, when I was fucking her—no, *making love* to her—it hadn't felt like it was Christina. It had felt like she was a whole different woman.

Somehow, she'd changed. I'd never have allowed myself to get close to someone like her, so innocent and good. But because she was Christina, because I knew she was cold, and evil...she was safe. So she'd slipped straight past my radar.

And being with her had changed *me.* I'd become more like the man I would have been if that day twenty years ago hadn't happened. That's why I'd bought her the dress and given her the necklace: it just felt right, as if she was the woman my mother and grandmother always told me I'd meet. And then I'd seen her in the dress and my heart just.... And then, when I realized she was in pain, I'd felt this overpowering, protective urge and swept her into my arms....

And then it was too late. I'd fallen for her.

Now, though, as I lay there watching her, the memories rose up, falling across my mind like cold shadows. *How could you do this?* Loving someone made me weak. Vulnerable. *You remember what happened!*

I leaned down and gently kissed the top of her head, the unease growing in my chest.

I couldn't be weak. I had to carry on. For the family.

But I loved her.

42

HAILEY

I SLEPT FITFULLY and the final few hours lay there awake, eyes open, staring at the window as the dawn filtered through the drapes. I wasn't sure which had shaken me most: the realization that I was in love with Konstantin, or the reminder that I was going to have to betray him.

Calahan must have been listening because, as soon as I got up and went to the shower, he came on my earpiece. Had he been on shift all night? I wondered how much sleep he was getting. "We've got a plan," he told me. "We need to get something to you. Walk to the coffee stand at the end of the street. The barista is one of our agents. Tell him your name and he'll put what you need in a coffee cup."

By the time I was dressed, Konstantin was up and dressed, too. I was worried that things might snap back to how they were, that he'd act like last night hadn't happened. But as soon as he saw me, he drew me to him, leaned down, and kissed me. It was tender but solemn and I could see the worry on his face. *He's still figuring it all out.* I'd try to give him some space. "I'm going to go down the street and get a coffee," I told him.

He shook his head. "Not with Ralavich around. I'll send a guard."

Ralavich. Just the memory of him made me shudder. It brought home to me how wrong Carrie had been, when she'd said these men were all the same.

I forced myself to focus on the mission. Sending a guard to get my coffee wouldn't work: what if he looked inside the cup? "Maybe you could come with me," I said. "It's a lovely morning. A quick stroll down the street...."

Konstantin's forehead crumpled. "I have things to attend to. And we have coffee here. Why would you want to—"?

God, he'd lived in a purely practical world for so long. 'Because it's *romantic!*" I insisted.

He blinked at me... and then softened and nodded. My heart lit up. This was all new to him, but he was *trying....*

And then icy reality crushed my heart again. He was trying... and I was being *romantic* to deceive him, to betray him.

We walked outside and down the long driveway. Konstantin looked around suspiciously as we reached the street: he made me think of a huge, protective wolf, sniffing the air. I wondered how long it had been since he left the grounds on foot.

But at last he nodded to himself and turned towards the coffee stand. And then he reached down awkwardly and—

My heart lifted as his hand closed around mine. *He really is trying.* And it *was* romantic. The freezing wind of the last few days had stripped most of the fall leaves from the trees but now it had dropped away and it was calm and peaceful, the street silent except for the scrunch of red and orange leaves under our feet.

We reached the coffee stand and I asked for a vanilla latte, giving my name as *Christina.* Konstantin went for a black Americano and we sipped them on the walk back, still hand in hand. We could have been any happy couple out for a stroll. *Why can't it just be like this?* Ever since Rufus was killed, I'd fought against criminals. I'd thought it was simple: they were bad guys, I was one of the good guys. But when I saw how Konstantin kept order on the streets, how he protected people...when I compared him to the *real* evil, people like Ralavich....

But of course it wasn't that simple. The FBI wasn't desperate to bring him down because he'd built an empire. There's always been organized crime in this city. We needed to stop him because his aggressive expansion was going to spin the city into a gang war.

"Why can't you stop?" I blurted, just as we reached the doors of the mansion.

He turned to look at me. "What?"

I pointed at the New York skyline. "You keep taking more territory, getting bigger and bigger. You already control over a third of the city. You're already the biggest. Why can't you stop there?"

He frowned, not angry, but concerned. "It never bothered you before."

"It bothers me now. When are you going to stop? When is it enough?"

His face fell and the pain flooded his eyes, chasing away any trace of blue. *God, what happened to him?*

"Never," he said at last. "There is no *enough*."

Then he bent down and kissed me. I grabbed onto his shoulders and clung on, wanting to extend the moment. But at last, he pulled away. "I'm sorry, I have to work," he told me, and walked inside.

I was left standing there with my coffee, the rising wind tugging at my coat. He was trying. He'd shown me a side of him that he'd never shown to anyone else. But he was still Konstantin.

I loved him. But I had to stop him.

I took my coffee up to our bedroom. As I sipped it, I was starting to feel something bumping up against the inside of the lid, blocking the flow. I pulled off the lid and fished the thing out, washing it off and then ripping off the protective plastic bag. I sat down cross-legged on the floor by the window to examine it.

It was a thin, pen-like thing made of white plastic, a bit longer than my finger. It had some sort of sensor at the "nib" end and a little LCD display about halfway along. It had a faintly medical feel, like a thermometer or...there was some other gadget it reminded me of, but I couldn't put my finger on it.

"I have it," I told Calahan. "What is it?"

"It'll get you into his safe," said Calahan.

It felt like my heart clenched tight in my chest and refused to pump. I snapped my head around to check the bedroom door was still shut and dropped my voice to a whisper, even though Konstantin was down on the second floor. "*I can't go in his safe!*"

The fear sluiced through me like ice water, numbing my limbs until they refused to move. I remembered the look in his eyes, when he'd caught me outside his office. If he caught me trying to get into his safe....

And his anger, and what he might do to me, wasn't even the worst part. The worst part was knowing I'd destroy everything between us.

Carrie came on the line. "We don't have a choice. Whatever he's involved in, whatever he paid that guy a quarter of a million dollars to do, it's happening the day after tomorrow. We have to find out what it is."

"Yes ma'am," I said miserably. I tried to tell myself that our happiness was only an illusion. It was all based on a lie. So why did risking it scare me so much?

Konstantin stayed in his office all day while I paced and worried. He even ate lunch in there. Finally, just as the sun was going down, he walked off downstairs. I rushed to the door...and then stood there on the threshold, gripping the door handle. "I can't do this," I said.

"Yes you can," said Calahan calmly. "I'll be with you every step of the way. I have a guy watching Konstantin through binoculars. He's downstairs talking to Grigory. If he so much as moves in your direction, I'll let you know and you'll have plenty of time to get out of there. Okay?"

I took a deep breath. "Okay." And I slipped into the study and closed the door behind me.

Everything about being in the room felt wrong. His huge, imposing desk and chair, the scent of his cologne in the air. This was *his* place, his private sanctum, the one place he'd made me promise never to go....

I hurried over to the safe. The quicker I did this, the better. "What do I do?" I asked, falling to my knees in front of it.

Calahan must have been scared too, but his voice was calm and comforting, exactly what I needed. "You know those movies where the guy opens the safe using a stethoscope, listening for the tumblers? Well, that's what this thing does. Just put the tip against the safe and start turning the dial. When a bar lights up on the screen, you've hit a number right."

I did as he said and started twisting the dial. I could feel the sweat forming between my shoulder blades. "Nothing yet..." A bar lit up. "Got it!"

"Now back the other way until you hit the next number."

I twisted the dial the other way. I kept glancing towards the door. Another bar lit up and I reversed direction again. "Where's Konstantin?" I asked, my voice tight.

"Still downstairs. Don't worry." But I could hear the tension creeping into his voice. It hit me that this was just like the hotel in Boston, except now *he* was the one helplessly observing and I was the one in danger. *How did everything get so backwards?*

The sweat was trickling down my spine in icy beads. A third bar lit up. I changed direction, my hand shaking. *Come on, come on!* A fourth bar—

There was a metal *clunk.* I looked up at the safe in disbelief, then tried the handle. The door swung open. Piles of cash, documents, passports—

A confusion of voices on my earpiece. Calahan's voice but quiet, as if he was turned away from his mic, and someone else, arguing with him. "What?" I heard Calahan say. "Where is he?!"

I jumped to my feet, sucking in a huge, panicked breath. I slammed the safe shut and locked the handle.

Calahan's voice, deafening in my ear as he shouted in panic. *"Hailey, get out! We don't have Konsta—"*

I raced towards the door. But just as I got there, it swung open and I was face-to-face with Konstantin.

43

HAILEY

IS EYES went from my face to the safe to the gadget in my hand. I saw the shock turn to disbelief and then to fury.

He grabbed for me.

The panic was total. It felt like being a child, caught by my parents. I wasn't thinking rationally, I just *bolted,* away from him and across the room, into the bathroom. All I could think of was to get rid of the evidence, as if I could somehow deny the whole thing as long as it wasn't there. I hurled the gadget into the toilet bowl and slammed the flush, holding it down. Konstantin arrived a second later and shouldered me aside. He shoved his hand into the whirlpool in the bowl but the thing slipped through his fingers. And then it was gone.

But it was too late. He'd seen it. He'd caught me in his office.

He slammed me up against the wall. The only thing worse than the fury in his eyes was the hurt. Oh, God, the hurt. *I never meant to hurt him.*

"*Who are you working for?*" he yelled, his voice shaking the walls of the tiny room. "Did the FBI get to you in the hospital? Did they offer you a deal?"

I opened and closed my mouth helplessly. There was no

explanation I could come up with, no way to talk myself out of it. But when I thought about telling him the truth, my throat closed up with fear.

He growled, took hold of my wrist and—

He *dragged* me. The shift was terrifying: that morning, we'd been a happy couple. Now I was a prisoner, not worth speaking to or even looking at. He marched all the way downstairs like that with me stumbling and begging behind him, desperate to stay on my feet because I knew he'd just pull me along the carpet if I fell.

Grigory stared at us as we came into view. Konstantin snapped orders to him in Russian. Grigory looked horrified and asked a question of his own, something short and desperate like *are you sure?* But Konstantin just nodded grimly.

Grigory went pale with fear. Fear for me...or fear that our affair was about to be discovered? *Oh God, what are they going to do to me?*

Together, they pushed me into the back of the car and we set off. No one talked. Even Calahan had gone silent in my ear, unsure if it was safe. Darkness had fallen and a storm was building, the dark clouds blocking out the moon. As we whipped through the city streets, Konstantin was just a motionless silhouette beside me. I couldn't see his expression until a passing car's headlights lit him up for a second. Then I wanted to throw up in fear. His face was back to that cold, emotionless mask, as if none of this, none of *us,* had ever happened. *How did it go so wrong, so fast?*

The car slowed. We were outside a nightclub that had some sort of horror theme: the front was lit up with flaming pentagrams and the line of people waiting to get in were mostly goths. Pounding industrial music, mixed together with recorded screams, shook the car's windows. I didn't understand. Why would they bring me *here?*

But we didn't pull up outside. We turned into an alley alongside the club and then around the back. Konstantin pulled me out and hauled me down a set of steps to a metal door, and then down a featureless concrete hallway lit by flickering fluorescent lights. He opened another, heavier door and pushed me through.

At one point, it might have been a cold storage room, where meat was hung and butchered. That would explain the drain in the floor. Someone had added a long mirror on one wall and there was what looked like a dentist's chair in the center. My stomach twisted as I saw the leather restraints dangling from it. We were directly below the nightclub: the music and screams shook the ceiling.

I knew what this was. An interrogation room. One where screams wouldn't be heard.

Konstantin left and slammed the door behind him. My legs had gone shaky and I fell to my knees beside the drain, unsure if I was going to be sick...

As I knelt there, I remembered the earpiece. If there was any hope of lying my way out of this, I had to get rid of it. But I assumed I was being watched through what had to be a one-way mirror, just like I'd watched Christina in our interrogation room. I put my face in my hands and managed to claw the tiny earpiece out of my ear and drop it down the drain, making it look like I was crying. And I *wanted* to cry. I wanted to scream at myself for volunteering, for falling for him, for trying to *do* something instead of staying safely behind the camera where I belonged.

The door opened. The man who stood there wasn't Konstantin.

He was in his fifties with thinning sandy hair and a crumpled white shirt. He had the same lean look as Grigory—a man who used to be in the military, and has kept in shape. But his eyes were utterly different. They were too old for his face. They were too old for anyone's face.

"Please sit," he said, nodding at the chair. His Russian accent was heavy, his voice sad.

I didn't move. "Who are you?"

"I am Maxsim." He gave me a smile that had long ago been sapped of any warmth. "I used to work for the FSB. You know what that is?"

I nodded. Russia's security agency.

He was carrying a folding table and a briefcase. He set the table up next to the chair and put the briefcase on top of it. "Please," he said, waving at the chair. "Sit."

I still didn't move. I knew what this was but my brain was rebelling against it. "What are you going to do to me?" I whispered.

He sighed. "I am going to ask you some questions." He looked around at the room. "Is what I do here. Unusual, that it is girlfriend I am questioning." He sighed again. "But...not *so* unusual." He opened the briefcase. From my position down on the floor, I couldn't see what was inside it and I didn't want to. He nodded at the chair. "Sit."

I shook my head.

He came over to me, grabbed my wrist and hauled me over to the chair. When I saw what was in the briefcase, I wanted to throw up. I recognized most of the tools from the dentist's office.

"Please," I said. I was suddenly breathless and however hard I sucked in air, it didn't seem to be enough. "You don't have to do this." I knew there was no hope for me, now. I couldn't hold out for long against the pain, but as soon as Konstantin knew the truth, he'd kill me.

Maxsim forced my arms down onto the arms of the chair and buckled them in place.

"Please," I said, fighting against the panic and losing.

Maxsim pressed my feet against the footrest and buckled my ankles down too.

"*Please!*" My voice was cracking.

Maxsim picked up a pair of pliers.

And it began.

44

KONSTANTIN

I WATCHED through the one-way mirror, palms sweating as they pressed against the glass. I'd been here before, several times. I didn't enjoy it but sometimes it was necessary. This, though...this was different.

Christina gave a howl of pain that rose higher and higher. My toes curled in my shoes and I wanted to be sick. Maxsim had the pliers deep in the back of her mouth, pulling hard on a molar. "Which agency?" he was asking. "Which agency do you work for?"

He pulled at a different angle and Christina wailed, the sound echoing around the room and crawling down my spine.

She deserves this. She betrayed me. And it was far worse than if it had been one of my guards. She'd made me fall in love with her! That was the worst kind of deception.

And yet... when I looked into her eyes, I couldn't believe she was some seductress, sent to tempt me. She was too shy, too awkward, too *good.*

Maxsim put down the pliers and picked up a drill. He gave the trigger an experimental squeeze and it came alive with a high-pitched scream that bit into my ears.

I knew I had to be strong. I'd been weak and look where that got me....

Maxsim raised the drill to her mouth. She started to buck and thrash in the chair, the restraints digging into her soft skin. God, she suddenly looked so vulnerable—

The drill's note changed as it found a tooth. Christina screamed.

Be strong. One second passed. Two.

I suddenly turned around and threw open the door. Sprinted down the hallway and into the interrogation room. Maxsim saw me coming and pulled the drill from Christina's mouth a split second before I grabbed him by the collar and hurled him across the room. "*Get away from her!*" I bellowed. "Can't you see she doesn't know anything?!"

As he hurried away, I fell to my knees in front of a sobbing Christina. My hands fumbled at the restraints, freeing her ankles and wrists. My stomach lurched when I saw the red marks on her pale skin where she'd strained against them. How could I have done this to the woman I loved? Of *course* she hadn't betrayed me. I took her hands in mine, trying to rub the marks on her wrists away. "Christina, I—" I wanted to say I was sorry, but how could *sorry* make up for what I'd done?

And however much I wanted to believe she was innocent, I still needed an explanation. "Christina, please, you have to tell me." My voice wasn't angry, now, it was pleading. "Please: what were you doing in my office? What was that thing?"

45

HAILEY

I SAT THERE PANTING, close to hysteria. I couldn't taste blood, but one of my teeth ached and throbbed and if I didn't find some way to explain, Maxsim might come back and it all might start again. I gripped his hands. His face swam behind my tears, but I could see him: that other Konstantin, the one who loved me. The man he'd been before something tore his life apart and left him so utterly cold. A normal man who just wanted normal things: not an empire, but a wife, a job, a family....

I suddenly realized what the gadget reminded me of.

"It was a—a p—pregnancy test," I sobbed.

He froze. The guilt washed over his face, obliterating any last traces of suspicion. "What?" he whispered.

"I missed a *pill*," I sobbed, my throat raw from screaming. "And I was worried and I needed to do the test and our bathroom was being cleaned and so I thought of the bathroom in your office, it was just for a *minute*—"

He had his hand over his mouth in horror. "But why didn't you just tell me?"

"Because I was *scared!*" The fear was recent enough and real enough that I didn't have to fake the emotion. "I thought you'd be mad that I'd messed up! And then you *were* angry and you brought me here and he was hurting me, he was—"

Konstantin suddenly grabbed me and wrapped me up in his arms. I pressed my face to his chest and it all came out in huge, wracking sobs, my tears soaking his shirt. The emotions were real, the fear and the hurt. The fact I was chewing myself up on the inside for lying to him only made me cry harder.

At last, he gently released me and pushed back so that he could look at me. "I wouldn't have been angry, if you'd told me about the test." He took my hands again and squeezed them. "I don't ever want you to be scared of me again."

I nodded, still shaky.

"Christina," he said quietly. "Are you pregnant?"

And I drew in my breath because, even though he was doing everything he could to make his voice level and neutral, I could still hear the hope in it. There was a part of him, buried deep and never normally revealed, that really, *really* wanted a family.

"No," I whispered. The guilt was slowly ripping my heart in two. "The test was negative."

He nodded quickly but I saw the flash of disappointment in his eyes. Then he was gently lifting me out of the chair and cradling me against his chest. He carried me like that all the way to the car, ignoring Maxsim's questions and just barking *Home* at Grigory. He held me like that the entire way home and then carried me up to our bedroom.

He set me down on the bed only long enough to run me a bath. Then he carefully undressed me and lowered me into it, kneeling beside me while he gently washed the sweat from my body and the hot water eased the tension in my muscles. The pain in my tooth was starting to ease, but he gave me a painkiller to help. Then he wrapped me in a fluffy towel and dried me, and only then did he lay me on the bed and make slow, tender love to me.

It was the first time we'd been properly private: there was no earpiece anymore, no one listening. When he whispered in Russian and English in my ear, it felt intimate on a whole new level. I hadn't realized how important it is to have secrets.

The feeling started when he kissed me. It got stronger as he fucked me and became a certainty as we came together. As he spooned me in the darkness, I *knew*.

I'd had enough.

I loved this man.

I was on his side, now. It wasn't me and the FBI versus him, anymore. It was me and him versus them.

For the first time, I dared to think it: *what if I just never go back?*

That's crazy. I couldn't just... could I?

I pulled his arm tighter around me. As I drifted off to sleep, I didn't know what I was going to do, but I knew I wouldn't betray him again.

But when I woke, a storm was howling outside... and he was gone.

46

KONSTANTIN

I WAS PACING THE HALLS, brooding and furious. Outside, the wind was screeching over the roof and rattling the windows, a monster ready to tear the house apart. I knew how it felt.

I'd got up and dressed in a suit because I knew I wouldn't be sleeping again. It wasn't that I'd had the bad dream. The bad dream was terrifying, but it motivated me, kept me focused on what was important.

I'd had the *good* dream again. More vivid, this time. More real. Like before, I'd been with Christina, somewhere green. I'd woken and stared down at her, aching for her, aching for a different life. One where I could be a husband... a father. That's what had made me get up. That's what had me pacing the halls, enraged at myself. I'd let this whole thing get out of control.

I'd been weak. So, so weak. I'd let her get close to me, I'd fallen for her, and now I was having stupid ideas, ideas like a *family!* I knew what that sort of thing led to. A woman made you vulnerable. A child, doubly so. I'd been blinded by emotion, but now, alone with time to think, I could see it. I was risking everything I'd built, everything I'd promised them, that night.

A noise, behind me. I turned to see her standing there in just her panties and a sheet, the thin material wound around her like a toga, the moonlight painting her pale skin silver. God, she was beautiful. For a second, I just wanted to tell her everything was okay and go back to bed with her. I could feel myself weakening. *This is why I can't be around her!*

"What's going on?" she asked. "Why are you dressed? It's the middle of the night!"

I couldn't explain. I shook my head.

She stepped closer and took my hand. "What is it? Talk to me!"

I wanted to. I wanted to share everything with her. But I can't talk about what happened that night. And the more I opened up to her, the closer we got, the harder this would be. If I didn't want history to repeat, there was only one thing I could do.

"Christina," I began, looking at the floor, "I think—I can't be with you."

She drew in her breath. She shook her head in denial, but, as soon as I looked up and she saw my expression, she knew it was true. She dropped my hand as if scalded. "You're *breaking up with me?!*"

I started to say *no...* but I couldn't.

"Now?" she asked, incredulous. "In the middle of the—After we just—"

I cursed. I had no idea how to do this, I only knew it had to be done. "Victoria can help you pack," I offered. "Grigory will take you anywhere you want to go—"

But she gave a hurt little cry and I stopped talking—I was just making it worse. "Christina," I said, reaching for her.

"No," she said, shaking her head. "No." And then she was off and running, down the stairs and into the hallway, and then the howl of the wind rose as she threw open the door and ran outside.

Shit! Should I go after her? Not go after her? I had no idea how to deal with something like this.

Then I realized where she was going, and how much danger she was in.

And I bolted down the stairs and ran after her into the storm.

47

HAILEY

W HEN I GOT OUTSIDE, the wind was so strong it made me stumble sideways. It stole my breath and tried to rip the sheet away from me. But I regained my balance and staggered on into the darkness. If I lost myself thoroughly enough in the undergrowth, maybe the truth wouldn't find me.

The wind made the long grass ripple: it felt like I was running through the surf, out into the ocean. The storm had already stripped the last of the leaves from the trees, turning them into dark-boned skeletons. They creaked and groaned in agony as their branches were bent further and further, finally snapping and pinwheeling across the ground.

I raced into the glasshouse. It was sheltered, there, but the howl was replaced by a high-pitched whistle as the wind tried to force its way in through a thousand tiny cracks. It reminded me of Maxsim's drill and I pressed my hand protectively against my cheek as my tooth started throbbing again.

I pulled the sheet tighter around me for warmth as I walked down towards the far end of the glasshouse. I didn't have a plan. I just wanted to hide, to put off the inevitable for as long as possible—

The door opened. "Christina!" Konstantin's voice.

I didn't answer. I couldn't face him. I pushed on into the shadows. I heard him cursing, trying to close the door, but the wind kept sucking it out of his hand and he gave up. "Christina!"

I kept moving, but then I reached the glass wall at the end of the room and the moonlight lit me up. I heard him run forward as he saw me and I had no choice: I turned around.

I hadn't realized that I'd started crying but I could feel the hot tears running down my cheeks. "Why?" I blurted. "Why... *now?* Just when we were—"

He sighed, exasperated. But not at me, at himself. "That's not what we *are,* Christina. You and me, we've never been that. Both of us just forgot, for a while." He sighed and ran a hand through his hair and I glimpsed the scar on his forehead. "You always understood before!"

I shook my head. "Well I don't understand *now.*"

The wind rose outside, the whistling rising in pitch and then dropping as it changed direction. Konstantin looked up, worried. "Please, Christina! It's dangerous in here."

Christina. The name cut me to the core. I wasn't the woman he thought I was. It wasn't *me* he'd fallen in love with, it was her. I shook my head, my eyes swimming with tears.

"*Golub,*" he pleaded. *"Please!"*

And I softened. I took a step towards him. And—

The sheet suddenly lifted and the dusty soil on the floor rushed around my feet as the wind suddenly sucked the air out of the glasshouse. The door flew all the way open, straining on its hinges. And then just as abruptly, the wind changed and the door slammed closed with a bang that shook the whole structure.

The first pane popped loose from the roof a few feet to my left. I saw it fall in slow motion, shining bright in the moonlight and perfectly flat until it smacked into a table and shattered, spraying shards of glass at waist height. I screamed as something stabbed into my hip but more panes were already falling. Some fell flat, some swung down and dangled for a second before slicing down like falling swords. Some fell from the roof, some from high up on the walls. The door slam had started a chain reaction: as one pane fell, the change in weight made the ancient metalwork bend and flex, releasing more panes. Glass was falling all around me and exploding into vicious, deadly shards, the echoing crash of it almost continuous. I bent low, trying to protect my face—

Konstantin slammed into me and bore me to the ground on my back, hunkering down over me to protect me. Pane after pane smashed on his broad back and shoulders, but he didn't seem to care. At last the rain of glass began to slow... and finally, it stopped.

He gingerly turned and looked up at the ceiling. Most of the glass was gone, but one pane was dangling from its frame overhead. He winced as it slipped free and fell, edge-on. But it was on our side, it would miss us—

I glanced down and my insides went cold. It would miss *him,* but somehow, in the chaos, one of my legs had wound up kicked out to the side. I frantically started to pull it back—

The pane of glass sliced deep into my thigh and the sheet bloomed red with blood.

48

KONSTANTIN

"GRIGORY!" I bellowed, but the wind snatched my words away. I was sprinting through the trees, Christina's body cradled in my arms. She'd passed out before I even got her out of the glasshouse.

"Grigory!" I ran through the long grass. The bitter wind was chilling both of us: I could feel her going cold in my arms. Worse, my chest and stomach were slicked with hot wetness. The life, pumping out of her.

I rammed open the door, almost taking it off its hinges, and into the hallway. "*Grigory!*" I yelled. And this time he heard and came running around the corner, stumbling in shock when he saw Christina's limp body. "*Hospital!*" I snapped, and we ran together down the stairs to the garage.

In the back seat of the car, I held her on my lap. I tried to rouse her but she wouldn't wake up. Grigory kept glancing in the mirror at Christina, his face as pale and drawn as mine. "Run the lights," I told him.

I'd made a mistake. A horrible mistake. I'd thought that there was nothing as important as the promise I'd made, years ago. Nothing more important than my family, my legacy, my empire.

There was.

If I could just get her back, I'd do everything she wanted. I'd tell her everything, share all my secrets.

Her body seemed to relax. The blood soaking my shirt started to cool. I couldn't find her pulse. "Drive faster," I snarled at Grigory. The street lights blurred wetly. "Drive faster!"

49

HAILEY

L IGHTS, cold and stark, blasting through my eyelid shone in. "Ma'am, do you know where you are?"

I couldn't speak. My tongue was limp and dry and moving it was like trying to lift a mattress with one finger. Why was I so weak?

"BP's 90 over 60," yelled someone. "She needs blood."

"Her name is Christina Rogan," said Konstantin's voice. I could tell how worried he was because his English was disintegrating. "She's AB-negative."

Why would Konstantin know that? Then I realized: for the Bratva families, getting shot was an occupational hazard. Grigory, Konstantin, Christina...they probably all knew their blood types, in case they needed to be patched up by some backstreet doctor.

"Check the records, just to be sure," someone ordered.

The sound of fevered typing. The lights dimmed as someone leaned over me, comparing my face to a photo. "Yep, that's her. Records say she *is* AB-negative."

"OK, grab some."

Running footsteps disappearing into the distance. A thought coalesced in my brain, making me uneasy, but it was blurry and indistinct and I couldn't make sense of it.

Someone was digging their fingers into my leg and it hurt like crazy, but I couldn't raise the energy to scream. I heard someone move in close to the other side of me and smelled Konstantin's cologne. Then a big hand lifted mine and squeezed it. I tried to squeeze back, but I was too weak.

Footsteps pounded towards us. "Got the blood!"

This time, my stomach lurched. That was *bad.* That was *wrong.* But my brain still wouldn't work properly—I couldn't figure out why I was scared.

"Get it in, her pressure's dropping."

The metal feet of a drip stand rattled against the tiles as someone struggled to hang a bag on it.

That fear again, shapeless but real. With a monumental effort, I managed to crack my eyes open. I could see the bag swinging above me, heavy with blood.

Christina's type of blood. But—

But not mine. I was O-negative. My brain finally came awake. *The wrong blood will kill me!*

Someone had hold of my arm. A needle pricked at me. I tried to pull my arm away in panic.

"She's waking up!"

"Get the damn IV in, she needs the blood!"

A heavy arm pinned mine to the bed. Then the stab of a needle going in and the sticky pressure of a dressing securing it in place. "Line's in!"

No! Stop! I tried to yell a warning, but all that came out was a groan.

Konstantin's voice. "What's wrong with her?"

"She's just in pain."

A pull on the IV needle as the tube from the bag was screwed onto it. "Blood's going in!"

No, no! I started to thrash. Strong hands held me down. "Ma'am, we're trying to help you! Lie still!"

Over the doctor's shoulder, I could see the blood coursing down the transparent tube towards my arm. *No!*

Konstantin leaned over me. "*Golub,* what's wrong?"

The blood reached my arm—

Moving my injured leg made it feel like the glass was stabbing into it all over again. But I cocked it and *kicked*—and felt one toe just catch the drip stand. My arm exploded in pain as the IV was tugged and then the whole thing was tipping—

"Catch it!" someone yelled. But they were all busy trying to hold me down and—

There was a wet slap as the bag hit the floor.

"Goddammit!" snapped a nurse, glaring at me. "Bag's burst. And that was the last AB-negative we had."

"Then get me some O neg!" yelled the doctor.

O neg. O neg is fine. I slumped on the bed, my eyes closing.

50

HAILEY

T HEY KEPT ME in the hospital for the whole of the next day. I spent most of the time sleeping, recovering from the blood loss, but whenever I woke, Konstantin was by my bedside, watching over me.

They discharged me the following morning, the 18th. As Konstantin pushed me to the car in a wheelchair, a man hurried across the hallway without looking and slammed into me. Konstantin glared at him, protective, and he stammered an apology... and as he moved around the chair, I felt him discreetly slip something into my jacket pocket. *He must be FBI.*

I knew what he'd slipped me, but I didn't touch it. Not yet.

Konstantin had Grigory drive us into Manhattan and then to somewhere I recognized, though I hadn't been there in years. Battery Park, at the southern tip of Manhattan. You can look out and see the Statue of Liberty and Ellis Island.

He lifted me out of the car and carried me. I told him that I could walk, or at least limp, but he wouldn't allow it. He carried me all the way to a bench, looking out over the water, and then sat down beside me.

It was still early and autumn mist was rolling across the water, but you could still see Lady Liberty rising up out of it. It was bitterly, *bitterly* cold and that made my tooth start aching again. "What are we doing here?" I asked.

He was staring out at the water. "I need to tell you my story. You need to understand why I—Why I'm *me.*"

I nodded, eyes wide.

He took a deep breath and then huffed it out in a white cloud. It was so cold, I wasn't sure how long we'd be able to stay sitting there. "My father was Nikolai Gulyev," said Konstantin. "He ran half of St. Petersburg for the Russian mafia for over twenty years. A hard man, but fair. He fell for a secretary who worked for one of his companies."

"Your mother," I guessed.

"My mother. He married her and they had three boys: Pavel, Stefan, and me. We were the richest family in St. Petersburg. Growing up, I didn't want for anything. I had the best tutors, a huge house to play in, a horse...." He shook his head. "Things were different, back then. There was more honor. We always knew there was danger, we had guards, but we never thought...."

Konstantin did something I'd never seen him do before. He closed his eyes and bent forward, as if in respect or prayer. The wind started to howl, scouring our exposed skin as it blasted across the water, but he didn't seem to notice. When he spoke, he didn't open his eyes.

"There was a new gang in St Petersburg. Small, but brutal. They didn't pay any attention to the rules of the *Bratva,* the brotherhood. They had no honor. They..."

He paused for a moment, his jaw set hard. I reached out and touched his shoulder, my chest going tight with tension.

"My brothers and I had just arrived home from school," he said in a rush. His accent was getting stronger, the edges of the words rough. "My mother was in the dining room, planning the formal ball we held each year. And suddenly there was a crash as the front door was kicked open. Eight men, and their leader had brought his teenage son along, a kid no more than eighteen. They started killing. The guards first, but then the rest of the staff... the cooks, the maids.... The whole house was running in blood."

"I was fifteen. My brothers were eleven and eight. They took us upstairs and locked us in a room that had no windows. My mother, they took to the bedroom next door."

I slid my hand across Konstantin's back, trying to comfort him, but his body was like cold rock. There was no comforting him from this.

"My brothers were crying. I... was crying. I kept telling them that soon, it would be okay because my father would get home and then he'd unleash unholy hell on them. I told them, *these fucking idiots don't know what they've done.* I told them, *we'll watch as father executes every last one of them."* He paused. "I didn't realize that they *wanted* my father to get home. That's what they were waiting for."

His eyes opened and he stared out across the water towards the Statue of Liberty, but I knew he wasn't seeing it. He was in a mansion four thousand miles and twenty years away. The Russian in his voice was even stronger, now. "When my father got home, they took him upstairs. We heard him pass our door and we banged on it, telling him we were there, and he shouted for us to be brave. Then they took him into the bedroom with my mother and..." He swallowed. "And then a few minutes later, we heard her start screaming."

"Oh God." I wanted to be sick. "Konstantin—"

"You see, my father offered them money. Told them where the jewelry was hidden, opened the safe for them, told them they could take all the cars. But that isn't what they wanted. They wanted to *take over.* They wanted to take control of everything, all of the family's businesses, legal and illegal. And of course he refused. So they started to rape my mother, right in front of him."

I couldn't speak. I just gripped his arm and hung on in a death grip.

"He loved her. He loved her, and us, more than anything else in the world. And when they said they'd torture us, too, cut our fingers off one by one... he broke. He gave them everything. It took all night and into the next morning: they had him calling banks in

Switzerland, approving transfers, signing over his companies. They'd bribed lawyers and blackmailed people at his businesses so that everything could be witnessed and signed. We'd never be able to undo it. In one night, we lost everything... and they went from a small-time gang to running half of St. Petersburg."

"When it was all done, they told us they were releasing us. They let us out of the room and we ran to our parents. My mother was crying but trying to be strong. She tried to pretend she was okay, but we knew she'd been.... And her face was covered in bruises. Some bastard had beaten her while he—" Konstantin squeezed his eyes shut in disgust.

"They drove us out of town and up to a bridge over a river. It was January, thick with snow and far below zero. The sun was just coming up and the river was white with floating hunks of ice. We got out of the car and...." He closed his eyes again. "Nataliya was there. And Mikhail. And Evelina and Feodor." He had to stop for a moment and take a breath before he could explain and when he spoke again, his voice was raw with pain. "My cousins, Christina. Every one of my cousins. And their parents. People who had nothing to do with crime, the only thing they'd done wrong was to be related to us."

"It wasn't enough that they'd ruined us, they had to destroy us. They had to end the Gulyev line so that no one could come back and take revenge on them."

I clapped my hand to my mouth. I'd suddenly realized why Konstantin had never mentioned any brothers. The cold and the bitter wind that whipped at us were forgotten: they were nothing, now.

"They made us watch as they gunned down all of our relatives and threw the bodies into the river. Then it was our turn. The leader of the gang didn't do it himself. He got his teenage son, a fat, obnoxious little prick, to do the killing, said it was a rite of passage— one day, the gang would belong to him. And the little bastard was happy to help."

"He started with my youngest brother, Pavel. My father was begging, pleading. He knew he'd made a mistake, he knew he'd given up everything, for *nothing*, he didn't even care that he was going to die, he just wanted them to let his children live. But the teenager shot Pavel, right in front of him. And then he shot Stefan. And then he got me to kneel down on the edge of the bridge, because it was my turn. I knelt down. I didn't cry. I knew my father would want me to be strong. I could hear my mother sobbing. I heard the shot and there was pain, and then I was falling...."

Konstantin put his hand to the back of his head. "The teenager who shot me had been drinking our vodka, and he was showing off. He was laughing and joking, taunting my father, and his hand was shaking from the cold. The gun must have moved away just a little as it fired. The bullet only scraped my scalp."

He shook his head. "It shouldn't have mattered. The fall should have killed me. It nearly did: my head hit a chunk of ice as I went into the water—"—he pushed back his hair and showed me the scar on his forehead—"—that's how I got this. But somehow, I survived. I floated there for a few minutes. I was in shock: I didn't even notice the cold. Then a body fell from the bridge. My mother. And finally, another. My father."

"I wanted to swim over to them. I knew they were dead, but I just wanted to hold them. But I knew the gang might look down and see me so I just had to float there, playing dead, until I heard their car drive away."

"I started to come out of my daze. I looked around. I was floating in a mass of bodies: everyone I'd ever cared about was dead around me, The cold began to sink in and it was...." He shook his head. "It was cold like I'd never known it. The only reason the water wasn't freezing was that it was moving. Every time it slowed, I could feel the ice crystals trying to form around me. But the air was even colder. When the wind blew on my wet skin... agony, like a knife cutting down to the bone."

I suddenly understood why he'd brought me to this freezing place. This wasn't a story that could be told at the mansion, or in the warmth of a bar. He'd needed to feel at least a hint of that brutal cold.

He felt so guilty, for having survived, that he'd needed to punish himself just to be able to keep talking.

"The air was so cold, so painful, I just wanted to sink under the surface to get away from it," he said. "Letting go would feel so good. But...." He turned to me. "I could feel *this.*" He showed me his ring. "It was my father's. He gave it to me on the way to the river, when he thought they'd only kill him. And my mother, just before they shot *her,* she pressed her necklace into my hand. Now, those two things were all that was left of our empire. And *I* was the only Gulyev left." He looked at me and the pain in his eyes was heartbreaking. "They were all *dead.* My entire family was *dead.* If I let myself die...."

"There'd be nothing left," I whispered, my vision swimming with tears.

"So I made a decision. A promise. And I swam to the bank, pushing my way through their bodies. I hauled myself out and started walking. It was several miles into town, crunching through the snow. By rights, the cold should have killed me. But I wouldn't let myself stop walking."

"I finally found shelter in a bus station on the outskirts of town. The next morning, everything sunk in. I had no money, no home, and if the gang found out I was alive, they'd kill me. But I'd decided: I was going to take back everything they'd stolen from me. So I took a different name and began."

"I had to start at the very bottom of the Bratva, as a gutter rat picking pockets. I lived on food other people threw away. But I worked my way up. Built my own gang and started taking my family's territory back one street at a time. It was ten years before I dared to take the name Konstantin Gulyev again. Another five, and I'd taken our half of the city back. Then I came to New York. And...."

I finished the sentence for him in my mind. *And I just kept going.* His whole adult life had been about rebuilding his family's power and carrying on their legacy. He had nothing else. That was why he had to take over the whole of New York. That was why it was never enough.

He looked towards the Statue of Liberty. "I swore I'd never let myself get close to anyone. I'd seen what could happen, if you allowed yourself to feel. I never loved anyone...." He turned to me. "Until you."

My cheeks were wet with tears and my throat was choked. "And the other gang?" I asked. But I already knew what he was going to say.

"Their leader was a man called Olaf Ralavich," said Konstantin. "He was killed a few years ago and control of his empire passed to his son. The teenager who killed my family. Dmitri. Dmitri Ralavich."

I broke and threw my arms around him, burying my face in his chest. I understood, now. I understood why he was so cold, so isolated, why even sex had been stripped of its emotion and safely locked away in the dungeon. I understood why everything in the mansion was so old and why he'd clung onto traditions like the annual ball: he was trying to recapture all that family heritage that had been torn away from him. I understood why he wore the ring and why he'd had it made into the hardware key for his laptop: he knew he'd never, ever take it off.

The necklace. He'd given me the necklace. I was *that* special to him.

And God, the way he'd reacted when he thought I might be pregnant: he'd glimpsed a chance for his family to have a future. I even understood why he'd wound up with Christina: he'd wanted someone cold and heartless so that there was no danger of him falling for her. And then I'd come along and—

He pushed me gently back and frowned at me. "I don't understand how you've changed. But ever since the accident, however hard I try..." His shoulders hunched and I saw his whole body tighten in frustration. He grabbed my hand and squeezed it. "You make me weak," he said helplessly.

I put my other hand over his and squeezed back. "That's not weak," I said breathlessly.

He stared at me for a long time, battling with himself...and finally he sighed and nodded and we threw our arms around each other and sat there hugging. The wind was picking up, howling across the water and blasting across our backs. But we were impenetrable, our fronts pressed together to form a glowing core of warmth the cold couldn't steal.

"I don't want to have any secrets from you anymore," he said, his cheek pressed to mine. "Ask your questions about my business and I'll answer every one."

My chest contracted. This was it: everything we'd wanted when I'd volunteered for this mission. I could ask him what he was planning for the 18th: God, that was *today!* I could get all the information we needed and then call in Calahan and arrest him....

But I didn't want to. Not anymore.

"Go on," said Konstantin gently. "What do you want to know?"

I had to finally make the decision that I'd been struggling with since the night before. I took a deep breath, inhaling his warmth, the scent of his cologne...and I made my choice.

I wasn't going back to the FBI. Not ever. And that meant I could know nothing, because if I had information, the FBI could bring me in and force me to testify against him. "I don't need to know," I told him. "I trust you." And as soon as I said it, I realized it was true. "I know you're honorable. You're not like Ralavich, you don't murder innocent people."

He hugged me even tighter. And then he helped me to my feet, put his arm around me, and supported me all the way back to the shelter of the car.

When the doors *whumped* shut and the howl of the wind was suddenly cut off, it was a shock. I sat there with my skin throbbing and my toes tingling from the warmth. As the car pulled away, I was still trying to come to terms with what I'd decided. *I'm not going back. I'm not FBI anymore. I'll never see Calahan or Carrie again....*

"Tell me something about you," said Konstantin.

I looked at him, startled. His expression was more open than I'd ever seen it. *He's....* My heart melted as I realized: *he's trying.* He hadn't had a real relationship in twenty years and he was trying to make it work, for me.

"Your father," he said. "Tell me about him."

I thought of my childhood. The three fathers I'd had: my real dad, the artist. The abusive step-dad who'd made my life a living hell. And the mentor who'd become like a father to me. I wasn't sure if I could revisit all that: the wounds were too deep. But if things were going to work with Konstantin, I had to be honest with him, just like he'd been with me. I tried to start talking, but the memories welled up and the pain blocked my throat.

"He lives on the Upper East Side, yes?" said Konstantin gently.

I stared. *What?!*

"You visit him, every few weeks."

And the pain turned vicious and sharp. Oh God: Christina's father was still alive! She'd already told Konstantin about him, which meant now I could never tell him about my real childhood. Even if we were together until the day we died, I'd never be able to share what happened. Reality sank in and it was crushing. I wasn't FBI anymore but I'd still have to lie to him, every single day.

"We get on well," I said, trying not to choke.

When we got back to the mansion, I told him I was going out to the garden for a while, even though the cold made my tooth ache. I needed to think. I needed to figure out if I could really do this. Being with Konstantin meant living a lie for the rest of my life and turning my back on everyone I'd ever cared about. My stomach lurched as I realized: *I'll never see my mom again, except as a stranger.*

And did we really have a future together? He wanted a family. If he kept going on his current course, taking over New York and triggering a gang war, our kids would grow up knowing nothing but violence.

I needed help. And there was only one person I could talk to.

I pulled out the earpiece the FBI agent had slipped into my pocket at the hospital. I'd gotten so used to wearing one, but now when I put it in, it felt alien and wrong. To my surprise, I could hear someone already talking on it as I pushed it into my ear. "—ailey? Hailey, are you there, *please!*" It was Calahan and he sounded frantic.

"I'm here," I said.

He didn't ask if I was okay, or ask where the hell I'd been, or demand to know why it had taken me hours to put in the new earpiece. That's how I knew something was very wrong. "Christina!" he snapped. "She escaped!"

"What?!"

"Hailey, *she's on her way to you!"*

51

HAILEY

I SPRINTED through the overgrown garden, ducking low branches and crashing through bushes. If Konstantin saw her, if she told him I was an imposter.... "What happened?" I yelled.

Calahan sounded as breathless with panic as I was. "We had her at a safe house. Two guards. She seduced one of them, stole his car. We're tracking its GPS. She's only a few streets away from you."

"Stop her!"

"We're in pursuit, but we're not going to get there in time!"

I reached the back door of the mansion... and realized I didn't have a plan. I knew I had to intercept her before she talked to Konstantin but what the hell was I going to do with her?

"Hailey, she's there! She's outside the mansion!" yelled Calahan.

I cut through the staff area, dodging maids and cleaning staff as I raced to the front of the mansion. I stumbled to a stop by the front door and wrenched it open—

The guard outside turned and looked at me in surprise. I scanned the driveway: no sign of Christina.

The guard was still frowning at me. I looked up at him. "What?" I asked.

He shook his head in wonder. "How did you get changed so fast?"

My eyes widened. *I missed her!* I turned and bolted up the stairs. Burst into our bedroom. A dark-haired woman spun around and—

The room seemed to rock and tilt under my feet. That sickening shift in reality, again. I was looking at myself.

Christina's eyes narrowed. "*You!*" She was panting: she must have raced up here just like I had.

I put my hands up defensively. I had no idea what to say or what to do. *Why the hell has she come here?* If she exposed me to Konstantin, the FBI would have to rush in to try to save me. Maybe he'd kill me before they got there, maybe he wouldn't, but either way they'd recapture Christina and she was facing serious prison time for the drugs they'd found in her car in Italy. By coming here she'd pretty much guaranteed she'd be caught. Why hadn't she just driven to Mexico and disappeared? With any other woman, I'd have thought it was for Konstantin, to get her man back. But I knew she didn't love him. So why?

A creak from the stairs. My heart jumped up into my throat and Christina gave me a cat-like grin. "I could fucking kill you," she told me savagely. "But I'd rather watch him do it."

I wasn't ready for the raw emotion in her voice. *Maybe I was wrong. Maybe she does love him?*

And then, before I could say anything, Konstantin's voice came from the landing. "Christina?"

My eyes went wide as I saw Christina's mouth open. *No no no—*

"In here!" yelled Christina. "Come in, I've got something to show you!"

I heard Konstantin's heavy footsteps coming down the hall. It was all over. He'd see the two of us and kill me. Unless—

"We'll cut a deal with you," I whispered frantically.

Christina frowned. "What?"

"Walk away," I told her. "Walk away *right now* and don't tell him and—and—we'll drop all charges against you. You'll be free!"

Carrie exploded on my earpiece. "*What the hell are you doing?! You don't have the authority to make that kind of a deal!*"

"It's the only chance we have!" I snapped.

Carrie muttered and cursed. Then, "Okay!"

I looked at Christina. "The FBI agrees." I glanced at the door. I could hear Konstantin right outside. "Just walk away," I hissed. "We won't come after you. Please. *Please!*"

She glared at me suspiciously, unsure if it was a trap. Then she seemed to see something in my expression and she frowned in amazement.

I flushed. *What does that mean? What did she see?*

The doorknob twisted. It was too late for Christina to hide: she was right out in the middle of the room. But I was next to the closet. I darted inside and pulled the door shut.

And prayed that she'd take the deal.

52

HAILEY

I STOOD THERE in the darkness of the closet, my nails digging into my palms. I heard the bedroom door open. Braced myself for Christina to tell him the truth—

"You changed clothes," said Konstantin uncertainly. "Is that what you wanted to show me?"

"No," I heard Christina say. "This is."

Shit! I threw up my hands defensively, expecting her to pull the closet door open—

But nothing happened. The door wasn't all the way closed and I peeked through the crack—

Christina was standing right in front of Konstantin, her t-shirt and bra pulled up to her neck, her breasts bared to him. She shook her shoulders, jiggling them at him. He grinned, looking confused but pleased. I felt a sudden stab of jealousy.

Then it got worse. She reached up, took his cheeks in her hands and—*no! Stop!*—

She drew him down into a kiss.

The jealousy swelled and rose: I realized just in time that I was reaching for the closet door, about to throw it open, and had to force myself to stop. Christina's kiss was nothing like one of mine. It was open-mouthed and lewd, and she moaned like a porn star as she did it, molding her body to Konstantin's and grinding against him. She turned him so that she was looking towards the closet over his shoulder, then opened her eyes and stared right at me, her eyes gleaming with victory.

I felt ill.

She finally released him and he stared down at her, wiping his lips and frowning. "You seem...different," he said.

"Why don't you go and work," she told him. "I'll put on something sexy and come and find you, and we can go down to the dungeon." She leaned close and whispered in his ear, just loud enough for me to hear. "I'll let you do *horrible things* to me. In fact, I'd love it if you—" She lowered her voice even more, but I saw Konstantin's eyes widen in shock. The *bitch!* She was setting me up!

She patted Konstantin's arm and he left, still looking confused. I emerged from the closet and glared at her. She gave me a smug grin. "Don't be so uptight," she told me. "You might even enjoy it."

I scowled, then glanced at the door. *Just leave!*

She walked right up to me, then leaned in close. I flinched back, but she was already pushing back my hair and peering into first one of my ears, then the other. The earpiece was discreet, but you could see it if you looked carefully. She found it and smiled, nodding to herself. Then she clamped her hand over that ear and whispered quietly in my other one, so that only I could hear.

"*I know why you really made that deal,*" she told me.

Then she drew back and stared into my eyes to see my reaction. And I felt myself flush and look away, confirming it: I was in love with him.

She grinned victoriously and strutted out of the room. I ran to a window at the rear of the mansion and watched. If I hadn't known to look for her, I never would have seen her slink out of the back door and slip into the undergrowth. I followed her to the edge of the grounds... and then she was gone.

I let out a massive sigh of relief. *It's over.* I had to sit down on the bed for a second: my legs were shaky with adrenaline. God, just ten minutes before, I'd been out in the garden soul-searching about whether I was doing the right thing. But having my new life nearly ripped away from me had woken me up. *I nearly lost him!*

I took a deep breath and stood up, then started hunting through the closet for some lingerie to put on. I found a pretty bra and panties set, black with silver thread along the edges. I stripped off and pulled it on and as I dressed, I pushed all my doubts down inside. I'd never see my mom, Calahan, Kate or Alison again. And *Carrie!* I'd be betraying all the trust she'd placed in me. She'd be heartbroken.

I'd never be able to talk to Konstantin about my real past. I'd have to lie to him every day.

But it was worth it, to be with him. My new life started *now.*

The bedroom door suddenly opened and Konstantin marched in. "I couldn't wait," he told me, his voice thick with lust. He put one hand under my ass and scooped me up, being careful of my injured leg. "I'm going to take you downstairs," he muttered, "and I'm going to give you exactly what you asked for, you dirty little *shlyukha.*"

I flushed scarlet. I was distracted, half-worried and half-curious about what Christina had set me up for, and just so happy that we were finally together, I did what I always did when I was embarrassed. I pushed my glasses up my nose. And when my finger didn't find any glasses, I realized what I'd done and froze... which made it way worse.

I stared at him, my finger still against the bridge of my nose.

He was staring right back at me and his face was turning pale.

No. No, he can't remember. No! It's such a small thing! No, NO! Not when we were so close! I finally managed to whip my finger away. But it was too late. That one tiny slip had opened a crack in the dam and behind it was the pressure of all his suspicions: every way I'd been different to her, since the very beginning. I watched his face fall, his happiness turning to shock and disbelief as the truth broke free.

He knew.

53

HAILEY

THE FLOOR seemed to drop away from under me. This was the nightmare scenario I'd lived in fear of since day one, but the reality was so much worse than I'd imagined. I stood there staring up at him, my mouth moving but no words coming out. If he'd had any doubts, the guilt on my face ended them.

He grabbed me by the shoulders and twisted me, searching in my ears just as Christina had. But when he found the earpiece, he pulled it roughly out, flung it on the floor and—

His heel crushed my only link to the outside world, grinding it into plastic shards against the floorboards. I drew in a horrified, shuddering breath and then his hands were on my shoulders, slamming me up against the wall. "*Hailey?!*" he hissed.

I swallowed, panting in fear... and nodded.

He stared at me, stunned, looking at my face, my eyes. Shock made his Russian accent thicken. "*How?! How do you look like her?*"

"Pl—Plastic surgery," I said. I felt as if I was drowning, had to choke the words up through thick, cold dread. But the fear of what he'd do to me wasn't the worst part. The worst part was the horror in his eyes, the shattering of all the trust he'd put in me.

He was shaking his head, barely able to speak. I'd grabbed hold of his forearms and I could feel his muscles going rock hard with rage. "Is she—Is Christina *dead?!*"

"*No!* No, she's fine. That was her, in the bedroom, a few minutes ago. We had her in custody, but she escaped. We let her go, she's fine!"

"You're... *FBI?*" He spat the letters.

I nodded. The horror, the *disgust* in his eyes made it feel as if my heart was crumpling in on itself, imploding into a tiny, icy little nugget of black.

He pushed away from me and staggered back across the room. He ran one hand through his hair, slowly shaking his head. "You—Jesus, since the *accident!* The *shoes!* That's why the shoes didn't fit. God, in my office. The pregnancy test."

He opened the drawer of his bedside table and stared at something inside. His body blocked my view as he picked it up. Then he slowly turned around.

A handgun, blunt and angular, huge even in his big hand.

"Konstantin," I said, my voice shaky, "Please—"

He looked at me and my words died in my throat, my legs going rubbery under me. His eyes were *so cold,* a cold without hope. I'd seen that look before, when he was going to throw Ralavich's man off the roof. I reached out towards him, trying to calm him, but I didn't get past the first letter of his name. "K—"

"*I trusted you!*" he roared. His voice shook the room and I flinched and went silent. He started to advance, the gun raised.

I backed away, unable to take my eyes off the gun's gaping, inky-black muzzle. Konstantin *never* used a gun. I hadn't even known he owned one. He always used his fists, like with Ralavich's man on the rooftop. I tried to force words out of a throat gone sandpaper-dry. "K —Konstantin," I managed. "Just let me—"

"*Suka!* Traitorous *blyád'!*"

"*Please!*" My back hit the wall and my stomach lurched. There was nowhere left to run. I threw up my hands as if that could stop him, my eyes welling with tears. "*Please!*"

He pressed one hand between my breasts and pinned me to the wall. He put the muzzle of the gun against my forehead, the metal shockingly cold. I could see my own terrified eyes reflected in the gun's chrome. And suddenly, I knew why he was using a gun. He loved me. He couldn't hurt me with his own hands, couldn't bear to put them around my neck and squeeze the life out of me. He needed the gun to make it distant and emotionless.

His eyes were wet. "*Izmennik.*"

I didn't need to speak Russian. The meaning was there in his expression, in the disappointment in his voice: *traitor.*

I closed my eyes.

And heard him pull the trigger.

54

KONSTANTIN

A BOOM like the end of the world. Then utter silence. *She's gone.* I'd closed my eyes as I did it, unable to watch. I couldn't bear to open them again.

It was several seconds before I felt it: a finger tentatively brushed the hand that pinned her to the wall. Then her fingers closed around mine and squeezed tight.

We both opened our eyes at the same time.

We were staring at each other from six inches apart. A few inches to the left of her head, there was a smoking hole in the plaster.

Something inside me had rebelled, as I'd pulled the trigger. I'd jerked the gun aside at the last second.

"Damn you," I whispered. "Goddamn you for making me weak."

I dropped the gun and it fell to the floor with a dull *thunk.* A thousand different ways to kill her flooded my mind, but none of them would work. How can you kill the person you can't do without?

"I love you," she said.

"Shut up!" I snapped.

Three little words... they shouldn't have done anything. I was shaking with rage, wrapped in ice a mile thick and as hard as diamonds. And yet the words breezed straight through, simple and innocent as the butterflies in her goddamn garden and hitting me right in the heart because—

I turned away. I couldn't look at her. Because the words sounded true and if I looked into her eyes and they *were* true....

"I do," she said, and sniffed back tears. "It's true. I'd decided, I'd changed sides, I wasn't going to go back to them, I was going to stay here with you!"

"Shut up!" My words were like weapons, trying to tear hers from the air so I didn't have to hear them. "You lie to me! You tell me nothing but lies, all this time, and you expect me to believe you?!"

"Look at me," she whispered. Her voice had changed and it was more than just the tears. It was slower. More *country*. It was the voice I'd heard in my hotel room in Boston. Her *real* voice.

I shook my head.

"Look at me," she begged,

I shook my head again. I was trying to stoke my anger higher, so I could do what needed to be done. She was lying. I had to kill her and then call Grigory in here and find a way to dump the body—

"Konstantin," she sobbed, the tears overwhelming her. "Look at me, *please!*"

My whole body was screaming at me not to. *Its lies, all lies....*

I looked. Just for a second. But a second was too long. Once I looked, I couldn't look away. Her eyes were swimming with tears and I saw—

Innocence.

Goodness.

And not a trace of deception. She loved me. She really did love me.

The feeling rose up inside me, expanding, filling me up. It cracked the ice into a million shining shards.

I pulled her towards me. My palms slid on her tear-wet cheeks and then my lips came down on hers.

55

HAILEY

I'D BEEN THROUGH so many emotions in just a few minutes: panic, guilt, fear. And now, as he tilted my head up and kissed me, *hope*. It was a tiny, fragile flame: if I even breathed too hard, it would go out. But it was there. I opened under him, desperate to show him this was *right,* this was *real.*

He was savage, kissing me with the full force of his anger, wanting to hate me. But I didn't pull away, I stood there and took it, letting all the rage and hurt boil down into me, *Yes. Yes, I lied to you. I lied to you and I'm sorry.* My hands were on his sides and I could feel his body tighten and tighten as he fought with himself: he was a hair's breadth from hurling me across the room, picking up the gun again and shooting me. I sobbed and kissed and prayed....

And at last, I felt his body relax. He gave a low growl and settled into it, one hand burying itself in my hair, the other sweeping down my back and clutching my ass, pulling me into him. The kiss changed, turning soft and slow... and *deep.* He sought me out and explored me. He'd told me all his secrets, but he didn't know *me* at all. *Who are you?*

I answered, opening up to him, hiding nothing. I was the woman he'd met back in Boston, the one I'd been trying so hard to hide.

And he liked it. The kiss began to move and change, taking on a rhythm, firm presses of that hard upper lip, and slow strokes of the lower one. The room filled with our panting.

He finally broke away and stared at me, his chest heaving. "Glasses," he said at last. "In Boston, you wore glasses."

"They fixed my eyes," I said. My voice sounded weird and unfamiliar. I'd gotten so used to Christina's.

He stared at me for another few seconds. "I liked you in glasses," he told me.

A big, hot wave crashed through me. He'd liked me even before—

He put a hand between my breasts and pushed me back against the wall, then scowled down at me. His voice was like granite, telling me *this is how it is going to be.* "If you ever, *ever* lie to me again—"

"I won't," I said meekly.

He stared at me silently for a few seconds. Then he looked down at the crushed earpiece on the floor. "They won't just let you walk away," he told me. "As soon as they realize you're not loyal to them, they'll come in here and take you from me.

I went cold inside. I couldn't let that happen.

"There's only one way this works," he told me. "Come away with me, right now."

My eyes widened as I realized what he meant. "To—"

"To Russia, yes. In six months, a year, we can come back. But for now, we have to get far away from them."

My stomach lurched. I'd be turning my back on everything and everyone I knew and loved. But we'd be together. It only took me a second to decide.

I nodded.

"Pack a bag, *quickly.* We might only have minutes. I'll have the jet made ready."

He gave me one last kiss and hurried off. I stood there frozen for a second, struggling to come to terms with how much had changed in such a short time. My eyes fell on the bullet hole in the wall. We'd come *that* close....

I shook it off, ran into the closet, and grabbed Christina's suitcase.

I started throwing in clothes. I felt different. *Lighter.* Even my tooth had finally stopped hurting. *This is actually happening. Everything's going to be okay. We're going to be—*

A phone rang. But not Christina's phone, or Konstantin's phone. I didn't recognize the ringtone and it sounded muffled. On the second ring, I lifted up the suitcase because it sounded like the phone was underneath it. But the ringing lifted, too. The phone was *inside* the case.

I opened up the secret compartment Calahan had shown me. And underneath my FBI badge and my gun, I found a pocket. With shaking hands, I pulled out a cellphone, attached to a power bank that had kept it charged. It had been sitting there this whole time, and there was only one person who could have hidden it there.

I pressed the button to answer the call and put the phone to my ear. "Hello?"

"Hailey," said Calahan. "What's going on?"

56

HAILEY

"I'M OKAY," I said quickly. But then my throat closed up. How could I possibly explain? How could I tell him I was turning—I felt sick—*traitor* and running away with the enemy?

I'd underestimated him. "The phone's a secret," he said. "No one else knows about it. When you went off the air, procedure says I should have called in the cavalry and rushed in to get you. But...."

And I heard it in his voice: worry, frustration... and just a hint of jealousy.

He already knew.

"...but if there's something you need to tell me, first...." He left it hanging in the air, a plea for me to come clean.

I closed my eyes, mad at myself. This was *Calahan,* my friend. Of course I had to tell him. I took a deep breath and then it all came spilling out: my attraction to him, even before the mission, what happened in his hotel room in Boston, how we'd fallen for each other, how he wanted me even now he knew who I was. "He's taking me to Russia," I finished breathlessly.

I heard the rasp of his palm rubbing his stubble. "Hailey," he started.

"I know. I know what you're going to say, I haven't forgotten what he is. But if you knew him like I knew him...." For once, I used his first name. "Sam, I love him. And he loves me."

I heard Calahan's chair creak as he rocked back in it and imagined him sprawling there, hands over his eyes as he debated.

I held my breath.

Calahan sighed. Cursed. "Go," he said at last. "But make it fast. I'll cover for you as long as I can but Carrie and the others will figure it out soon."

"If they find out you covered for me, you'll be in trouble," I said.

"Wouldn't be the first time. Go. *Go,* Hailey, go and... be happy."

I heard that tiny pang of jealousy in his voice again and my chest tightened. *He deserves to be happy, too.* "Thank you," I whispered. And ended the call.

Less than five minutes later, we were in the Mercedes, speeding towards the airport. There was no sign of pursuit yet but Grigory wasn't taking any chances and had his foot hard down. Meanwhile, in the back, Konstantin was on his phone, looking up the number of a Russian government contact who could help me arrange an emergency, last-minute visa. I dug out my own phone so I could call her.

Weird. My phone was off. I turned it on and waited for it to boot, trying to remember why I'd turned it off. Then Konstantin was reading me the number and moments later I was speaking to a woman in Moscow, painstakingly spelling out Christina's name, the address of the mansion, her passport number, and date of birth... the woman was polite and efficient but the questions seemed to go on forever and we were nearly at the airport before we were done. I thanked her and sat back in my seat with a sigh of relief. Then we were pulling up outside the terminal and hurrying past the crowds. Konstantin went in front, his size and attitude clearing a path for me. Thanks to it being a private flight, we breezed straight past check in and security and we were jogging across the runway towards the jet when my phone rang.

I stared at it in confusion. I recognized the number: Calahan. But why would he be calling me *now?* To try to change my mind? Or to warn me the FBI were moving in? I put the phone to my ear, still running. It was loud, out here, with planes roaring overhead as they came in for landing, and I had to shout. "*What is it?*"

Calahan was panting, frantic. It sounded like he was talking from a moving car, but I couldn't make out the words.

"*What?*" I yelled.

"*Arrest him!*" repeated Calahan. "Hailey, everything's changed. You have to arrest him!"

57

HAILEY

I STUMBLED to a stop. Ahead of me, Konstantin kept running. I pressed the phone hard against my ear, shutting out the din of the aircraft overhead. "What?" I asked. "What do you mean, what's changed?"

"The photo you sent, of Grigory putting that case into the trunk of his car?"

Now I remembered why my phone had been off. I'd shut it down when I was hiding in the basement garage, just after I'd taken the photo. And the last few days had been a non-stop rush: I hadn't turned it back on since. The photo must have been sitting in my outbox and it had sent as soon as I'd turned my phone back on. Even as I'd been running away with Konstantin, I'd been unwittingly sending one last piece of evidence to the FBI. "What about it?"

"There was a model number on the case. I ran it through the computer. Hailey, it's a Russian sniper rifle, designed to punch through bulletproof glass. That's what Grigory was delivering for Konstantin. That's the "tool" the guy you met at the shopping mall needed."

It made sense. One of Grigory's jobs was managing weapons for Konstantin's men. He was the perfect person to get hold of a rifle and deliver it. My stomach lurched: I already knew what Calahan was going to say next.

"Hailey, *it's an assassination*. Konstantin paid that guy at the shopping mall a quarter of a million dollars to murder someone!"

I shook my head. "No!" Ahead of me, Konstantin had realized I wasn't with him, and had spun around to look. He frowned, worried, as he saw me standing there on the phone. "He wouldn't do that,' I said. "Not cold-blooded murder." But a creeping dread was spreading through me.

"That's *exactly* what he'd do. Hailey, this is Konstantin Gulyev! He wants to take over the city and if he's trying to kill someone protected by bulletproof glass, someone so important it costs a quarter of a million—"

"...it must be one of the other crime bosses," I finished for him. Killing one of them would trigger the gang war the FBI feared, the very reason I'd been sent to take Konstantin down in the first place. I wanted to throw up.

"We're on our way," Calahan said. I heard the screech of tires in the background. "But we won't get to the airport in time to stop him. *You* have to do this."

Konstantin was running back towards me, now. "What's the matter?" he called. "What's going on?"

The dread reached my heart, my lungs. I couldn't breathe. Calahan was still talking, telling me to *do it, do it now,* but my arm went limp and I dropped the phone to my side and just stood there, staring at Konstantin as he approached.

I can't.

But I had to. I could accept what Konstantin was but I couldn't be party to *this,* to cold-blooded murder and the war that would follow. Hundreds of innocents would die in the crossfire.

Unless I did the unthinkable.

Konstantin reached me and put his hands on my shoulders. "Hailey! What's the matter? Who's on the phone?"

The dread changed to hot, jagged pain. *I'm so stupid.* Everyone— even him—had warned me about *men like him* and I'd ignored them.

I'd believed a criminal could be honorable. Carrie's voice rang in my head. She'd been right. I'd forgotten who I was. I'd forgotten I was FBI.

My vision swimming with tears, I felt for the secret compartment of my suitcase and shoved my hand inside.

Konstantin's voice was gentle but panic thickened his Russian accent. "Hailey! We have to go!"

Tears welled and heated and then, as my fingers found the grip of the gun and closed around it, they spilled free and started running down my cheeks.

He stared down into my eyes, his own eyes icy blue and full of worry. I remembered telling him at Battery Park that I didn't need to know his secrets, that I trusted him. *How could I have been so wrong?*

He gripped my shoulders hard. "What's the matter? *Hailey!*"

I pulled out the gun and pointed it right at his face. "You're under arrest," I panted through my tears.

58

HAILEY

THE FBI OFFICE should have felt like home, but being back there felt... *wrong.* The buzz of conversation, the smell of bad coffee... even my gray FBI suit felt scratchy and alien. I stared at the paperwork on my desk, undisturbed since I'd flown off to meet Konstantin. I'd been gone two weeks. It felt like a lifetime.

I needed to be busy, so I wouldn't think, but there was no more surveillance to be done. Not now our quarry was a prisoner downstairs.

Prisoner. Every time I closed my eyes, I saw the look on Konstantin's face when I'd arrested him. There was a party atmosphere at the office: *we did it, we caught him.* Someone had opened a bottle of champagne and was pouring glasses. It made me want to break down and scream.

I'd lost him. I'd torn us apart forever, betrayed him in the cruelest way possible, just after he'd spared my life and given me a chance.

But I'd had no choice. Had I?

There was no one I could talk to. The FBI agents all thought I was some sort of hero, sympathetic about *what I must have had to go through* at the mansion. I needed Calahan, but he was being debriefed and might be hours. He'd managed to cover for me, claiming that I'd alerted him to Konstantin making a run for the airport.

After an hour, I couldn't take it anymore. I went down to the interrogation rooms, careful on the stairs because I was still wearing three inch heels. I'd changed clothes because I wanted to leave Christina behind as fast as possible, but I hadn't had any spare shoes at the office.

I found Carrie in the observation room, staring through the one-way mirror into the interrogation room. I hesitated in the doorway, keeping my eyes off the mirror. I'd come down here to see Konstantin but, now that I was here, I couldn't face seeing him.

Carrie saw me, marched over and pulled me into the room and then into her arms. "Good job," she told me. "*Very* good job." Her voice was shaky with emotion.

I squeezed her back. The mirror was behind me, now, and the hairs on the back of my neck were standing up: I could feel Konstantin's brooding presence in the room beyond. *I'm not going to be able to turn around.*

Carrie pushed back from the hug and studied me. "I know it can't have been easy," she said carefully. "I'm glad you're back with us."

I said nothing. While I'd been at the mansion, she'd heard enough over the earpiece that she must at least suspect that I'd fallen for him. But she was letting me come home, all sins forgiven, because I'd delivered her the prize.

I nodded. "It's good to be back," I said weakly.

Carrie looked over my shoulder, towards the one-way mirror and Konstantin. "He's not talking," she told me bitterly. "Not a goddamn word."

What?! "That makes no sense!" I looked at the clock, panicked. "The email said the assassination would happen at 1pm. That's in two hours. We have enough to pin it on him. If he lets it happen, he's going to jail for twenty years!" I felt ill: I'd wanted to stop a gang war, but the thought of Konstantin caged in a tiny cell until he was an old man.... And if the assassination went ahead, the war would still happen.

Carrie shook her head, scowling. "Maybe it's worth it to him, to see one of his rivals fall."

I turned that over in my mind. It didn't feel right. Konstantin had a sense of honor. I still had trouble believing he'd murder one of his rivals in cold blood. But even if that was true, he wouldn't want to rule New York from prison. Why wouldn't he cut a deal and help us stop the assassination? With his lawyers, he could be out in five years instead of twenty.

I had to see him. My chest so tight I could hardly breathe, I slowly turned around.

A huge, hot lump rose in my throat. They'd chained Konstantin's wrists and ankles and then chained them together, like he was some kind of animal. He sat there in silence, glowering at the mirror. I knew he couldn't see us, but it felt like he knew I was there. His eyes burned into me. *Why did you do this to me?*

I felt tears prickle at the corners of my eyes. *I'm sorry!* "Let me have five minutes with him," I told Carrie. "Maybe I can get him to talk."

Carrie turned and frowned at me, searching my face for any shred of deception. But I had no ulterior motive: I just wanted to stop the assassination and the gang war that would follow, the same as her. If I couldn't, everything I'd sacrificed would have been for nothing.

"*Please,*" I begged.

"Five minutes," she told me.

～

I opened the door. He looked up and saw me and—

He turned his head and looked away, glaring at the mirror. It felt like someone had punched me in the gut. *Of course he hates you. What did you expect?*

I closed the door and walked over to the metal table. The room was so quiet, I could hear the hiss of air as he breathed, each exhalation shaky with rage. I pulled out my chair, the legs scraping on the tiles, and sat down.

"Please," I said. "You have to tell us who's going to be assassinated. Is it Luka Malakov? Angelo Baroni?" But he didn't react, wouldn't even look at me. "Please! I want to help you!"

At that, he finally turned his head. But the raw fury in his eyes almost made me want him to look away again. I wilted under that glare, crumbled under it. *I'm sorry! I'm sorry!*

"Why won't you talk?" I blurted, close to tears. "Co-operate, you could be out in a few years instead of...I don't want to see you spend your whole life in jail!"

Without thinking, I reached across the table and grabbed his hand. He looked down and a bolt of fear went through me as I realized what I'd done. He was a prisoner and I was meant to keep my distance. Even chained, he could easily break my neck if I let him get hold of me. I went to draw my hand back—

And then I remembered the first time I'd ever taken his hand, in the back of his car, and how shocked he'd been. *No one's ever done that before. No one's loved this man.*

He needed someone to love him now.

So I left my hand where it was. Trusting him not to hurt me.

And when he looked up and met my eyes, I could see a flicker of blue in all that cold gray. He still loved me, whether he wanted to or not.

"Please," I said again. "Talk."

He shook his head, but... the blue expanded and there was a hint, just a *hint,* of warmth as he looked at me. He turned away, trying to hide his weakness. But I'd seen it. He still cared about me, and the reason he wasn't talking was—

Oh God.

The reason he wasn't talking was *me!* Even now, even after everything I'd done to him, he was trying to protect me. He knew that if he talked to the FBI, it would eventually come out that I'd been running away to Russia with him. My career would be over: they might even charge me with something. "No," I said frantically, "No, I won't let you rot in jail just so that—"

I broke off, staring into his eyes. I'd just remembered that Carrie was listening from behind the mirror. I leaned in and put my lips to his ear. "Thank you," I whispered. "But I can't let you do that. Tell us about the assassination. Cut a deal. I'll take my chances." He shook his head. "*Please!* There'll be a gang war, innocents will die. I know you don't want that!"

He lifted his head and put *his* lips to *my* ear. Even now, the feel of him there, the sound of his voice, sent a hot rush straight through me. "Even if I didn't care about you, *Golub,* I can't tell them what they want to know," he told me. "And if you really love me, you know why."

I heard the door bang open behind me. "That's enough!" snapped Carrie.

Konstantin's head snapped up and he glared at his nemesis. She glared right back at him. "Mr. Gulyev," she said, "if you won't cooperate, *fine*. When the assassination happens, I'll charge you with conspiracy to murder and put you in a deep, dark hole for the rest of your days."

I slowly stood up, my hand still on Konstantin's. My eyes stayed locked on his as the realization hit me. I *did* know why.

I hadn't been wrong about Konstantin. I'd been right. He wasn't a cold-blooded murderer.

He couldn't tell the FBI about the assassination because he wasn't behind it.

Someone had set him up.

59

HAILEY

I POUNDED up the stairs three at a time, too frantic to wait for the elevator.

Carrie had warned me, just before I went undercover, about forgetting who I was. And the whole time I'd been in the mansion, I'd been worried she was right: was I forgetting I was Hailey? Was I turning into Christina?

But I'd had it wrong. That whole time, I'd been *me*. It didn't matter what I was called or what I looked like. The person who'd fallen for Konstantin had been *me*. And it had been *me* he'd fallen for. And the one time I'd gone against who I was, the one time I'd ignored my gut and tried to be a hard-nosed FBI agent, was when I'd arrested him.

I'd betrayed the man I loved and now he was going to jail for the rest of his life for something he didn't do.

No he isn't. Not if I have anything to do with it.

I burst out of the stairwell and sprinted along the hallway. Found the correct room and threw open the door without knocking. Calahan was at a desk, being debriefed by two other agents. All three of them looked at me.

"*I need you!*" I blurted, my voice raw and shaking.

The other two agents scowled at being interrupted. "It'll have to wait," said one. "We're in the middle of a—" He was cut short by Calahan pushing back his chair. "Agent Calahan, you can't just—" Calahan got up. "Goddamn it, Calahan, don't you dare—"

Calahan walked out, shutting the door behind him. Then he turned and looked down at me, ready to help. *God bless this man.* I led him downstairs and out to the garden: It was the only semi-private place in the whole building. A cold wind was whipping across the open space, sending anyone not in a coat hurrying for shelter. But Calahan stood unflinching, one hand on my shoulder. "What is it?"

I took a deep breath. "Konstantin isn't behind the assassination. Someone's setting him up."

It was the last thing he expected to hear. So many emotions crossed his face in just a few seconds. Shock. Then disbelief. Then anger, that Konstantin had fooled me with a lie, and pity for me that I'd believed it.

"Hailey..." he said gently.

"*No!* Listen to me! *It's not him!* Someone else is behind it and they're framing him!"

Calahan shook his head. "Then why doesn't Konstantin just tell Carrie that?"

"Because she'd never believe him! No one will! Except me." Calahan gave me a look. "I know how it sounds, but I know him. He wouldn't just murder someone in cold blood, not even one of his rivals." The wind blew my hair across my face and I shoved it angrily back. "He's better than that!"

"Hailey, all the evidence points to him. Hell, *you* found it! You saw the emails he sent to the assassin. You even delivered the money for him. You saw Grigory getting hold of the gun and heading off to deliver it, all on Konstantin's orders."

"That's just it, it's too perfect! You really think someone as smart as Konstantin would leave that trail? Emails right there on his own laptop? *Really?!*"

Calahan crossed his arms and scowled. But one thing about

Calahan, he's a champion for the truth. He doesn't gloss over something just because it's inconvenient. "No," he said at last.

"Someone else organized this whole thing." I told him. "They played us. We were *meant* to find this evidence, but we were meant to find it after the assassination had happened."

He glared. I was getting through to him, but he still wouldn't buy it. He'd had too many years fighting bad guys to side with one. He was willing me to back down. And a month ago, I would have. But a lot had changed. *I'd* changed. I crossed my arms and stared right back at him. "He's done plenty wrong," I said. "But he didn't do *this*."

Calahan narrowed his eyes, rubbed his stubble..., and finally sighed. "Even if you're right, what can we do? The assassination's going to happen in less than two hours! We've warned Malakov and Baroni that there's a possible threat to their lives: that's all we can do."

"We need to stop it happening! We need to clear Konstantin's name! The only way to do that is to find out who's really behind it and that means...." I hesitated. "We're going to need Konstantin's help."

Calahan's face fell as he realized what I was suggesting. He grabbed my shoulders. "Are you *fucking insane?* Helping a prisoner escape: that's not just your career over, that's *federal prison* for the *rest of your life!*" He shook his head. "You can't even be sure you're right. What if he *is* guilty?"

He glared down at me, determined to make me change my mind. His hands were unconsciously squeezing my shoulders and I could feel that protective need rolling off him in waves, like all he wanted to do was pull me to his chest and wrap his arms around me.

I looked up into his eyes. "Sam," I said, my voice shaky. "I love him. And I know that means I'm compromised. But it also means I know him. And he wouldn't do this."

He glared. This was about more than just wanting to protect a friend. There was jealousy in his eyes, too. I was asking him to put his career, even his freedom on the line, to help the other man. My stomach knotted. I hated asking him to do it, but there was no other way.

"*Please,*" I whispered. "I can't do this without you."

Calahan scowled and looked away, cursing. I held my breath....

"Fuck it," said Calahan at last. "Carrie's been trying to fire me for years. Might as well go out with a bang." He sighed and met my eyes. "What's the plan?"

60

KONSTANTIN

TWO AGENTS were interrogating me—or trying to. They were playing good cop, bad cop while I stared at them, silent and impassive. In another few hours, it would all be over. A shot would be fired from a rifle and they'd put me in jail for a murder I had nothing to do with...but at least Hailey would be spared. She'd be able to continue at the FBI, a good person doing good work.

I didn't hate her. I'd tried to but I couldn't. She'd done what she thought was right and I could see how much it had hurt her.

At that moment, the door flew open. *Hailey?!* Even in her shapeless gray suit, she was so beautiful it hurt. She had a man with her, a big guy with stubble who looked like he'd slept at his desk. "Change of plan," she announced to the two agents. "We're taking the prisoner upstairs. Going to question him somewhere more civilized."

"What?" Both agents stood up and the one who'd been playing bad cop got in her face. "That isn't procedure! Does Carrie know about—"?

"It was her idea," said Hailey coolly. "If you want to argue with her...."

The *good cop* agent backed down, but the *bad cop* one squared his shoulders. "I will," he muttered. He marched out and the other agent hurried after him.

Hailey ran over to me. "Get up," she told me. "We're getting you out of here."

I stood, blinking at her. It was only when the stubbled guy produced a handcuff key and my chains fell to the floor that I realized what was happening. Then I grabbed Hailey, lifted her into the air, and crushed her against my chest. "*Golub,*" I breathed.

"I'm sorry!" she said into my chest. "I'm sorry, I was wrong—"

"*Sweet,*" interrupted the stubbled guy, his voice dripping with sarcasm. "But we've got about three minutes until those guys get up to our boss's office and discover they've been played. So unless you want us all to spend the rest of our lives in jail, *move!*"

I saw the anger in his eyes. *He hates me. So why is he helping?* Then I saw his gaze drop to my hands, where they stroked Hailey's back. He glared at them as if he was trying to burn them off.

That's why he was helping her. And that's why he hated me. I felt jealousy stirring in my own chest, hot and possessive.

Hailey pushed back from me a little and saw what was going on. "*Two* minutes," she said, her cheeks flushing red.

The guy gave me a curt nod and I nodded back. *Later.*

We ran. Out into the hallway. Up the stairs to the first floor. We slowed as we reached the crowded lobby: the alarm might be raised at any second, but if we walked too fast, it would arouse suspicion. I could glimpse daylight and freedom through the glass doors of the building, only thirty feet away.

"Isn't that—Wait, is that *Konstantin?!*" a guard asked as we passed.

"Yep. Lawyers got him off on a technicality. Go figure," Hailey told him, not slowing her pace. We were twenty feet from the doors. *Fifteen—*

A klaxon started to blare. All around us, the guards' radios came to life. I heard *lockdown* and *Konstantin* and *Hailey Akers* and *Agent Calahan*

"*Run!*" yelled the stubbled guy and we sprinted for the doors. A guard charged in front of us, drawing his gun, but I shouldered him out of the way and we burst out into the open air. A shabby-looking car was parked right outside the doors and we dived in, Hailey and me in the back and the stubbled guy—Agent Calahan, I presumed—behind the wheel. We were thrown back in our seats as he stamped on the gas and then the FBI building was shrinking in the rear view mirror.

"They'll be looking for my car," Calahan muttered to us over his shoulder. He didn't try to hide the anger in his voice. "Hold on. I've got to switch it."

He took the next corner without slowing down, then another and another, until our stomachs were churning and we were deep in a maze of narrow streets. He finally pulled into the open doorway of a garage and screeched to a stop. "Wait here," he snapped, and got out.

Hailey and I looked around. To our left, two guys were stripping a BMW of all its valuable parts. To our right, a man was grinding the identification numbers off a Mercedes while another guy fitted fake license plates. *A chop shop.* And Calahan seemed to know the men and know how to deal with them. First it was fist-bumps and hugs, then he pulled out his wallet and finally, when they still seemed reluctant to help, he shrugged and spread his arms wide. I couldn't hear what he was saying, but I could guess. *Wouldn't it be awful if the FBI got a tip-off about this place....*

I started to warm to the man.

In less than five minutes, we were driving out in a fresh car: a piece of junk compared to what I was used to, but no one was looking for it and that made it more valuable than any limo. "You planned that well," I allowed.

Calahan didn't turn around, but he glanced at me in the rear view mirror. "Not my first time breaking the rules."

When a few miles had gone by without any sign of pursuit, he pulled over and sat back with a sigh. "There. We're clear." He twisted around in his seat and scowled at me. "Now you better hope you can fix this thing—"—he glanced at Hailey—"for her sake."

I nodded. I understood what they'd both done for me. They were fugitives, now. And if the assassination happened, they'd be going to jail. We had to stop it, and clear my name.

But there was something I had to do first. Something I couldn't wait any longer for.

I grabbed Hailey by the waist and dragged her across the seat and into my lap. I pushed her hair back from her face, my fingers tangling in the soft strands, and kissed her.

61

HAILEY

THE AIRPORT. The arrest. The interrogation. The rescue. This was the first chance we'd had and I hadn't realized how much I needed him until I felt his hands on me. As he pulled me onto his lap, I was already stretching up to kiss him, my mouth searching, my hands clutching at his shoulders. Then I felt the hard press of his lips, spreading, demanding, and the pleasure crashed through me, rolling down my body in an electric ripple.

I gasped, frantic and panting. His hands slid over my back and ass and mine traced the muscles of his arms, feeling their warm strength through his suit. We both had to reassure ourselves that this was real, that we were back together.

I didn't know what would happen next. But I knew I wouldn't let anything separate us again.

When we finally released each other, I was weak and fluttery. I just wanted to cuddle up to his chest, my head on his pec, and nestle there for a week. Nothing in the world ever felt so good.

"So what now?" Calahan's voice broke the silence.

Shit. My head jerked up and I looked towards the front seat.

He wasn't glaring at us angrily. He was staring straight ahead, out of the windshield. That was almost worse, somehow: he couldn't bear to look. The guilt welled up inside me and I untangled myself from Konstantin. I'd always known there was something, something more than friends, but he'd always crushed it, as soon as it started. *Oh, Calahan....*

"We need to find out who set me up," said Konstantin. "We have less than an hour."

Calahan finally turned around in his seat... and nodded. The tension was still thick between the two of them, but we had to put it aside and focus or we were all going to jail.

"If you didn't send those emails, hiring the assassin and arranging everything... who did?"

"Maybe you were hacked," said Calahan.

I shook my head. "It had to have been someone inside the mansion. They told Grigory to get hold of the rifle and deliver it."

"I don't understand. No one can get into my laptop," said Konstantin. "It's encrypted, you need my ring to get in."

That was true. I knew from experience how hard it was, I'd barely managed it and I'd been sleeping with him. How could anyone else— *Shit.*

A truck thundered past, rocking our parked car, but I just sat there, staring at the other two without seeing them.

"What?" asked Calahan.

I didn't answer. The suspicion was rolling through me like an oily fog, chilling me as it settled into my bones.

"*What?*" demanded Konstantin, gripping my arm.

I hadn't ever considered it. I'd spent so much time feeling guilty.... I looked in the rear view mirror, at the reflection of Christina's face. *Oh God....*

I looked at Konstantin. "What if I wasn't the only one betraying you?" I croaked.

His brows knitted.

I turned to Calahan. Everything was reversing in my mind, every assumption we'd made since the very beginning. "Our whole plan was to impersonate Christina," I said. "We were so busy thinking about me being the imposter, me not getting caught, we just assumed she was innocent. But what if Christina's behind this whole thing?"

Calahan and I stared at each other. I'd gotten so used to being Christina, the idea made me feel physically sick, as if *I'd* done it. I'd thought I'd been impersonating Konstantin's lover. What if I'd really been impersonating his worst enemy?

"No," said Konstantin, but his accent had thickened with worry. "How would even Christina get into my laptop?"

"The same way I did," I told him. "Wait until you're asleep, then use your ring."

Konstantin stared at me. "You did that?"

I nodded and hung my head, the guilt eating me up.

"But you barely managed it once," said Calahan. "Christina would have had to have been on his laptop night after night, checking for mail, organizing things...."

Konstantin suddenly put a hand to his face. "*Chert!* I'm so stupid!" When we twisted to look at him, he sighed. "When Christina arrived at the mansion, I started to sleep soundly. There were no—" He glanced at Calahan, uncomfortable. Even now, he didn't want to appear weak.

"Go on," said Calahan. And I was surprised at how gentle his voice was.

"There were no nightmares," Konstantin said through gritted teeth.

Calahan just nodded as if he understood.

Konstantin rubbed at his cheeks. "The vodka. Every night, she and I would have a glass—"

"She was drugging you!" I breathed. Suddenly, it was all making sense. I imagined her sitting next to him in bed, the glow from the laptop screen lighting up her face as she wrote emails pretending to be him. *That's* why all the emails about the assassination had been filed away in a hidden folder: not to hide them from me, to hide them from *him!* I let out a groan.

"What?" asked Calahan.

"She was so *smart!* That email she sent, organizing the payment at the shopping mall: *I will send a woman. Don't discuss things with her, she's just the courier.* She knew law enforcement would find those emails eventually. She set it all up to look like it was Konstantin organizing things, and she was just a pawn. And we bought it completely."

I groaned again as I remembered sitting in Battery Park with Konstantin and him offering to share all his secrets with me. I could have found out then that he knew nothing about the assassination, but I'd put our relationship ahead of my job. *This is all my fault!*

Konstantin was shaking his head. "But how did she convince Grigory to get hold of the rifle for the assassin? He must have known that order wasn't coming from me."

I winced. Of course: he didn't know. "Grigory and Christina were —" I swallowed and looked at Calahan. He, too, was avoiding Konstantin's eyes.

"*What?*" demanded Konstantin, sensing something was up.

"Christina was having an affair with Grigory," I said quietly.

"No—" Konstantin shook his head, his face going pale. "Grigory's been loyal to me for *years.* He wouldn't be involved in...."

He trailed off as he saw my mournful expression. Even Calahan looked sympathetic. Konstantin let out a roar and thumped the car's ceiling, hard enough to leave a dent.

"It wasn't Grigory's fault," I said quickly. "It wasn't just sex, he was in love with her. I think ever since she came to the mansion. Christina saw that and used it: *she* seduced *him.* Told him she'd run away with him, all he had to do was help her frame you."

Konstantin was staring at the ground, his shoulders rising and falling as he panted in anger. At last, he raised his head and looked right at me. "I don't care about Grigory," he said. "I don't care about Christina. But I do care about—Did Grigory—" His voice caught and he had to look away and take a deep breath. "You were impersonating Christina, did you have to—"

I grabbed his hand. "*No!* He kissed me, just once, before I could stop him. That's all. I never slept with him."

Konstantin sighed and relaxed and a big, unexpected glow soaked through me. It was me, not Christina, he cared about.

"This is why Christina was so scared, when we ran into her in the lobby and she realized you were going to impersonate her," said Calahan. "This is why she escaped and came to the mansion. She was worried you were going to find out about the assassination and stop it." His forehead wrinkled. "But then why did she take the deal and walk away?"

I looked at Konstantin. "Because she could tell I—" I swallowed. "That I was in love with him." Even now, even with all that was going on, saying it out loud was a heady thrill. And Konstantin just stared right back at me, the blue in his eyes fiery, and squeezed my hand and nodded. Then I swallowed and hung my head. "She could see I was past investigating anything. She could see I'd switched sides."

I closed my eyes and just slumped in despair. *I had the real villain right there, and I let her go because I was so desperate not to lose Konstantin—*

Someone grabbed my *other* hand and squeezed it. I reluctantly opened my eyes and saw Calahan. "We'll get her," he told me. "And find out who she's working for."

I looked between the two men. Things definitely weren't resolved between them, but there was a sort of truce, for now. And with all three of us... maybe we *could* catch her. I nodded.

"Where would she go?" Calahan asked Konstantin. "Friends? Relatives?"

"Her father," said Konstantin. "She visits him once a week. He lives on the Upper East Side."

Calahan shook his head. "Remember when you went to the shopping mall and I checked Christina's records to see if there was a photo of her mom? Both her parents are dead."

Another lie. But—"She *did* go to the Upper East Side every week, though. I found a parking pass in her purse for an apartment complex called Barlow Heights."

"Probably meeting the person she was working for," said Calahan. "Checking in, getting orders. She could be hiding out there now!"

"But it's an apartment complex," I said. "How do we know which apartment?"

Calahan cursed under his breath and we stared at one another in frustration. It would be a thirty second job... if we had access to the FBI computer system. But we were fugitives.

"Okay," said Calahan at last. "I know someone who might be able to find out." He took out a cell phone. "A hacker group. They're the best, and I know one of them. If I can reach her."

"*Her?*" Konstantin sat forward and narrowed his eyes. "She is one of the *sisters?*"

Calahan looked thrown, but nodded.

"I know one of them also," said Konstantin, sitting back in his seat. "They *are* the best." He glanced at me, then looked almost embarrassed. "She sneaked into the mansion. *Downstairs.*"

To the *dungeon?* That was a story I was going to have to make him tell me. But it could wait.

Calahan's call connected. "Li—*Mary?* It's Calahan."

A woman's voice, with a New York accent. "You need a favor."

A man's voice in the background, richly Texan. "He *always* needs a favor."

Within a few minutes, the phone was on speaker and we were listening to keys rattling. The woman typed so fast, it was almost a continuous buzz. "Most of the apartment rentals look legit. But there's one, apartment 502, that's rented by a company in Panama."

Calahan sighed. "So you can't give us a name?"

"*Pfft.*" The woman sounded offended. "What do you think I am? I'm tracing it back...that's a shell company...*that's* a front...*hello!* It all leads back to a Russian company owned by...." Her voice darkened, as if she knew the name. "Dmitri Ralavich."

62

HAILEY

BARLOW HEIGHTS was a high-end apartment complex, a slab of white stone and glass ten stories high with balconies that overlooked a shimmering blue pool. By the time we reached the fifth floor, it was twenty minutes to one.

Calahan lifted his foot to kick down the door of 502 but Konstantin got there first, lowering his shoulder and charging it like a bull. The door crashed to the floor...and there was Christina in a low-cut crimson dress, hair and make-up immaculate as always, throwing clothes into a suitcase. Getting ready to run.

"Hello *darling,*" growled Konstantin.

Christina looked at us and cursed. I could see her eying the door as if wondering if she could break past us and run. I shuffled sideways, making sure her way was blocked, and we glared at each other: an unsettling effect, like frowning into an enchanted mirror.

"How long?" Konstantin snapped. "How long have you been working for that bastard? When did Ralavich turn you?"

Christina blinked at him... then threw back her head and laughed. "*Turned* me?" She gave him a withering look. "You still don't get it, do you?"

"Get what?" I said tightly. I could see how her legs were tensed: she was trying to distract us so that she could make a move.

"Ralavich didn't *turn* me," she said scathingly. "He *created* me."

What?!

Christina smirked at Konstantin. "He found me, dancing at a strip club."

Konstantin was shaking his head, unable to accept it. "No—"

"He gave me money and fancy clothes. He made me into your perfect woman, Konstantin. Sexy and glamorous and as cold-hearted as you."

Konstantin had gone quiet, staring at her with raw hatred. She stepped forward and touched a perfectly-manicured finger to his lips. She whispered, but loud enough that all three of us could hear. "I wasn't dumped by my boyfriend by the side of the road. *I was waiting for you!*"

I glanced at Konstantin, open-mouthed. Both of us were reeling. The woman I'd thought was innocent, the one I'd felt so guilty about impersonating, had been betraying him the whole time. And I, the one sent by the FBI to betray him, had wound up loyal to him.

Konstantin grabbed Christina and slammed her up against the wall. "Who's going to be assassinated?" he roared. "Whose murder are you trying to pin on me?"

"Answer him!" I yelled. A hot, protective fury was washing through me. She'd played him from the very beginning, planned to bring him down...and *yes,* I'd started off doing the same—the irony wasn't lost on me. But I'd fallen for him, whereas she never had. I was trying to put right my mistake; she didn't display an ounce of regret.

Christina stared at him, impassive. "You think you can scare me? I work for Ralavich. If I talk, what he'll do to me is far worse than anything you can do."

Konstantin glared, but she was right. He'd never hurt a woman: he knew it and *she* knew it.

"It's a quarter to one," said Calahan from the doorway.

No! My chest closed up tight. It didn't matter that we'd found her. The assassination was still going to happen. Konstantin would still be blamed: it was his word against hers and all the evidence still pointed to him.

"Is it Luka Malakov?" asked Konstantin frantically.

But Christina's face didn't move. God, *I* wanted to hit her! Konstantin was going to go to jail for the rest of his life.

"Is it Baroni? Is it Angelo Baroni?" demanded Konstantin.

Christina looked serene.

"*Twelve minutes* to one," said Calahan, his voice grim.

It was all over. We'd lost. All she had to do was keep quiet and wait for our time to run out.

"Is it one of the other Malakovs?" asked Konstantin. "Vasiliy? *Irina?*"

I was watching her, just as I'd watched Konstantin for years. I'd spent weeks studying her, knew her face better than my best friend's. And my weird, detail-focused brain noticed something. I'd been watching for *guilt,* that tiny flicker that would tell me Konstantin had hit the right name. But instead, I saw something else. A movement, barely a tremble of the muscles at the corners of her mouth.

She was trying not to smirk.

We were on completely the wrong track.

And once I knew that, and put it together with the fact it was Ralavich behind all this.... framing Konstantin for murdering a mob boss wasn't... *enough.* Ralavich's cruelty was beyond words and he went for excess. He hadn't just killed Konstantin's father, he'd slaughtered his entire family. The target of the assassination had to be someone whose death would be a game-changer. Their murder had to be something that Konstantin's empire would never recover from.

There was something else didn't make sense. *One O'clock.* Why had the assassin been so specific about the time? I'd been around Konstantin long enough, now, to know that mobsters weren't that predictable. They were always racing around their empire to keep everything running smoothly. They didn't have a daily routine, like—

I had a sudden memory. Not an image: a sound. A clock chiming one. A woman's voice. *I always shut myself in here at this time—*

"It's Carrie!" I screamed.

Everyone—even Christina—turned to stare at me. In that half-second of shock, she forgot to control her face. I saw the fear in her eyes: I was right.

Konstantin was frowning at me. "Your *boss?*"

I was almost panting with fear. "She eats lunch every day at one pm. *Her office is walled in bulletproof glass!*"

"No," said Calahan. "That's crazy."

"It makes perfect sense! Carrie has had our team investigating Konstantin for years. He has the perfect motive to assassinate her. Add that to the emails and no jury is going to question it!"

"But *why?*" asked Calahan. "Why frame him for Carrie's death, why not kill one of the other mob bosses? Ralavich could kill two birds with one stone."

The implications were sinking in and they made me go weak and shaky. "Because.... *Oh Jesus.*" I turned to Konstantin, feeling sick. "If the FBI thinks you assassinated another mob boss, you'll go to jail. But someone else gets promoted within your organization and it keeps going. But if they think you assassinated *an FBI chief....*"

"National outcry," said Calahan. "They'll bring in a hundred agents, a *thousand.* They won't stop until they've dismantled every last piece of your empire. Every business you own, every street you control."

"They'll do in *two weeks,*" I said, my voice quavering, "what Ralavich couldn't do himself in two years. They'll wipe out the Gulyev name forever."

"And then Ralavich will come in and fill the vacuum," said Konstantin. "That's why he has so many men in New York. This is what he was waiting for. And the fires... the fires were to make people afraid, so they wouldn't dare protest when he takes over."

He released his hold on Christina. And that was his mistake. She ducked low, sprinted forward, and slammed into Calahan, sending him staggering backwards. He growled and regained his balance, started to grab for her—

And froze. We all froze.

Christina was holding Calahan's gun. She must have pulled it from his holster when she crashed into him. Now she had it pointed at Konstantin. She backed up a little towards the doors that led to the balcony, so that she could cover all of us.

"I'm sorry," she told him, her voice sugary-sweet. "But Ralavich will be here any minute: that's why I was running. He's mad at me because the plan went wrong. You were never meant to get arrested until after the assassination. If you actually stop it happening, it'll be even worse for me." She shook her head grimly. "I'll be in one of his fucking rape clubs by tonight."

"Cut a deal with us!" said Calahan quickly. "We can protect you!"

"No one can protect me from a man like him," Christina told him. "But if I kill you three, everything works out just fine. We can make it look like Konstantin paid you to help him escape, and then you killed each other in a fight over money. The assassination goes ahead, Konstantin still gets the blame for organizing it, the FBI still take apart his organization and Ralavich takes over. I'll be back in his good books. He might even reward me." She pointed the gun right at Konstantin's face.

My insides went ice cold. *No!* God, no, not Konstantin! I started forward, but the gun twitched towards me and I froze.

Konstantin looked at me and shook his head, determined to protect me.

"Pity poor Konstantin," said Christina. "Gets fooled by one fake, then falls for another."

Konstantin glowered at her. "This time," he said, "it *isn't* fake."

I drew in my breath. Christina's lips tightened in jealousy.

"And you," Konstantin told her, "are *not* my perfect woman."

And then he looked at me. And there wasn't a shred of the cold gray left in his eyes, just blue that shone with warmth and love. I felt myself *lift*... and out of the corner of my eye, I saw Calahan react, too. Just a tiny, heartbreaking, lowering of his eyes. *Acceptance.*

Christina gave a roar of fury. Her finger tightened on the trigger and—

Suddenly, I was charging at her, my guttural yell filling the room. I wasn't brave and I didn't know how to fight. I had no plan. I just knew I wasn't letting her take him.

Christina swung the gun towards me and I heard it go off. There was a hiss of air next to my cheek. And then I was slamming into her, my momentum taking us across the room. I was trying to push the gun up, away from my face. It went off again, deafening me, and we staggered on. She was in front of me so I couldn't see where we were going. There was a jolt as Christina's back hit something and I heard a set of doors swing open. Cold air engulfed me: we were *outside*—

"Hailey!" screamed Konstantin.

Christina hit the balcony handrail and we tipped—

And then we were falling through the air together, five stories up.

63

KONSTANTIN

SHE DISAPPEARED over the edge, dropped out of view....

And then she was just... *gone.* Icy fingers crushed my hammering heart to a dead stop. *No....* No, God, not again. It was sheer panic and loss on a level I hadn't felt since that day in the river.

Then I saw Calahan rush past me and I got myself moving. We reached the balcony at the same time, looked down....

And saw the twin splash as they hit the pool.

I turned and *ran,* sick with worry. What if hitting the water from that height had knocked her out and she was sinking to the bottom right now, water filling her lungs?

I pounded down the stairs, jumping the last few of each flight, pinballing off each corner, picking up bruises. But five flights still felt like it took an eternity. I found the hallway that led to the front of the building and sprinted down it. Crashed through a fire exit and—

She was kneeling by the side of the pool, panting. Her hair hung down in wet ropes. Her mascara had run in long streaks and that ugly FBI suit hung shiny and heavy from her body, streaming water. She'd never looked more beautiful. I picked her up and crushed her against me, the chill water soaking my shirt and then the warmth of her body against mine. "I thought I—" The emotion choked off my words. "I thought I—"

"I'm okay," Hailey panted. "We're both okay."

I looked down. Christina was lying on her back, unconscious. Her red dress was soaked through and askew, one breast almost exposed. But she was breathing. Hailey must have dragged her out of the pool. *That's so like her.*

Calahan ran up behind us. A few of the block's residents had heard the splash and come out to investigate, but he waved his FBI badge at them and they gave us some space. "We've got to go," he told us. "It's eight minutes to one!"

At that second, two black SUVs screeched to a stop in the middle of the street. *Shit!* Ralavich's men. Christina had said they were coming. And now they'd seen us.

The doors opened and men started to pour from the SUVs, all of them carrying guns. The residents screamed and ran back inside. We ran for cover, ducking down behind a row of parked cars. The men opened fire as they advanced and Hailey cried out in fear as the car windows shattered, pebbles of safety glass showering our heads. I pulled her tighter against my chest to protect her and looked furiously around. Calahan's car wasn't far away. We could maybe make it if we ran, but—

All of us looked at Christina. She lay unconscious, out in the open by the swimming pool. If we ran back and tried to carry her, we'd be easy targets. And we had to *go:* the assassination was minutes away. *Shit!* We all looked at each other, torn.

"We need her to testify!" said Calahan. "She's our proof!" He took two running steps towards her—

I growled and dived on him, knocking him to the ground. A bullet that would have taken his head off whistled over our heads. He scowled at me...then reluctantly nodded his thanks.

"Leave her," said Hailey.

Calahan stared at her. "*What?* She needs to go to jail!"

Hailey glared at the unconscious Christina. "Let Ralavich's men take her. Let *him* punish her. It'll be worse than anything a judge can hand out."

I blinked at her. Part of me agreed, but.... "When did you get so heartless?" I asked.

"When she tried to kill my man," Hailey said with feeling, and clutched me close.

Ralavich's men were almost on us. "We don't have a choice," said Calahan. "*Go!*"

And we ran, keeping low until we reached Calahan's car. As we pulled away, one last shot shattered our rear window. Then we were roaring down the street. The last thing I saw in the rear view mirror was Ralavich's men pulling Christina to her feet. I almost felt sorry for her.

Then I faced the front and put my arm around Hailey, drawing her protectively against me. She was safe, but she was still going to jail—we were *all* going to jail—unless we stopped the assassination. Without Christina's testimony, we had no proof I'd been framed. If an FBI chief died, there'd be no hope of anyone listening to our side of the story. And Hailey would lose a colleague... a *friend*.

We had to save Carrie. We had to save the woman who'd spent her whole career trying to bring me down.

"How long?" I asked, my voice tight.

"Five minutes," said Calahan.

64

KONSTANTIN

THE CAR screeched to a stop in front of the FBI building and the three of us leapt out. As we reached the glass doors, I cursed. Extra guards were on duty in the lobby. As we burst in, three of them moved to block our path, young and inexperienced, hands twitching nervously towards their guns.

"Get out of the way!" screamed Calahan.

The nearest guard shook his head. "We've got orders to take all three of you into custody."

"We don't have time for this!" Calahan started forward. "You've got to get word to Carrie. Tell her—"

The guard put his hand on his gun. "Agent Calahan, *remain where you are!*"

Calahan stopped and cursed, raising his hands. He looked over his shoulder at me. Then I saw him glance at Hailey and when he looked at me again, our eyes locked. He sighed and the rivalry between us faded away. "Tenth floor," he murmured, too low for the guards to hear. "Office at the end of the hall. I can give you a few seconds."

I nodded and readied myself. "Stay here," I told Hailey.

Her eyes went wide. "No—"

"I'm not letting you get hurt." I squeezed her tight, then pushed her gently behind me. And then I gave Calahan the nod.

"They're going to send me to Alaska with Kate for this," he muttered. And then he roared and charged forward, arms stretched wide. As the guards drew their guns, he slammed into them full force, taking all three to the floor. They were up and on him in seconds, but by then I'd already sprinted past them and was heading for the stairwell.

"*Stop!*" yelled a voice behind me. Then a gunshot and my suit jacket tugged as a bullet sliced through the flapping fabric, missing me by an inch. I heaved open the stairwell door and ran.

Ten floors, up this time instead of down. I went up them three at a time, heart pounding, muscles screaming. I had no idea how much time was left and I couldn't stop to check. By the eighth floor, my hamstrings and calves were screaming. Nine and I was staggering, sweat slicking my brow. Ten—

I stumbled out into the hallway. Carrie's door was dead ahead, what felt like a mile away. I growled and forced my legs into a run. As I neared the door, I could hear a clock chiming—

I burst through the door, almost taking it off its hinges. And there she was: *Carrie.* The woman who'd pursued me since the day I'd set foot in New York. The woman who'd sent so many of my men to jail. Her eyes widened as she'd recognized me: *him, here, in my office?!*

"*Get down!*" I yelled, but I didn't wait for her to comply. I slammed into her, carrying us both towards the floor—

There was the sound of breaking glass. A tight little hole appeared in the huge window, the glass frosting white around it. Something sliced into my arm.

And then we were sprawling on the carpet behind her desk, me half on top of her. She stared at me. Then she looked up at the fresh bullet hole on the wall, right behind where she'd been standing.

Credit to her, she didn't waste time arguing or asking questions. She slapped her hand over my injured arm, pressing to stop the bleeding. With her other hand, she heaved on the cord of her desk phone until it tumbled off the desk and fell down to her. Then she started yelling orders into it, telling her people to surround the building across the street.

It was almost five minutes before Calahan and Hailey arrived, accompanied by a small army of FBI agents. Calahan had a black eye and was limping a little, but he was grinning. "It's okay," he told us, offering me his hand. "Look."

I took his hand and heaved myself to my feet, then helped Carrie up. Through the window, we could see the sniper on the rooftop of the building across the street. He had his hands up, and armed FBI agents were advancing towards him.

Carrie looked at Calahan, then at Hailey, then at me. She crossed her arms. "Okay," she said. "I'm listening."

I gave a long sigh of relief and sat down heavily on the edge of her desk. Hailey ran over and threw herself against me and I wrapped her in my arms.

Everything was going to be okay.

65

HAILEY

ONSCIOUSNESS returned slowly. It was the cold that hit me first. I was lying on something hard and freezing and I could feel wind blowing across my body: was I outdoors? And the wind was chilling me more than it should, as if my skin was wet.

Then a smell that seared my nostrils and made me cough. *Chlorine.*

I opened my eyes and tried to focus, blinking away water. A towering slab of white rose above me. I heard shouts that sounded familiar, then a car start up and roar away, but I was too dazed to put it together. I stared up at the building.

A balcony. I fell from a balcony.

A man in a black suit stepped into my vision. Then another and another, surrounding me, all of them holding guns. "Get up," one of them commanded, but I just lay there, still stunned. His accent was heavy, Russian. *These are Ralavich's men.* But where were Konstantin and Calahan? I remembered the car I'd heard roar away. *But...* I fought the rising panic. *Come on, they wouldn't just leave me...*

One of the men reached for me. I shrank back against the concrete. *Do they know I'm FBI? Should I tell them or would that make things worse?* I glanced down at my suit, wondering whether to pull out my badge—

My suit wasn't there. In its place was a soaked red dress. I froze. *Why am I wearing Christina's clothes?*

The man grabbed my shoulder and hauled me to my feet. The top of the dress flopped down: the zipper at the back hadn't been fastened. I scrambled to fix it as they dragged me towards an SUV, not liking the way they were leering at me. "Wait, where are you—" I began.

They pushed me into the back seat and climbed in after me, trapping me between two of them. "We're taking you to Ralavich," one of them said. He shook his head, then gave me a cruel grin: *better you than me.* "You messed up. He's not happy."

Oh God. Oh Jesus, no... They thought I was Christina! I must have been knocked out, when we hit the water, and she'd quickly switched clothes with me. Which meant... *shit!* She must have run off with Konstantin and Calahan. She was being *me...* and she'd left me for Ralavich to find. "Wait," I told the men, my voice tight with fear. "Wait. I'm—"

And stopped. What was I going to say? *I'm not Christina, I just look exactly like her?* Even if they believed me, once they found out I was an FBI agent, they might just kill me.

I couldn't tell them.

The SUV started up and we roared off.

The horrifying reality of it set in. I was trapped living Christina's life. And the only person who could save me, the only other person in the world who knew we'd switched places... she was probably cuddling up to Konstantin right now.

66

KONSTANTIN

"AND THEN I ran in here," I told Carrie. "And you know the rest."

I was still sitting on Carrie's desk, with Hailey pressed tight against my side, her arm around my waist. I'd just given Carrie the short version of everything that had happened. She'd stayed standing throughout my entire speech and with me sitting, that put us eye-to-eye. We stared at each other, her face emotionless and unreadable. I knew she didn't want to let me go. This was the closest she'd ever got to putting me behind bars.

She could have claimed she didn't believe me, pinned the assassination attempt on me just to see me go down. But she was that rare thing: an honest cop.

"It isn't over between us," she warned me.

"I don't doubt it," I told her.

"I'm putting a hold on your passport. Don't try and leave the country... and you'll give us any help we ask for in tracking down Ralavich."

I nodded.

She stared at me for another long second. Then: "Fine. You're free to go." She turned to Hailey. "And as for you..." She looked between the two of us, her expression troubled. I could see how much she cared for Hailey... but an active FBI agent dating a known criminal? That couldn't be allowed.

"I'll make it easy for you," said Hailey. And she pulled out her badge and handed it to Carrie. "I quit."

I glanced across at her. *You're sure?*

She nodded and pressed even tighter against me. I stood up, wincing a little at the pain in my arm. The sniper's bullet had sliced a line across my triceps, not deep but painful. An FBI medic had put a dressing on it but had warned me to avoid moving it. I had no problem with that. The most strenuous thing I intended to do was hug Hailey. At least, until we got back to the mansion. Then I was going to fuck her all night long.

In the elevator, I hit the button for the first floor. As we descended, I stood staring at the button below it, the one for the basement. They'd told me that Grigory was down there, in an interrogation room. When I was arrested, he'd panicked, knowing his betrayal might come out, and he'd made a run for Russia. The FBI had stopped him at the airport and when he'd heard that the assassination had failed and that his beloved Christina was gone, taken off by Ralavich, he'd broken and confessed everything, which helped to prove our story.

He'd betrayed me. Slept with Christina. Plotted to kill me. But...part of me wanted to forgive him. Not now. The wounds were too fresh. But one day. Before Hailey, I wouldn't have understood, but now....

I looked across at her. Grigory had been in love. And love can make you do stupid things.

We reached the first floor and strode out through the lobby. This time, the guards stepped back and gave us a respectful nod. Calahan had run off to lead the search for Ralavich: a pity, because I would have liked to say goodbye. I was slowly growing to like the man.

Outside, one of my guards was holding open the rear door of the Mercedes. Hailey and I climbed into the back seat and we sped off towards the mansion. As the adrenaline slowly left me, I realized how exhausted I was. *I need a vacation.*

The idea would have seemed unthinkable a month ago, but now.... I'd never taken a real vacation, just business trips to Italy or London: endless meetings in darkened bars and hotel rooms while Christina shopped for clothes. Now, with Ralavich on the run, his plans foiled, maybe I could just...*stop* for a week or two.

I looked across at Hailey and smiled. The future was bright.

I reached out, took her hand and squeezed it. I was still getting used to doing that. It felt good.

But Hailey didn't react the way I expected. Instead of just squeezing back, she swung a leg across me, straddling me, being careful not to jar my injured arm. I blinked at her, smiling uncertainly. As her pubis ground against mine, I could feel myself getting hard. But this wasn't like her, she wasn't usually so confident.

She leaned forward and her breasts pressed against me through her wet blouse. I realized I could feel her nipples through the thin fabric. *She's not wearing a bra?*

Hailey leaned forward and took my earlobe between her teeth, biting gently. "Just sit back and relax," she breathed. "I'll do all the work." She rolled her hips and I groaned in pleasure—where had she learned to do *that?* I didn't care, it felt amazing.

I had a sudden vision of her falling from the balcony. I shuddered, then pulled her even tighter against me. "I thought I'd lost you," I muttered.

Her lips brushed my ear and I felt her grin. "It's alright," she said. "You have me back, now. Forever."

And she kissed me.

67

HAILEY

THE SUV headed west out of New York, speeding me away from the FBI, from my friends, from everything I knew. Ahead, storm clouds were gathering, blocking out the sun.

As we neared our destination, the men, who'd been chatting and joking with each other in Russian, gradually fell silent and began to glance at one another uneasily. Whatever was waiting for us, it scared the hell out of them.

Christina's wet dress had soaked every last bit of warmth out of me. I sat there numb and quiet, my head filling up with all the stories I'd heard about Ralavich from my friend Kate, who'd narrowly escaped him herself. Truly sickening stuff. Murder. Human trafficking. And of course his notorious *"rape clubs."* I was so scared, I wanted to throw up.

This monster believed I worked for him. And if Konstantin and Calahan had been successful, if they'd stopped the assassination, he'd blame me. My punishment wouldn't be death, not from what I'd heard. It would be much worse than that.

I started to panic-breathe. One of the men glanced round at the sound, meeting my eyes...and then just looked away, a trace of guilt in his eyes. As if he'd seen this a thousand times before. I felt my heart rate accelerating out of control. No rescue was coming, no rescue was *possible* because no one knew I was missing. I could disappear into Ralavich's nightmare world for years, *decades,* before he got tired of me and killed me.

And meanwhile, Christina would walk away scot-free and enjoy a life with Konstantin. Accepting his love, his new affection, and grinning behind his back, gloating at what she'd done. The thought of them together made me want to throw up.

We turned off the highway and I got a glimpse of fences and aircraft, then we stopped at a barrier. *Oh God, we're here.* Some sort of private airfield, way out of the city where Ralavich could fly in and out unobserved. The hairs on the back of my neck stood up and I felt sweat trickle down between my shoulder blades. A guard waved us through and then the SUV pulled up beside a big, gleaming white jet. A set of metal stairs had been positioned outside, leading up to the open door. I knew who was inside. *Oh God, oh God.....*

As Ralavich's men hustled me out, I lost it completely. My legs turned to rubber and I started shaking my head. "No," I told them as they towed me forward, one on each arm. "*No!*"

But they ignored me. Two of them pushed me over to the steps and then up them. Overhead, there was a roll of thunder and the rain began to fall, heavy drops that soon became a torrent. By the time they'd forced me to the top of the steps and in through the door, my half-dry hair was soaked again and water was running down my face, half-blinding me. I blinked and blinked again—

And there he was. *Ralavich.* I felt my knees buckle in fear. The man had a physical effect on me, but it was the exact opposite of Konstantin's magnetic attraction. It was as if all the evil inside him, had spilled out onto the surface, as a warning. That ruined face you couldn't look away from, the bones broken and never properly put right. Those piggy eyes that made you feel dirty when they looked your way. That body, flabby with fat but still intimidatingly powerful beneath his dark blue suit. He was slouching in a huge leather armchair that had been positioned at one end of the cabin, facing down its length. He must have thought he looked like a king in his throne room, but he didn't have any of Konstantin's regal presence. For all his money and power, he was just a thug.

It amazed me that once, like Carrie, I'd thought all these men were the same.

"Christina," he said, his expression unreadable. "Have you heard the news?"

The assassination. I held my breath, about to offer up a silent prayer—

But I didn't know what to pray *for.* If Konstantin and Calahan had been too late, if the assassination had gone ahead, then maybe Ralavich would let me walk free. But if that was the case, Carrie was dead, Konstantin was going to jail and probably Calahan with him. I couldn't—*wouldn't*—pray for that.

And if they'd stopped it? If Konstantin and Calahan had somehow saved Carrie? Then it was over for me. But Carrie, Calahan, Konstantin...they'd all be okay.

I squeezed my eyes shut and prayed.

I heard Ralavich get up and walk towards me. And then—

One side of my face exploded into pain. I flew sideways and my head bounced off the jet's curved wall. I crashed to the floor, my head ringing and my eyes stinging with tears.

One of Ralavich's men grabbed me from behind and hauled me back to my feet. The fury on Ralavich's face gave me my answer. *They did it.* Carrie was safe. Konstantin was free. *Thank God.*

Then Ralavich grabbed me by the throat and lifted me. My toes skittered on the carpet and then came completely off the ground and my whole weight dangled from my neck. My eyes bulged and teared, my face going crimson as my air was cut off.

But the flabby, clammy hand didn't crush inwards. He didn't squeeze hard enough to kill me, or make me pass out, because that would have been sweet mercy. He just held me there, letting my own weight press the front of my throat down into the C of his hand between thumb and forefinger, keeping me in a permanent state of near asphyxia: just enough air to still let me fight and thrash, but not enough to give me the strength to break free.

He'd mastered this, I realized, by doing it to countless other women.

"All you had to do was let him fuck you, and send some emails," he yelled, little flecks of spit splattering my face. I couldn't have answered, even if there'd been anything I could say. I could barely move any air into my lungs and my head felt like it was going to explode from the pressure he was applying, each heartbeat thumping and ringing through my skull. *Maybe he'll kill me accidentally.* I actually found myself hoping for that.

He brought his face closer to mine. "I'm going to make it slow," he told me. "When we get back to St. Petersburg, I'll start you off in the clubs we keep for the military brass and the politicians, the people who have to be so snow white in public but like to do horrible things to women. Then in a year or two, I'll move you down to the standard clubs, the ones where businessmen slap you, tear off your clothes, bend you over a desk and pretend you're that hot new secretary they fantasize about. And in another year, when you're not pretty anymore, I'll move you to one of the clubs at the port, the ones for sailors and dockworkers, where you'll be fucked for loose change, for a box of cigarettes, for whatever they have. And when you've been there long enough, when you think it can't get any worse, that's when I'll show up, and I'll break every bone in your body before I kill you."

"But before I give you to the politicians," he told me, his voice growing rough with lust, "I'm going to sample you myself." He hurled me into his leather armchair and then he was on me, his weight crushing me, his hands tugging at the dress, ramming the shoulder straps down over my arms.

I had to make him kill me.

There was only one thing this man hated more than women, and that was law enforcement. My lips moved silently as I struggled to make my bruised throat work. When he saw I was trying to speak, he stopped for a second and smiled, looking forward to hearing me beg.

I managed a rasping whisper. "*I'm not Christina.*"

Ralavich and his men froze, then looked at each other in shock.

They had no idea how to react. Then Ralavich burst out laughing, an ugly, cruel noise. *Is that the best you can do?*

"*I'm FBI,*" I rasped.

The laughter stopped.

"*My name is Hailey Akers. The accident... they gave me plastic surgery to look like her....*"

Ralavich stared at me for a moment. Then he leaned down to speak in my ear. I lay there sobbing and limp. *Please believe me. Please get angry and kill me—*

His lips moved against my ear, like a pair of cold, wet worms. "I actually hope that's true," he told me. And I gave up and just wept, because now there was no hope at all—

There was a *thump* and the whole plane shook. Something soft but heavy had hit the fuselage from the outside. Ralavich and his men looked up, startled. Then another *thump,* even harder. His men raced towards the open door to look. I craned my head up. Turning my bruised neck was agony, but I managed to look out of a window and saw two guards slumped on the runway outside. They'd been hurled like toys against the plane.

Ralavich's men reached the door just as Konstantin stepped through it. They retreated uncertainly, pushed back by his sheer, intimidating presence.

Konstantin turned and saw me half-lying on the seat, dress askew, Ralavich atop me with his knee between my thighs.

I'd thought that I'd seen Konstantin angry: when people threatened his people, his empire. I suddenly saw that those times had been nothing. They'd been cold rage. This came from deep down, scalding and eternal.

This was love.

He didn't yell at Ralavich or snarl threats at him. His eyes said it all. They said, *you will not leave this plane alive.*

I saw all the color drain from Ralavich's face and neck. He scrambled to his feet and pulled me against him as a shield, one arm hooked around my throat.

"*How?*" I asked.

The pain in my voice made Konstantin tense. His scowl deepened and he wiped the edge of his finger across his lips, as if removing an unpleasant taste. "*I knew,*" he told me.

My chest went tight with emotion. *He knew!*

Konstantin turned to Ralavich. "And then I made that bitch tell me where he kept his jet."

Sirens wailed in the distance. Flashing red and blue lit up the gloom outside. Konstantin hadn't come alone.

The door to the cockpit flew open, startling us all. The pilot stared at the standoff, his eyes wide with fear. "The Feds are here!" he yelled. "Get that door closed, I'm getting us out of here!" He slammed the cockpit door and we heard it lock. A moment later, a rising howl came from the jet's engines, deafening because the door was still open. The plane lurched, making everyone stagger, and then began to move off down the taxiway. The boarding steps toppled over with a crash.

Ralavich backed away from Konstantin, using the arm around my neck to drag me with him. I pulled and clawed at it, but he was terrifyingly strong and my struggling only made him cinch it tighter, cutting off my air until my hands and feet started to feel numb and heavy. "Kill him!" Ralavich spat to the two guards.

I froze as both guards put their hands under their jackets to draw their guns. But then they looked uncertainly at the moving plane. *If they put a hole in it,* I realized, *we can't take off.* Leaving their guns in their holsters, they ran at him instead. I felt Ralavich's arm relax a little. The men were professional bodyguards, both well over six feet and loaded with muscle, and there were *two* of them....

The first one came within reach. Konstantin grabbed his shirt, swung him sideways and slammed him headfirst into the wall. The man slumped to the ground and the second guard faltered and stopped. Konstantin glared at Ralavich. *You. I'm coming for you next.*

The arm around my neck tightened again.

Outside, I could hear shouting and gunfire. From what I could glimpse through the windows, Konstantin's men were fighting Ralavich's, and the FBI were arriving right in the middle of it. Then I saw Calahan, gun drawn, running alongside the plane as it picked up speed. He was trying to climb on board, but the open door was a good ten feet above the runway and without the steps, there was no way up. We were on our own.

"A hundred thousand," Ralavich told his guard, his voice tight with panic. "A hundred thousand dollars if you kill him."

The guard's eyes narrowed and he ran at Konstantin, knocking him back and landing a flurry of punches. Konstantin gave a sudden grunt of pain as one hit his right arm. He hit back, but each time he used his right arm, he winced. A red flower of blood was spreading across his white shirt. He must have been injured, and the fight had opened up the wound. He threw another punch, but it was slower, weaker, and the guard blocked it easily.

A chill spread through me. Konstantin was going to lose.

Still gripping me tightly, Ralavich ventured nearer to the fight. "Did you know that I was the first to rape your mother?" he taunted.

Konstantin tensed... then grunted as he absorbed another few blows, weakening fast. I struggled helplessly against Ralavich's arm. *No! No, please!*

"I was the one who beat her," Ralavich told Konstantin. "I kept punching her because the slut wouldn't tell me how much she loved it."

Konstantin's lips drew back from his teeth and he tried to launch himself towards Ralavich, but was knocked back by another punch to the face.

"It's how I lost my virginity," said Ralavich. "They say you never forget your first time." He looked down at me. "I think that's how I developed my tastes."

Konstantin gave a yell of rage and dived forward again, but as soon as he dropped his guard, he took another punch and staggered back.

The pilot's voice came over a speaker. "Close the fucking door! We need to take off!"

Ralavich pulled me towards the open door. Outside, the taxiway was a blur beneath the wheels: the pilot was racing towards the runway to take off. Calahan was sprinting to keep up with the plane, his clothes soaked from the rain and his chest heaving with the effort. But he was starting to fall behind. For a second, we locked eyes and I could see the raw fear and frustration there. I was about to be lost to him forever, spirited off to Russia where I'd disappear into Ralavich's network.

Calahan moved his gaze, looking over my shoulder and into the plane. I twisted my head to look... and gave a moan of horror.

Konstantin had been forced back against the bulkhead, panting, his face pale and sweaty with pain. He was absorbing blow after blow, each one weakening him a little more. Any second now, the guard would knock him to the floor and then it would all be over. He looked at me and then past me, outside, towards Calahan. I followed his gaze—

And saw something pass between the two men. Calahan nodded to Konstantin, his eyes furious and desperate, putting all his faith in the man who'd been his enemy, lending him his strength.

Konstantin looked at me. I saw those blue eyes harden, determined—

Konstantin bellowed in rage and drove his right fist into the guard's face hard enough to lift him right off his feet. The man crashed to the floor, but something fell free from under his jacket and went spinning across the floor towards me. *His gun!*

Ralavich reacted first. He let go of me and crouched, his hand clawing for it. Konstantin took a step towards the gun but he was shaky, his lips drawn back from his teeth in pain and blood dripping down his injured arm: that punch had taken everything he had. *He's not going to get there in time!*

Ralavich's fingers wrapped around the gun. I ran over to Ralavich but what the hell could I do? He was twice my size and I was staggering around in the ridiculous heels I'd bought to look like—

What would Christina do?

I lifted my foot and stamped my heel down on the back of Ralavich's hand as hard as I could. He howled in pain and his fingers released the gun. A second later, Konstantin kicked it out of the open door.

I staggered back out of the way. Ralavich got to his feet, clutching his hand, and the two men faced off.

Konstantin's eyes grew cold. I drew in my breath. He'd waited twenty years for vengeance. Now Ralavich had no more guards, no more protection. I knew how this would end.

So did Ralavich. As Konstantin stalked towards me, he lunged to the side and grabbed me—

And threw me out of the plane.

68

KONSTANTIN

M Y WHOLE WORLD changed in half a second.

I'd dreamed of this day for twenty years. The fantasies had been all that had kept me going in the early days, when I'd lain awake at night starving and freezing, too poor to afford food or shelter. Later, my hatred had helped me build my empire. Every deal, every block of territory, was one step closer to killing him. Ralavich had always been too well guarded, too well hidden for me to get to. But I'd always known this day would come. My path had always been clear.

And then, suddenly, that path was torn in two.

I shoved Ralavich aside and leaned out of the door and into the rain, my heart slamming against my ribs. For a second, I couldn't see her. I searched the pavement as it rushed by beneath us, my chest tight and my hands crushing the door frame, terrified I was going to see her battered, bloody body—

Then I looked back, along the plane. Hailey was lying on the wing, behind and below the door. She was moaning in pain and I could see blood on the white wing, just beneath her head: she must have really hit hard when Ralavich threw her. But she was alive. And Calahan was sprinting after us for all he was worth. The wing was only eight feet or so off the ground, once he got there he could help her down....

Then the plane swung around, turning off the taxiway and onto the runway. I glanced up and saw what was right behind Hailey. *Oh God. Oh, no*—

"*Hailey!*" I screamed. "*You have to jump down! Now!*"

She gave a weak moan and tried to press herself up to sitting, still dazed. I could see a nasty gash on her forehead where she'd hit her head. Behind her, I saw Calahan curse as he, too, realized the danger. But he was still too far away—

The plane finished its turn and stopped at the end of the runway. And then—

It started as a deep whine that rose inexorably higher and higher. My tie flapped, then snapped tight, tugging at my neck. Rain stung one side of my face as the drops were sucked horizontally by an unmatchable force.

"*Hailey!*" I screamed again.

This time she came awake and pushed herself up to her hands and knees. The roar behind her made her turn her head—

I saw her whole body freeze as she stared straight into the gaping maw of the engine. Even as she looked, her hair streamed out towards it and her clothes snapped taut. Then *she* was moving, sliding backwards across the rain-soaked wing.

She was going to be sucked straight into the engine.

I whipped around. Ralavich had retreated further inside the plane, too far away for me to grab. He gave a victorious grin. We both knew that as soon as I went out there, he'd slam the door and I'd lose him forever.

I could lunge at him, kill him, and have my revenge. Or I could save Hailey.

I had to make a choice. My past or my future.

The engine noise built to an excruciating howl as the pilot throttled up. The plane rocked against its brakes, gathering itself like an animal about to leap. Outside, Hailey was slipping back, back across the wing, her fingers searching for grip against the slick metal—

It was no decision at all.

I launched myself through the door and landed on the wing, grunting as the jolt sent a bolt of fresh pain through my arm. Behind me, I heard the door slam and seal shut.

I started to crawl forwards towards Hailey, stretching out with my hands. But she was being sucked back too fast, fingernails clawing at the wing. She let out a shriek as the pilot extended the flaps and the wing changed shape beneath her: God, we were going to take off any second! The engine howl changed in note and the roar became agony, like someone trying to force a metal bar into your ear canal. Hailey's body began to lift from the wing as the engine reached full power. *No. No, no no*—

I launched myself forward and grabbed for her. My fingertips missed hers by a half inch.

She slid and slid... and then her fingers hooked into the groove where the flap joined the wing. The suction drew her up, stretching her body in a diagonal line, her feet towards the engine. I hooked my toes under the front edge of the wing and stretched forward as far as I could but I still couldn't reach her. She screamed but the noise was lost in the deafening roar. Rain was pounding at her face, making her splutter and screw her eyes shut, and I could see every muscle in her arm standing out as she fought to hang on.

Calahan finally reached us. He ran underneath the wing, stretching up to grab hold of Hailey's wrists—

The pilot released the brakes and we shot forward. Calahan barely leaped out of the way in time and was left behind in a second. Now, as well as the suction of the engine, we were being clawed at by the wind rushing past. I stretched as far as I possibly could, but my fingertips still didn't quite meet Hailey's. And we were quickly picking up speed. Soon, we'd be moving too fast to jump off.

I glanced up. Ralavich was at the window, gloating.

Hailey was a little to the right of me. There was only one way to reach her.

I lifted my right foot, so that I was only hanging on with my left. Instantly, the suction pulled me diagonally across the wing, stretched out from left toe to right hand. And that gave me the vital few inches that let me—

My hand grabbed hers. She stared at my injured arm in horror, eyes locked on the blood soaking through my shirt, but I nodded. *It's okay.*

And I pulled.

Pain. Pain like I hadn't felt since the frozen river, but this was fire instead of ice, blazing up through every tendon, commanding me to let go. But I had Hailey's hand in a death grip. The engine's suction tore at her, trying to snatch her from me, but I wasn't going to let it have her. She meant more to me than revenge, more than my past—

More than my empire.

Inch by inch, I dragged her forward across the wing. The engine was sucking in the air so fast there was none left to breathe, and my lungs ached and screamed. I couldn't hear anymore, the roar so loud that it had gone beyond noise: it was just a battering agony and a total lack of any other sound.

I stared right into Hailey's eyes and *pulled.* The pain in my injured arm doubled, trebled, but the world was whipping past faster and faster, it had to be *now.* I yelled and *pulled—*

And then she was next to me and I wrapped my arms around her. There was no time to say anything, and no way would she have been able to hear me over the engine. So I just looked at her and nodded. *Trust me.*

And I rolled us over the front edge of the wing.

I was praying that my body was heavy enough, and that we'd fall fast enough, that we'd fall out of the engine's suction before it could suck us in. But as we fell, I could feel us being pulled back, back, the underside of the wing racing past above us. As we cleared the wing, we seemed to hang in the air for a second, the engine sucking us up while gravity sucked us down.

And then I felt us begin to fall. I hugged Hailey tight to my chest—

My back hit the pavement, so quick and hard I felt the shock but not the pain. We bounced, spun.... I saw glimpses of red and blue lights, storm clouds, the plane racing away from us... then we hit again and this time the pain lit up one whole side of my body from ankle to shoulder. Another bounce, my stomach dropping away as we rose into the air... and then we slammed down and rolled, over and over, and all I could do was clutch Hailey close and pray she'd be okay.

We finally came to rest by the side of the runway. I knew I was panting because I could feel my chest heaving, but I couldn't hear my breath. I couldn't hear *anything.*

I opened my arms and legs, releasing Hailey from her protective cocoon. She struggled to her hands and knees. Moving. Talking, even though I couldn't hear her. *Alive!* The cut on her head was bleeding and she was covered in bruises but she was okay.

That's when the pain started to hit me. Not just my arm, but my legs, my ribs. There didn't seem to be anywhere that *didn't* hurt.

I managed to roll over. At the far end of the runway, Ralavich's plane rose into the air and banked away, rising towards the clouds. Hailey moved into my view, staring up at the plane in horror. Her expression said it all. *He got away!*

I took her hand with my good arm and squeezed it. *It doesn't matter,* I mouthed.

I drew her down for a kiss as red and blue lights surrounded us.

Nothing else mattered.

Only her.

EPILOGUE

Hailey
Six Weeks Later

W E'D BEEN DRIVING for several hours, taking turns. We should have been exhausted after all the traveling: it was mid-afternoon and we'd started our journey the evening before, an overnight flight and then another, much smaller plane to the tiny town where we'd rented the SUV. But we'd never been more awake. We were experiencing the opposite of white line fever.

We'd just crested another rise and I'd stopped in the road to drink in the view. It wasn't like I was holding up traffic: we hadn't seen another vehicle in hours. To our left, snow-capped mountain peaks clawed at the sky. To our right, the ground dropped away towards verdant green forest. And directly ahead, a sparkling river curled and twisted into a deep valley. The air felt different, here: bitterly cold but clean and fresh in a way that made New York air feel like it came from a bottle. It felt so good in our lungs, we had the windows wound down, even though it meant we had to huddle in gloves and thick jackets.

Alaska, I'd decided, was awesome.

Somewhere down there in the valley was our destination, but it was still too far away to make out. When we'd organized this over a video call, we'd been unsure if we'd be able to pull it off. It was late November and once the snow came, the track we were following would be almost impassable until spring. But we'd gotten lucky and the snow had held off. We had a week before we'd have to go back to civilization. Long enough for this visit, one that was way overdue. It had been almost two years since my friend Kate had left the New York FBI office for the tiny one in Anchorage, Alaska, with weekends and vacations spent out here in the wilds, at Mason's cabin.

We were truly in the middle of nowhere. We'd lost cell phone reception hours ago and there wasn't a telegraph post or a power line in sight. It was a little unsettling to think that, if we got into trouble out here, no one would find us for weeks or months.

Of course, *really* we were safe. If we didn't arrive, our hosts would come out looking for us. But it made me think how isolated Kate must have felt, doing this journey on foot, with no supplies and no back-up. Of course, she'd had *him*. Her protector, now her man.

I looked across at *my* man. "Last stretch," I said. "Maybe an hour. Want me to take it?"

Konstantin shook his head. "I'll take it. I'm meant to be exercising my arm."

I put the parking brake on and we walked around the front of the car to switch drivers. Six weeks on from the airfield, we were both still nursing injuries. We'd been incredibly lucky. The rain that had made the wing so slippery had also saved us: as we'd hit the runway, we'd skidded and slid rather than scraped. If it had been a dry day, we'd have lost most of our skin. Even so, we'd hit the ground hard. I'd cracked two bones in my ankle and still favored the other leg. Konstantin had come off worse: three broken ribs and a dislocated shoulder, but the worst damage was to his arm. Hauling me to safety and putting all that strain on it when it was already injured from the bullet had permanently damaged the muscle. He could still drive and write and pick me up, and physiotherapy was helping, but the doctors had warned that he'd never regain full strength in that arm. When they'd told us, I'd burst into tears.

But he'd just put a finger under my chin and lifted my head to look at him. "It's our weaknesses that make us human," he'd told me. And I'd thrown my arms around him and hugged him close.

Our hearing had taken several hours to return and it was weeks before the ringing in my ears went completely. One of the first things I'd heard, as I lay in a hospital bed, was Calahan's conversation with Konstantin, who was in the bed next to mine. Calahan had been muttering and his silhouette on the curtain had its shoulders hunched with embarrassment. I'd had to really strain to hear.

"... *special,*" Calahan had told Konstantin. "So you'd better not *mumble* her *mumble*—"

"I won't," Konstantin had said solemnly.

"Or I don't care how goddamn powerful you are, I'll—"

"*I won't,*" Konstantin reassured him.

And Calahan had stomped off. *Poor Calahan....* I knew we weren't right for each other, but I hoped he found someone soon. He needed someone as stubborn as him, someone who could break through all the walls he'd put up and help him lay his pain to rest. She was out there, somewhere.

Ironically, my mom had come to visit *me* in the hospital. Her health was much better, after her latest round of treatment, and I'd had a long phone call with her to prepare her for my new face. When she finally saw me, there was a lot of sobbing from both of us. But she finally sniffed and pushed back from me, then shook her head. "Doesn't matter what you look like," she told me firmly. "You're still *you.*"

To my amazement, she took to Konstantin immediately, describing him as *a gentleman.* I'd been worried at first, afraid she didn't understand what he was, who he was. But when I explained, she waved aside my concerns. "Is he a *good man?*" she asked.

"Yes," I said with feeling.

"That's all that matters."

Konstantin had offered to pay her medical bills, but it turned out he didn't need to. Word had gotten out about my shopping trip and once people heard that Christina Rogan, one of the best-dressed women in New York, liked to shop at my mom's boutique, the place had turned into one of those "undiscovered gems" that columnists love to write about. The shop had never been busier and my mom had to take on an assistant.

Grigory, broken-hearted, had testified against Christina. Without her influence, his loyalties had swung back to Konstantin and he'd refused to answer any questions about his employer. Konstantin hadn't said anything directly but I knew that had gone a long way towards letting him forgive his former bodyguard. Christina, meanwhile, was going to be serving a long sentence in a federal penitentiary for conspiracy to murder, attempted murder and the drug charges we'd first brought her in on. Grigory's sentence was looking to be a little shorter thanks to his cooperation. Finally, in a big win for the FBI, the arrest of the assassin had cleared up a whole slew of unsolved murders.

Konstantin and I crossed over at the front of the car and I kept going towards the passenger side... but Konstantin caught my hand and brought me to a stop, then pulled me back to him. "What?" I asked, startled. "What's up?"

"Nothing," he said. Those blue eyes looked deep into mine. "Nothing at all."

He smoothed his hand through my hair, pushing it back from my face. I'd stopped dying and straightening my hair and it was slowly turning back to its natural muddy brown frizz. He said he preferred it. I was dressing a little more like me, too, within reason. I wasn't going to stop wearing all the designer clothes, but it was nice to just throw on jeans and a sweater sometimes, like today. I'd even got some glasses with plain glass lenses so that I could wear them again. Mainly for him. In the bedroom.

We still had both kinds of sex. Slow, romantic, candlelit sessions in the bedroom, teasing each other for hours, and incredible, intense sessions down in the dungeon where he'd bind me and take me, again and again. But the BDSM was even better now we could cuddle afterwards and the romantic sex was even more fun with the occasional bit of kink thrown in.

The mansion had changed a little, too. My father's paintings were now framed and hanging on the walls and we'd cleaned up the mess the storm had made of the garden, and restored the glasshouse. I'd insisted on keeping the garden wild, though, as it should be.

We turned towards the view ahead of us and just stood there, leaning against the hood for a moment. Without looking, we reached for each other's hands and squeezed.

He wouldn't have been capable of this, a few months ago. He wouldn't have understood just standing and looking at something beautiful, wouldn't have tolerated the distraction from building his empire. But he'd changed. He walked in the garden, sometimes, not just with me, but *by himself,* as if he actually enjoyed it, and that was huge. One day, maybe he'd even make friends with the cat.

He pulled me closer and slipped an arm around my waist. We didn't have to say anything. We could just sit there and *enjoy,* in silence, something I'd never been able to do with any man.

An hour later, we pulled up at the bottom of a path that led up the steep side of the valley. That was as far as the SUV could go: from here on out, we'd be on foot. Two people were waiting for us, one a giant who stood even taller than Konstantin, the other—

Kate *whumped* into my chest and threw her arms around me. I'm not tall, but even I was looking over the top of her head. "I'm so glad you made it! We have everything ready. I mean, the cabin's not big and you're on the floor, but there are furs and a comforter and I'm sure you'll be fine, and Mason went hunting, there are venison steaks for dinner, I hope you're hungry, was your flight okay, sometimes it gets choppy—"

I was starting to realize that, other than Mason, Kate had been a little short on people to talk to, up here. Over the next week, we were going to get all the hospitality she'd been saving up for two years. I squeezed her tight.

We loaded up with a backpack each and started up the path. As well as our own supplies, we'd brought a few gifts. A bottle of red wine for tonight and—

Kate fell in beside me and whispered in my ear. *"Did you—"*

I grinned and opened the top of my backpack. The entire top third was stuffed with bags of gourmet coffee, straight from the city.

Kate squeezed me. *"Bless you!"*

Konstantin

The next day, I woke up to the sound of nothing. Even at the mansion, there was the distant sound of traffic and the faint hum of the air conditioning. Here, there was just silence and it was strangely relaxing. I wouldn't have believed, a few months ago, that it was possible to just slow down and switch off from my empire, but then Hailey had changed me in all sorts of ways. I felt better. I slept better. And my dreams were only good.

Hailey didn't know it, but sometimes, in the garden, when I was sure that no one was looking, I let the cat sit on my lap.

I was... *happy.*

She stirred next to me and cuddled sleepily into my chest. I leaned down and kissed her cheek. I'd deliberately made this vacation all about her: seeing her friends, doing something she'd always wanted to do. Being Hailey, she'd worried that that was unfair. "Isn't there anywhere *you* want to go?" she'd asked.

But there honestly wasn't. I'd spent so long being completely focused on my work, I didn't *have* a bucket list. Or, to be truthful, friends. But that would come with time. We had our whole futures ahead of us. For now, I was happy to be anywhere she was.

In the hospital, I'd made it clear to Hailey that if she wanted to reverse Christina's decision and rejoin the FBI, I'd understand. But she'd immediately shaken her head. "I'm not like Calahan or Kate," she told me. "They were born to be agents. I fell into it. There's something I've always wanted to do more." And she'd told me her dream.

Today would be the first step towards realizing it.

After an enormous, country-style breakfast, we hiked out into the forest, Hailey laden down with her camera gear. Mason led us through the trees without GPS, without even a map. I knew he did this for a living, guiding tourists, and before Kate he'd spent years up here, surviving on his own. But I was still amazed at how well he could navigate.

When we reached the spot, Hailey lay down on her front and got comfortable, putting her water bottle, snacks and camera lenses all within easy reach. I watched in amazement: it was the first time I'd seen her do it and it was like watching an animal nest. "This is how you used to watch me?" I asked.

She nodded. "For two years."

We stared at each other. She bit her lip. I felt that electric thrill, the one that never went away, the one that made me feel like a teenager. Hailey was good for me. Literally good, the balance to my bad. It was still a turn on but it was far more than that. She completed me, in the same way my mother had completed my father. She tempered me. I might never be *good* but, with her influence, I wasn't ruthless.

"I wish you hadn't stayed in the distance so long," I told her. And kissed her.

She'd asked me, *when is it enough?* When would my empire be big enough, when would I have enough money, enough power? And the answer was *never* because I'd been clawing away at the world, trying to fill some void the death of my family had left. But now I had Hailey. She was the answer. I looked at her. *This is enough.*

I'd stopped trying to take new territory. The truce between the gangs would remain and New York would continue to have three kings, not just one. It was better, that way. If one person had that much power, it opened the possibility that someone like Ralavich could take over, with no one able to overthrow him. Better that the three of us kept each other in check.

The FBI preferred it, too. Now that Carrie Blake had seen how Ralavich operated, she'd come to realize that there were worse people who could fill my shoes. When I'd reassured her that I'd stop my expansion, averting a gang war, that had placated her even more... and I *had* saved her life. Of course, officially she was still working to bring me down. But, as she'd told me at the end of my lengthy debriefing, "Right now, I have bigger fish to fry."

It wasn't just that Ralavich had kidnapped Hailey, or burned down buildings in the heart of New York. He'd tried to manipulate the FBI into doing his dirty work for him. That alone would have put him at the top of their Most Wanted list, but throw in the attempted assassination of an FBI chief and the anger was being felt all the way to Washington. Carrie had been summoned to DC twice, including for a meeting with the State Department and President Matthews himself. Ralavich had gone to ground in Russia and the Russian government was stonewalling, but President Matthews wasn't taking no for an answer and I had a feeling it was only a matter of time.

I had mixed feelings about him being brought to justice. I still wanted him dead for what he'd done to my family. But the hatred didn't consume me, anymore. It wasn't the most important thing in my life, and neither was my empire.

Hailey drew in her breath. I followed her gaze.

I saw the mother first, cautiously sniffing the air and making sure things were safe. Then the father, strong and protective. And then—

Three bear cubs, each small enough to pick up in your arms, gamboling and tripping over their paws and rolling on the ground. Hailey snapped picture after picture and as I leaned over her shoulder and looked at them flashing up on the screen, I felt my throat go tight. She was going to be an amazing wildlife photographer, one of the greats. It was the details she noticed: the look of gentle chiding the mother gave her cubs as she nudged them for roughhousing, the way the father nuzzled the mother's neck as the cubs climbed on his back. After a while, Hailey drew back from the viewfinder and just watched with me.

This. This was what was important. Not empire, family. Not death, life.

I'd already decided that I was going to ask Hailey to marry me. And after that, we were going to raise a new generation of the Gulyev family. They'd grow up in America, not Russia, and they'd follow whatever path they wanted. Maybe the Gulyev crime empire would end with me. But the family would continue.

That first day, we saw a moose and a beaver and a huge, lumbering black bear. As the sun started to go down, we began the hike back to the cabin. Hailey was strangely quiet. I slipped my arm around her waist and pulled her close. "Something wrong?"

"No," she said firmly. "Everything's perfect. That's just it, I worry that...."

I stopped, letting Kate and Mason walk on ahead. "What?"

She sighed. "I just keep thinking: we came so close! When everyone thought Christina was me, if you hadn't realized, she'd still be being me *now,* she'd be living this life with you, and I'd be—"

I put my hands on her shoulders and looked her in the eye. "I *did* realize," I told her.

"But what if you *hadn't?*"

"There is no chance that I wouldn't have. I knew as soon as I kissed her. Just as I knew something was different the very first time I kissed you."

"But *how?* I mean, was she harder or softer or more tongue, or—"

I took her cheeks between my hands and kissed her. Slow and deep and with every bit of love in my soul. I felt the tension flood out of her. And when the kiss ended, I told her, "*That's* how. It didn't matter that she had your face, or your clothes. I wasn't in love with her. I was in love with you."

THE END

Konstantin first appeared as a minor character in *Kissing My Killer.* Alexei, a Russian hitman, is sent to kill Gabriella, a hacker. But when he looks into her eyes, he can't pull the trigger...and the two are forced to go on the run together.

The story of Kate and Mason can be found in *Alaska Wild*.

Agent Calahan teams up with reclusive genius Yolanda to catch a serial killer in *Hold Me in the Dark*.

Find all my books at https://helenanewbury.com

Made in the USA
Las Vegas, NV
14 February 2023

67542210R00194